MW01601462

SPIRIT OF ELM

CHILDREN OF ICE

BY

MICHAEL VILLA

ILLUSTRATIONS BY ERIANA MIRABAL

Published by Avaleer Publishing Co.

Bethesda, Maryland

To learn more about the author and his other works, visit www.spiritofelm.com

Library of Congress Control Number: 2020914948

ISBN-13: 978-0-9967233-3-6

ISBN-10: 0-9967233-3-1

10 9 8 7 6 5 4 3 2 1   20 21 22 23 24 25

First Edition, September 2020

ACKNOWLEDGMENTS

Graeme Shaw was a friend of mine who is no longer with us today. He loved to call me "The Professor" and would always ask me what I was up to. He was the first person to request a mailed copy of my story, and he constantly asked how the next book was coming along. He would joke and tell me he would be my butler and drive the car when I became a big author. I unfortunately couldn't finish the second book in time for him, and I badly wish now that weren't the case. I shouldn't be sad, though. He often told me to eat a spoon full of concrete and harden up, so I will take his advice to heart and get straight to work on the the next book.

Thank you, Graeme, for everything you have done.

TABLE OF CONTENTS

Tea, tea, what a splendid brew
To have with someone like you.
Such moments were truly rare
To enjoy without a care.

On a hill full of flowers,
We sipped together for hours.
Miss Squirrel brought snacks to eat,
Some bitter and some quite sweet.

The old hound stood guard proudly,
And the kitten purred loudly.
There were other dear friends too,
All who came just to see you.

I told tales of every kind,
Or shared worries on my mind.
You listened to what I said,
Until the sky turned plum red.

Then the foxes and the mouse
Helped walk us back to the house.
There you were tucked into bed,
And dreamed soundly in my stead.

Tea, tea, what a splendid brew
To have with someone like you.
Such moments are truly rare
To recall without a care.

SPIRIT OF ELM

CHILDREN OF ICE

CHAPTER ONE
CAMPFIRE STORIES

O n a cold, cloudy night, a group of soldiers sat around a fire, telling scary tales to one another to pass the time. Some enjoyed poking holes in the stories, while others silently listened as they ate elk stew out of tins. Most of them had young faces except for their leader. Sitting towards the center of them all, Captain Malcolm Riff was an older man with worn eyes, a scraggly beard, and a much less jovial air about him.

"And to this day ... I've never set foot in that lake again," said a somewhat hoarse soldier named Thomas, concluding his tale for the evening.

Everyone lightly clapped, and he playfully bowed in return.

"It's my turn now, right?" said Riff, and everyone around him grew quiet in an instant. He took a moment to collect his thoughts before continuing. "When I first came to the country's scar, I met an old man in the town square. He was sitting on a bench, humming a song to himself with his eyes closed. He was kind of small, and his skin looked like dry leather — too much sun over the years. I had a lot to do that day and hurried past him without a second thought, but he suddenly spoke up.

"'Be careful,' he warned me with a light smile on his face. 'The fields in the west are haunted by evil spirits.'

"Being polite, I humored him and asked what they looked like, and he laughed.

"'I've heard all kinds of rumors about them,' he explained to me, so it was difficult for him to say which were true and which were not. He did believe there were some similarities, though, between all the rumors. He told me: 'The spirits have skin as hard as stone and their claws are sharper than any blade. They walk on all fours and rarely open their eyes ...'

"He had trailed off, and I was going to use that as my chance to say goodbye, but then he stood up while adding something more. He said, 'They let out shrill cries at night, angry that man would dare try to steal their home....' Such an ominous thing for him to say, I thought, yet his pleasant expression hadn't changed one bit.... With nothing more to tell me, he turned to leave, waving goodbye.

"At the time I didn't think much of what he had said, guessing it was just the settler's way of scaring newcomers like me for fun. We got orders the next day from headquarters to investigate a case of crops being damaged along the western edge of the borderlands, very close to where we are now. I still remember arriving there in the middle of the day and seeing all those pumpkins in the fields smashed to pieces. A friend of mine laughed it off, telling me what a waste of good food it was. I smiled, agreeing with him. We paid little attention to the large paw marks stamped into the soil and told the farmers to put a scarecrow up. They pleaded for us to at least stay the night, but it was getting too cold for that. We lied and told them we were too busy to help them.

"In the days that followed, reports kept coming in, each case similar to the one we'd been sent to investigate earlier in the week. It was annoying for us to be sent all over to deal with some pests. The captains were sure it was just a pack of red wolves or something roaming through, so the problem would pass soon enough. There'd been, I think, a few of those animals spotted somewhere north of here ... but they weren't the real culprits.

"By the end of the week, stacks and stacks of reports began to flood in, telling us the damage was getting worse. The things responsible had begun destroying more and more of the farmers' property with each night that passed, toppling fences and tearing apart barns. There was this one image that always bothered me, even now ... Inside a report was a photo of a mound of wood and debris stacked who knows how high, and at the top was a skinny scarecrow with a pumpkin for a head. I think it was then that I knew that whatever was doing all this was mocking us and the farmers, laughing at our pathetic little scarecrow.

"Soon, the few people stubborn enough to remain began disappearing from their homes. We weren't sure if they were being kidnapped or murdered, but we were dispatched with the orders of making whatever was causing all this to stop. Twenty-one of us were assigned to a farm that stood a little west of town. We arrived there late in the day when the sun was close to setting, so we immediately made a campfire and quietly waited. The farmer and his wife were kind to us, offering food and warm blankets, but I don't think we ate anything that night. No one wanted to admit it, but we were all afraid of being out in these fields after seeing those reports. None of us were laughing them off any longer.

"Right when I was about to light a cigarette — it must have been after midnight by then — anyway, I heard a shrill cry come from the fields. I was going to turn to see what it was, but I got bashed in the head from out of nowhere before I could even look. I got hit so hard that I slammed into the ground, stunned. There I then lay ... barely conscious as I listened to everyone begin fighting some kind of monstrous creature. They fired their rifles over and over at it, but the monster didn't seem bothered in the least. It rampaged through our tiny camp, felling anyone in its path with its enormous claws. My head was throbbing, but I was able to somewhat make out the shape of its ugly body. It walked on all fours, and its skin looked incredibly rough and hard.

"When the monster was sure it had won at last, it howled wildly over the fallen. I wanted to run after hearing such an awful sound, but I was still too dazed

... or maybe just too scared to move.... I thought my heart stopped when the spirit was answered a few seconds later by several other howls in the distance, crying what I imagined out of joy. Then, just as I was about to fall unconscious, I heard a familiar voice let out a hoarse laugh before saying, 'Didn't I warn you spirits live here?'"

Riff paused to take a moment to light a cigarette in the campfire's flames. He looked as calm as could be, but his new recruits were on edge thanks to his story, instinctively listening for any eerie sounds nearby. Some hugged their riffles, while others wanted to ask if the story was true. Riff wasn't finished, though, having a little more to say.

"The next morning, I woke up alone," he continued. "None of the other soldiers' bodies were there but my own. The farmer and his entire family were nowhere to be found either. The barn, fields, fences — everything was in pieces. Later on, a squad found me and helped me get back to town. I then reported what happened, but I kept the spirit stuff out since they would have thought I was crazy. I lied and just said I was knocked out without seeing a thing.... I'm still not entirely sure what happened that night, but I know I hate coming to this place."

There was one recruit who couldn't sit still listening to Riff. He was a slim young man pacing incessantly back and forth alongside the ruins of an old abandoned farmhouse they were using for firewood.

His hair was cut short and his body trembled from thinking about what the captain had just told them. He wanted to be brave, but his hands wouldn't stop shaking as they squeezed the buttons on his uniform coat. The nervous young man was none other than Andrew Glint.

"Captain," said Frank, who was a big, heavy recruit reclining, looking bored, "if your story's really true, why haven't we heard about anything like that happening here before?"

Riff nodded.

"That's a pretty good question," he replied. "A little after I made my report, the attacks strangely stopped, and I never learned why."

"That seems convenient," Frank remarked.

"Yeah, it does," Riff admitted. "I'll add while I'm at it that the government buried most of what happened. It wasn't hard for them to do since nobody really cares about this place."

Much of his recruits murmured in agreement regarding that last point. Even Frank nodded.

"Hey, Andrew," said Riff, pointing at him with his cigarette, "you alright?"

Everyone turned their heads to look at Andrew, and he grew embarrassed from being singled out.

"I-I'm fine," he mumbled.

"Huh?" Riff barked back. "Come on, no one's gonna hear you like that. I keep telling you to speak clearer for a reason."

"Try not to scare Andrew too much, Captain," said Thomas, "or he might start crying again."

Everyone laughed; even Riff let a smile slip. Andrew glared at them.

"I never cried!" he shouted in a somewhat high-pitched voice, but that just made his fellow recruits laugh harder.

Andrew stormed around one of the few chunks of the farmhouse's wall that still stood, trying to look defiant. Once out of sight, though, he crumbled down, ready to silently sob to himself.

Andrew had been a mess ever since the day he was shipped out. He had hoped that with his quiet, meek appearance, he would have gotten a calm guard post in some city, but he was now being traumatized in the wild frontier of Avaleer's western borderlands. The tiny handful of *towns* (he found them very undeserving of being called that) throughout these unending, overgrown fields had little to no technology, stability, or economic prosperity. The nights were too dark, and the days were too bright. Even worse, the food was just plain awful. The local farmers were simple folk with little to say, and the soldiers were crude and bitter. Really, there was nothing redeeming in Andrew's mind about this part of the world.

"Whose turn is next?" Riff asked. "Bill, you haven't told us one yet. Come on, make it good."

"What about Andrew?" Bill whined. He had a great smile that helped conceal his mean personality.

"Leave him be," said Riff.

"Yeah," replied Frank, "I don't want to know what goes on in his head. I want to be able to sleep tonight."

Everyone roared with laughter at that, thinking how true it was … except poor Andrew. He despised these men and how they enjoyed picking on him.

He angrily reared his head around the corner to yell at them.

"You all —" he began to shout, but then he stopped himself. He noticed that the tall grass behind his fellow recruits was rustling quite a bit, worrying him. Andrew said nothing, though, not wanting to sound like a nervous fool, especially if it turned out to just be some lively crows or field mice. Instead, he listened to the next story while silently observing.

"When I was a little boy," said Bill in a solemn voice, doing his best to set the mood, "I lived with my grandfather outside of Sotting, in a tiny village none of you have probably ever heard of."

"I thought you were from Maldwood?" a scrawny man named George remarked.

Bill smiled.

"Maybe," he joked. "Anyway, whenever my grandfather was busy working, I played outside in a small garden. It wasn't anything special, just a bunch of root vegetables and a few small pumpkins, but there was this great big ol' apple tree growing against the garden wall. I liked to climb up high and sit on a big branch, thinking I could spy on the whole village from up there.

Really though, I could only see over the garden wall at the neighbors. One day, while I was lying there on the branch eating an apple, I heard a young woman begin sobbing. I sat up and looked everywhere for her. Eventually, I caught sight of her right beneath me, huddled against the neighbor's side of the wall, crying hard to herself..."

Andrew was having trouble paying attention to Bill's story. His mind was entirely focused on the fields and their incessant rustling. He told himself over and over that he was just being paranoid. Spirits were made-up creatures, he knew that well enough, but Riff's story had done a masterful job of frightening the wits out of him.

"... The next morning, my grandfather woke me up and told me they found her body in the river. She had slipped and fallen running away in the dead of night. I knew it wasn't my fault, but I still felt guilty, you know? Like I could have done more for her ... I just hadn't thought she would go so far to get away from her family.... Later that day, I heard a woman sobbing. I thought for sure that it had to be her, that there had to be some kind of mistake, so I climbed the tree like I always had, but when I looked over the garden wall ... nobody was there."

As everyone then began to applaud the eerie ending to Bill's story, Andrew's eyes slowly widened from him knowing the rustling was growing in intensity.

"E-e-every-e-everyone, t-t-turn around, q-quickly!"

he nervously stuttered, but the gang of soldiers just looked at him confusedly.

"Andrew, quit your mumbling over there," said Riff, sounding annoyed. "What are you trying to tell us?"

"I think he said something's behind us," said Bill. "Hey, Andrew, you trying to scare us? You're pretty bad at it, you know that — ?"

Before any of them had the chance to make another crack at Andrew, a massive paw came crashing down on the campfire, snuffing it out. A few men shouted in confusion before Frank suddenly cried out in pain.

Andrew, having only seen the paw for just a brief moment, instinctively cowered behind the brick wall of the farmhouse. He listened to rifles fire over and over as more men wailed like Frank. Others yelled, trying to act strong, but all of the soldiers were helpless before the mysterious beast's wrath.

With a loud thump, something suddenly collapsed in front of Andrew. He was terrified, holding his breath in fear that it might be the beast itself, but then a small moan came from the figure in the dark, telling him it was one of his cohorts. He couldn't see well who it was, but the person in question next dropped something that made a clinking sound as it hit the ground. Andrew immediately crawled forward, hoping it was some kind of firearm. He felt around with his hands in the dirt until one of them brushed against a small, metal object. Picking it up, he squinted and rubbed his thumb along its body. The top swung open with a click, and he was certain then that it had to be a lighter.

The beast let out a hoarse howl. In the minute or so Andrew had spent searching for the lighter, the jeering camp had been reduced to a few lingering groans.

"Come on ... Come on," Andrew quietly moaned to himself with tears welling up in his eyes as his thumb flicked like mad against the lighter's wheel. He could hear the creature's heavy breathing somewhere behind him, sounding like it might be getting closer. He needed to be able to see, he told himself, if he wanted to think of a way to survive. Really though, his heart raced from him knowing any second his life was probably going to end without him able to do a thing.

As the beast let out a growl only a few feet away, Andrew cried aloud, "PLEASE, WORK!"

With those emotional words said, the lighter finally flickered on, letting out a warm wave of flames. They singed what was left of the house and shot out towards the field. Andrew was startled but equally amazed by this magical sight. The fire was purging his worries away. Peering around the corner, he saw the beast for what it was in this light: a large, four-legged creature with a body clad in an armor of clay scales. Its stone tail swayed heavily, almost beating the ground with each thump it made. Dust and cracked clay-like hairs made up its pointy ears. Its eye sockets appeared empty, but Andrew was sure it was angrily glaring right at him. With its uneven, chipped stone fangs bare and its claws dug deep into the dirt, this hideous beast looked anxious to kill the human standing defiantly before it.

"I-is that r-really ... a spirit?" Andrew mumbled to himself.

He remained frozen with fear, afraid to do anything, but the creature did not advance.

"It — doesn't like — fire," spoke a pained voice beside Andrew.

Looking down by his feet, Andrew was horrified to see that it was Captain Riff who had collapsed in front of him. He was lying in a pool of blood with a massive gash in his side.

Every so often the clay spirit looked side to side, growling at the flames. It took a moment, but it sank in for Andrew what his superior meant. Andrew clicked the lighter once more to be sure, shooting another wave. The creature's thick skin protected it from the heat, but the armor did nothing to stop its fear of the fire.

"G-go away!" Andrew cried out, standing up tall while flicking the lighter's wheel several more times. Wave after wave of flames then came pouring out, beating incessantly against the spirit's body. Eventually, fear overtook the spirit, and it turned and fled.

Once Andrew was sure the creature was gone, he collapsed to the ground and gasped for air. He could not believe he had survived. He silently thanked the lighter for what it had done for him. Then, bringing the flame closer to his face, he crawled to Riff and examined his wound more carefully.

"C captain," Andrew nervously mumbled, "we — we need to s-stop the bleeding. I need to d-do — do something before —"

"Don't bother, Andrew," said Riff, doing his best to act strong despite the horrible condition he was in.

"No, I — I can — w-we need to —"

"Shut up, and Listen!" Riff yelled over him. "You need to listen and not act like a crying nitwit for once in — y-your life —"

Riff started coughing hard, breathing heavily as a small bit of blood began trickling out of the corner of his mouth.

"Captain — !"

"That — lighter," Riff continued, forcing his words out, "is something special I earned years ago. Unfortunately, it never worked f-for me. I want — I want you ... to take it and — and promise me that you will burn my body and everyone else's too."

"No, but Captain," Andrew moaned, "you'll — you'll be fine. I'll bandage y-you right up —"

"Andrew," said Riff softly, staring at him with incredibly stern yet pleading eyes, "I-I don't want anyone to end up the same way my friends did ... they deserved better than that."

"What do you mean?" Andrew asked.

Riff remained silent for a moment, but then turned his head and struggled to point.

CHAPTER ONE

"Can you go get my bag, Andrew? I'd like a cigarette. I left them in m-my bag."

Andrew didn't understand what was going on anymore, but he nodded anxiously in response. He got up and dashed to the camp. He'd almost forgotten about everyone else, but he was firmly reminded upon seeing their lifeless bodies strewn everywhere. The spirit had been merciless in how it had dealt with his fellow recruits. With each body Andrew checked to be sure no one was left, he felt he was slowly growing numb to the sight of death. He found no comfort in such a depressing feeling, so he soon decided to quickly grab the captain's belongings and hurry back.

"Captain, I got your bag just like ... you ..." Andrew began to say as he entered the farmhouse, but sadly, he found his captain lying there lifeless, having already passed away. Andrew's eyes started to well up with tears, but he did his best not to cry ... Riff wouldn't have liked it.

Andrew sat down and rummaged through the bag until he pulled out a carton of his superior's cigarettes. Just once he wanted to try smoking one of them to see if they would make him any calmer like Riff had always been. He pulled a cigarette out, lit it, and breathed in hard, but then immediately coughed like crazy. It tasted like a stick of ash ... though he did find some solace in its bitter taste. Then, remembering what Riff had said, Andrew aimed the lighter and mournfully ignited his captain's remains.

Andrew proceeded to do the same for the rest of his fellow recruits. It would be a lie to say a part of him didn't loathe these men, thinking they got what they deserved ... but he still pitied them for not having his luck tonight.

Once finished, Andrew walked back to his chunk of wall and slumped down against it onto the ground. Then, hearing thunder, he looked up and saw storm clouds had gathered overhead. As rain started to pour down next, extinguishing the burning fields, Andrew closed his eyes and silently listened to the rain's lulling tune.

With a hard thump, Glint was jerked awake. He groaned in annoyance, wishing that he could remain asleep a little longer.

"Oh, up at last?" said an all-too-familiar voice beside him.

Several months had gone by since the night Glint had nearly died in the Wrivenworth factory. The world believed that he had been lost to the fire, but in truth, he had survived thanks to his assistant, Owen Thivalane. After escaping the factory, Owen had helped Glint recover in secrecy. The toxins were now gone from his body, but the burns were going to need far more time to fully heal. Just like his younger self in his dream, Glint had short hair again. From head to toe, he was bandaged, and he wore a hat and a long, heavy coat to protect his frail body from the stinging winter winds. It hurt to breathe at times, let alone move, but Glint did his best to endure.

For the last few days, he and Owen had traveled across the country by car, passing through the western borderlands and now several hours into the unchartered frontier beyond Avaleer.

"How are you feeling, Mr. Glint?" Owen asked, sounding annoyingly calm and polite as usual.

"Fine," Glint replied gruffly as he stared out the window.

The tall, wild grass was slowly dying away as the car pressed on. The fields were receding and gradually transforming into fractured earth devoid of life. Owen hadn't told Glint where they were going, and Glint never bothered to ask. He frankly was too tired to care. The only question permitted to float around in his mind lately was what motivated Owen to do all this ... though, a part of Glint was afraid to know the answer. Ever since the night of the fire, he had found Owen to be a somewhat frightening figure. Not just because of his random actions, but also because of how purposeful he acted in doing them. Nothing he did made sense, yet he moved as if it was all so clear, like he was seeing a bigger picture that normal men like Glint could not possibly comprehend.

"Oh, look," said Owen suddenly, pointing forward, "we're almost there."

Glint struggled to sit up and look more carefully, but upon peering out the windshield, he couldn't see anything unique that would indicate they had arrived anywhere. The grass was completely gone now, and small clouds of dust drifted by here and there. It all looked perfectly flat and empty without exception.

After a few more minutes, the car came to a gentle stop.

"One moment," said Owen, turning off the engine. He then opened his door and hurried out and around the front of the car to the passenger's side.

"I'll help you get out," he said as he opened the passenger door, but Glint immediately pushed himself up from his seat and took a few steps on his own. Owen actually looked a little impressed.

"You're doing much better, Mr. Glint!" he cheerily remarked, closing the door.

"Yes, I guess I am," said Glint, admiring the desolate scenery.

Owen next walked to the back of the car and opened the trunk wide. Glint in the meantime leaned against the car door with his hand while stretching his stiff body.

"So, why are —" Glint had to briefly stop to let out a hoarse cough, "w-why are we here?"

"Well," Owen pulled out a satchel and then shut the trunk closed, "today, I am going to introduce you to someone very special."

CHAPTER TWO

TOCK

G lint didn't understand at all what Owen meant by someone *special*.

"What are you talking about?" he groaned, sounding more like his old, grumpy self. "We're in the middle of a wasteland. There's no way anyone could live out here."

"That's true," Owen calmly replied. He then knelt down and brushed his palm against the ground, revealing a thin, worn line of stone buried in dust.

"Mr. Glint," said Owen, standing back up, "you, of all people, should be familiar with the stories behind Ravnell."

At first Glint was still confused, but, as a strong wind suddenly rushed by, his eyes slowly widened as the wind revealed more of the stone outline of where a building once stood. Glint anxiously stepped forward into the outline, looking all around.

7 ... 10 ... 12 ... he tried counting how many buildings once stood here.

"This is a tiny, now nameless town I stumbled upon years ago," Owen explained. "If you keep going deeper into the wastelands, you can find many more places like this."

"So this isn't Ravnell ..." said Glint, sounding a

little disappointed. "I guess the old capital would have to be a lot farther away than this … wait, you said it had been years, right?"

"Years?"

"Yes, years since you found this place, so how old were you when you first came here?"

"Um," Owen scratched his head, thinking for a moment, "I'm not sure."

"Not sure?" Glint repeated, raising an eyebrow.

"Well, it was a long time ago," Owen replied, shrugging. "If I had to guess, maybe I was around seven or eight years old then."

Glint was a little startled to hear that. He couldn't imagine what a boy at such a young age would be doing in a desolate place like this.

"So, what happened to this town then?" he asked next. "Did Elm do this as well?"

"I don't know," Owen quietly answered. "We'd better get moving, Mr. Glint. We can't spend all day here enjoying the view. Please, follow me."

With that said, he proceeded forward. Glint was annoyed at how vague Owen was being today, but he obediently followed after him to see where it was that Owen was so eager to go. They passed many outlines, walking to what Glint imagined was the heart of the town. There, Owen stopped in the middle of a rather large outline and knelt down like he had done earlier. This time, though, he pulled a metal-scaled glove from his satchel. After sliding his right hand into it, he dug his gloved fingers deep into the dirt. Glint watched without saying a word, knowing something would happen. A few seconds passed and then the ground slowly gave way, crumbling where Owen had prodded with his fingers. Eventually, a large hole formed, revealing a stone spiral staircase carved out of the ground.

"Let me know when you recognize where we are," Owen said playfully as he walked down the steps.

Following right behind him, Glint let out a weak cough in response. He had no idea how he could possibly recognize a place like this in the middle of nowhere.

Just as Glint's head passed the ceiling of the stairwell, the entrance began to seal itself back up. In a matter of seconds, the stairwell was completely filled with darkness.

"Hey," Glint shouted, grabbing Owen by the shoulder, "I can't see a — !"

Before he could even finish voicing his complaint, electric lights flickered on overhead. They weren't very bright, some struggling to stay on, but they did the trick for Glint.

"Is something wrong?" Owen asked, staring over his shoulder with a composed expression. Glint pulled his hand back while wearing a slight scowl.

"It's nothing," he said gruffly. "Keep going."

"Yes, right this way, Mr. Glint," replied Owen, continuing downward. "It shouldn't take us long, but if you feel tired, feel free to lean on my shoulder again."

"Shut up!" Glint snapped angrily, trying hard not to cough as he followed after him.

Together they descended to the bottom of the stairs and then walked along several narrow stone passageways until their path was blocked by a set of iron doors. They were etched full of markings, though Glint saw no theme or clear pattern to them. Pressing his fingers on the metal etchings to see how they felt, he also slowly realized there was no knob to turn or keyhole to unlock the heavy doors.

"What now — ?" Glint began to quietly ask, but Owen thrust his gloved hand forward without warning. Glint expected Owen's fingers to slam hard against the metal, but, to Glint's surprise, Owen's fingers instead sank through as if the door were made of water. Owen then slowly turned his hand, and the metal doors creaked open.

Glint noticed right away that something was moving on the other side.

"Careful!" he barked as he ripped his misshapen lighter out from his coat pocket and started flicking its wheel desperately. Little bursts of sparks came out, but no flames.

"It's alright," said Owen, placing a hand on Glint's arm.

The lights in the room beyond the doors flickered on, revealing a rusty humanoid machine standing before Glint and Owen. As it struggled to move, doing its best to slowly bow its head, Glint quickly realized that it was one of Silas's creations, and that fact alarmed him greatly.

"Why are we in some place owned by Silas?!" he shouted at Owen, pointing his lighter at him now. "What are you two planning — ?"

"This facility and its contents have nothing to do with the Wrivenworths," said Owen calmly, walking past Glint.

"That doesn't make any sense!" Glint shouted. "One of their machines is standing right there — !"

"I have someone with me that I would like you to meet," Owen told the horolock. The machine nodded in response, and Owen then proceeded deeper into the room. Glint, with his hand shaking as it clenched the lighter, felt unbelievably annoyed being ignored. He shoved his lighter back into his pocket and followed after Owen.

Nothing about the horolock still made any sense, but, once Glint bothered to actually look around, it slowly dawned on him that the machines and equipment throughout the room looked strangely familiar like Owen had mentioned earlier. After the two of them walked past several tables and a few tall piles of metal scraps, Glint found an odd, though nonetheless familiar sight: The middle of the room was taken up by a black stone archway nearly identical to the one he had seen months ago in Moss Hill.

"Where are we?" Glint mumbled.

As the horolock yanked on levers and activated

several consoles along a wall, the black stones in the arch began to glow blue. The light grew stronger, and eventually the stones let off pulses of electricity, discharging over and over until the discharges connected with one another. The energy then began to meld together and become a solid, fluid substance contained within the arch. Glint was entranced by what was happening, having never experienced such a sight before.

"No time to waste, Mr. Glint," said Owen cheerily.

"Huh — ?" Glint began to say until a sudden push to his back sent him falling straight forward into the blue wall of energy. He tensed up, ready for the shock of his life, but within seconds, he was flat on his face, sprawled against the ground.

"What ... what happened?" Glint groaned, rubbing his sore nose. "Why'd you push me?"

After a few seconds crawled by without an answer, Glint tiredly rolled onto his side in frustration.

"Answer me, or I swear I'll — !" he began to angrily shout, but as Glint's eyes searched for his assistant, he grew silent. He was startled to see that not only was Owen nowhere to be found, but the room Glint was lying in had completely changed.

Instead of being in a cramped lab underground, Glint was now somewhere much brighter, much grander in scale. It looked to him like a library at first glance because two enormous rows of wooden bookshelves were towering over him. Each and every shelf was nearly overflowing with books, tomes, scrolls, boxes, and stacks of papers. Many more writings were piled in heaps on the floor, waiting for their turn to be properly shelved. The bookshelves spanned a great distance and reached an absurd height, but the vaulted stone ceiling far above was even higher. Here and there, a large circular window dotted the ceiling, letting in the afternoon sun to push back the library's shadows.

"Are you … Owen's guest?" a sharp, chillingly clear voice suddenly whispered in Glint's ear. Glint shuddered in fear at hearing that, looking to his side for the source, but nobody was there.

"Yes, he is," Owen answered out of the blue.

Glint jerked his head around and found Owen standing right where Glint had fallen only a moment ago.

"Follow me, Mr. Glint," said Owen, quickly helping Glint stagger to his feet before walking ahead.

Glint was absolutely confused by just about everything now, but he refrained from speaking out of fear. He chose instead to obediently follow behind Owen down the aisle of bookshelves.

Glint tried to keep his mind busy at first with reading the spines of books they passed, seeing if he recognized any of their names, but every so often, a distant clicking and clacking could be heard around them. The new sounds were somewhat eerie and distracting for Glint because he had no idea what was making them. Fortunately, he and Owen soon reached the end of the bookshelves, and Glint's mind became occupied by two enormous stone columns they passed between. He marveled at their size but noted that they were badly damaged, worrying him that they might no longer be strong enough to hold the weight of the ceiling above. With several more columns in the distance, together they formed the circular heart of the library, and in the very center sat a tall, warped, metal throne coated in rust.

"Here we are, Mr. Glint," said Owen softly as he came to a stop at the foot of the throne.

Glint stopped as well, less so because of Owen and more so because he finally noticed that someone was sitting on the throne. The person was draped in rags and wrapped in heavy chains. Glint saw thin, metal fingers resting on the throne's arms, making him think for a moment that it might be another horolock, but Glint also could see the figure's chest heave and breathe like a human being's would. His head hung low, hiding his face from view. Glint wasn't entirely sure, but, from the way the rags draped flat against the throne, it seemed this individual didn't have any legs or feet.

"I am sorry to say," said Owen, speaking louder than a moment ago, "but the spirit in Moss Hill was destroyed."

The cloaked man's fingers clenched and his body moved to sit up, but, as the chains seemed to tighten, he relaxed.

"I had not planned for that to happen," he told Owen in that same clear, cold voice Glint had heard earlier. "Such a waste of potential."

"It is a shame," Owen concurred, "but as you have told me several times before, we still have plenty of spares to take its place."

"Yes, but that spirit was the most receptive ... how is that inventor doing?"

"You mean Silas, sir?" said Owen.

"Yes, him," replied the cloaked man. "I can only observe so much on my own from here."

"Well, his work seems to be coming along nicely, actually," Owen explained, sounding almost surprised to admit it. "The horolocks are starting to function properly and follow commands without issue. I've tested them myself."

"No needless changes planned, I hope?" said the man.

"Nothing I would consider significant enough to worry about," Owen answered.

"Good. I do wish he would be quicker, but I can't ask for much more, can I?"

"I doubt you could from him."

As these two chatted with one another like old friends, Glint had been quietly listening while his thumb instinctively flicked over and over against the wheel of his lighter, but ever since the night of the factory, the lighter had not been able to produce a flame.

"You've never brought company before, Owen," the

man said next, pulling up his hunched head to look Glint over more carefully.

Glint naturally looked up at the mention of the word "company," but he was disgusted to see such pale, inhuman yellow eyes staring back at him.

"Who are you?!" Glint yelled, no longer able to control his temper. "What is this place and why am I here, Owen?! ANSWER ME — !"

Glint started having a coughing fit, having pushed himself too hard. Neither Owen nor the cloaked man spoke as he wheezed hunched over; they patiently waited for Glint to get his coughing under control first. Once he had done so and looked up again, he saw those yellow eyes had thinned as their owner's head tilted to the side, resting on his knuckles.

"Andrew Glint ..." said the cloaked man, "your appearance has changed a great deal, but I recognize that fiery anger you like to wear. Like my old friend, Elm, whom you burned alive, I am a caretaker as well. I am the master of a spirit and one of the shapers of this world ... boy."

Glint felt a freezing chill wash over him from hearing such an answer.

"I have had many names over the centuries —" two colossal horolocks poked their heads out from around the columns, "— but you may call me 'Tock.'"

Similar to how he felt when he fought Elm, Glint was overcome with a mixture of wonder and fear from knowing he was standing before an incredible being.

The quiet library had come to life, with gears and cogs throughout the structure working in unison to turn once more. While the two gargantuan horolocks remained still, dozens upon dozens of normal-sized ones crawled out from everywhere. Some carried long iron mallets, jagged saws, and other tools as they climbed up and down the shelves like a ladder, while others went about organizing the books. Several more stepped forward to present themselves before the single caretaker they all served.

"Ho ... where did all that fervor go?" Tock remarked at Glint, almost mockingly. "Are you that in awe of the great workshop of Ravnell?"

"R-ravnell?!" Glint practically yelped, looking even more startled than before. "We're in Ravnell?"

"You didn't tell him, Owen?" Tock asked.

"No, I did not," Owen replied. "I thought it would be fun to surprise him since he is so interested in this city."

Tock nodded.

"Still playing the role of a fool...." he remarked. "To be clear, Andrew, I don't hold a grudge over Elm's death. He had grown so old and weak over the years ... if you hadn't done it, I would have killed him myself."

Glint wasn't sure if that was really supposed to make him feel relieved.

"W-why am I here?" he asked, unknowingly continuing to click his lighter out of nervous habit.

"I've kept an eye on you for some time," said Tock.

"At first it was out of curiosity, but time and time again, you surpassed my expectations. So much so that — silence, please."

In an instant, every machine throughout the workshop froze perfectly still.

"That's better ... you surpassed my expectations so much so that I wanted to learn more about you. Your excellent work as a spirit hunter, your rise through the government, and even your recent investigation of Moss Hill led me to believe you could be a valuable ally. The night you fought Elm, Owen thought we should leave you there to die, but I thought it would be such a waste, so I sent him to help you."

Glint was startled to hear that. He naturally looked over at Owen for some kind of admission of guilt, but Owen didn't seem troubled in the least.

"Andrew," Tock continued, "this world is built on a lie that I wish to correct as one of its caretakers. I'm close, very close to achieving my goal, but I need help from capable men like you.... Give me that lighter and I will have it fixed," said Tock as a horolock walked up to Glint. "I can see it's damaged, but you have taken very good care of it. A man like you has a role to play far grander than anything you could ever imagine."

Glint was hesitant at first to hand over his lighter to the machine, but, as Tock's words sank in, a rare smile grew across his face.

"I swear, you're as long-winded and vague as Owen, you know that?!" he howled with laughter and a few coughs. "I-I think I understand a little bit, though. You have some kind of big plan in mind and want my help, right? That's fine," Glint dropped his lighter into the horolock's outstretched hands, "I have nothing better to do now, so just tell me what you need done."

Looking smug, Glint then waited to see what this master of spirits had in store for him.

CHAPTER THREE

HAPPY FAREWELL PARTY

H oward, do you know where we're supposed to go next here? I can't remember if we're supposed to turn left or right at the apple carts up ahead ... Howard?"

It was the middle of the day and Tawton was teeming with life as usual. Leon and Howard were both carrying crates full of wine bottles and wedges of cheese as they walked through the city's busy streets. Their hair had gotten longer and Leon was an inch taller, but Howard's habit of reading wherever he went hadn't changed in the slightest. While Leon was struggling not to bump into anyone with his crate, Howard somehow kept his eyes on an open book without taking a single misstep.

"Hey ..." said Leon with a yawn, "are you listening?"

"Yeah," replied Howard halfheartedly.

Leon rolled his eyes, having a hard time believing that.

"Alright," he said, "then which way do we go at the corner up ahead?"

"We turn right," Howard answered with ease. "I'm almost done with my chapter, so let me finish it — wait, stop."

Howard suddenly stopped.

"Hmm?" said Leon, coming to a stop as well.

"Show me the list again," said Howard, quickly putting his crate down on the ground and then sticking out his hand.

"Oh — um, hold on," replied Leon, putting his crate down too. He then pulled out from his pant pocket a folded piece of paper and handed it to Howard, who unfolded it and began to read:

1. Three bottles of Coal Ridge to the Dead Cannery

2. Two bottles of Orange Fin to the Southern Importers (remember to be extra polite and not look the owner in the eye)

3. Three bottles of Savra and half a wheel of Evermold to the Empty Bowl (new shop towards the end of the pier)

4. Pick up an order from Thomas's Glass House

5. Two bottles of Orange Fin, one Rising Night, and two wedges of Krispshard to Dreming Manor (it's the large building close to the cavern's edge)

6. Pick up a dozen lemon cookies and two loaves of fen bread (give the baker the extra bottle of Coal Ridge as a gift)

7. And please pick up the tools at Mr. Quirbly's shop

"Did we miss something?" Leon asked.

"I don't think so," Howard answered, studying the list carefully to be sure. "For some reason, I thought we needed to pick up tea leaves, but Louis didn't write anything about that. We just left Thomas's shop in the middle of town, so ... all we need to do is go right here, pass through the Gem Market, take another right, and then keep going until we reach the cavern's edge. It shouldn't take us too long, I think."

"Lead the way," said Leon, motioning with his crate now back in hand.

After making the turn at the corner and walking down a few blocks, Leon and Howard entered the Gem Market. This part of the city was particularly aggressive and fast paced. Useful ores and precious stones hidden throughout the Weathered Mountains were mined and then brought here to be sold. Merchants could often be seen loudly touting their goods as customers quibbled over prices. As Leon and Howard navigated through the dense crowds, they found two old men standing inches from each other's noses, haggling hard over an enormous pile of coal.

"I can only offer you 40 gold pieces for this quality of coal," the thinner, more stern-looking of the two explained to his merchant adversary.

"40?!" the much larger, much fatter bald merchant howled back, seeming insulted by the offer. "I might as well burn the coal myself for that kind of price!"

"You can bluster all you want," said the old customer, gesturing towards the crowd around them for their support, "but we both know I'm right. The best I can offer is 40 —"

"50," the merchant bluntly countered, crossing his arms.

CHAPTER THREE

For a moment the two old men silently glared in frustration at each other while the crowd murmured over who would give in.

"… I'll offer 40 —"

"50."

"Come on now, it's 40 —"

"50."

"40!"

"50 GOLD PIECES — !"

"40 AND NOT A GOLD MORE, YOU SWINDLER!"

"SWINDLER?!"

"THAT'S RIGHT, YOU HEARD ME!"

"Come on, Leon," said Howard (Leon had stopped to watch this bout between two grizzled veterans of the market). "We don't have all day."

"I want to see who wins, though," Leon replied with somewhat pleading eyes, but Howard looked up from his book, glaring to show how serious he was. Leon grumbled but hurried along.

Once they had worked their way through the market, they found themselves on a much quieter road that snaked parallel with the mouth of the cavern. There was plenty of room between the boys and the edge, and the open sky was easily visible over their heads. With the winter season coming, the sun was setting much earlier, so Leon and Howard were able to watch it on their way to their next stop.

Along the road was a hill that overlooked the cavern's edge, and at its very top sat a tall house. The home was old, a little worn, but fairly sizable, and it had an asymmetrical design to it, something Leon thought made it look unique. The pointed roof was covered with round, slate shingles. The siding was wood, the foundation stone, and most of the windows were tall and thin. A turret protruded from the front left corner while a porch wrapped around the house's right. There were lights on throughout, and a lamp glowed beside the front door.

"Is this the right place?" Leon asked as he and Howard walked up the front steps.

"I think so," Howard replied. "Louis mentioned that it was near the historic district where all the old build-ings are —"

Leon, without a moment's pause, put his crate down and then swung the large brass knocker of the front door hard, thinking he needed to put some effort into it if he wanted to be heard through such a thick wooden door. He knocked loudly several more times and then stepped back to wait for an answer. Howard looked appalled by what Leon had just done. Before he could say anything to admonish him, though, a rather frail, distinguished old gentleman answered the door.

"How may I help you boys?" he asked, but then, noticing the crate of bottles by Leon's feet, he quickly answered himself, saying, "Oh, you are employees of Louis's, I'm sure of it."

"Yes, we are here on behalf of the Sleeping Cheese to make a delivery," said Howard, nodding politely. Not wanting to seem ill-mannered, Leon quickly imitated his friend's courteous gesture.

"Wonderful, my name is Abel Clive," said the old gentleman, happily introducing himself. "I serve the Dreming family. Please, come in."

Leon and Howard both nodded politely again and then followed Abel inside. Upon entering, Leon was somewhat reminded of Tim's home: Everything was a bit messier, but there were books and objects every-where throughout the two-story foyer. There were many paintings of all different sizes hanging on the walls; bowls filled with precious metals and gems were openly on display in a windowed cabinet; and the skeleton of a large tailed beast stood in the corner by the stairs, looking down at those who came to visit. The items in this collection felt grander and brighter than what Tim had owned, as if they were meant more to brag about their owner than simply tell stories of the past.

"If you two would please wait here a moment, I just need to have a quick word with Master Dreming," said Abel. "It shouldn't take long at all."

"We're not in any hurry, Mr. Clive," replied Howard.

"Good, I will be right back then."

Abel then walked to a pair of stained glass doors at the far end of the foyer. He opened one door, stepped inside, and then gently closed it behind himself. Once Leon was sure he heard the door click shut, he put his crate down on the floor and began to stroll about, admiring the room more closely. He walked past a sofa and stopped in front of a tall bookcase filled entirely with red leather books that had caught his eyc. Each book's spine was embossed with gold numerals, but none of them had a title. Leon reached out to —

"Hey, Leon," Howard suddenly spoke up.

"I didn't touch anything," Leon quickly replied, waving his hands in the air. "I was just looking."

"That's not what I was going to say," said Howard, "but yeah, don't, or you'll probably break something." (Leon scowled, not liking that jab.) "Anyway, I want to ask you something."

"Go ahead," Leon yawned.

"Are you really sure you want to come with me?"

Leon stopped eying the books' spines and turned to see Howard looking at him with a serious expression on his face.

"You mean to Pradow?" Leon asked.

"Yes," Howard answered, "I still don't think you've really thought it through —"

"I have," said Leon, wearing a serious expression as well now. "Your boss knows a lot about spirits, right?"

"Yeah," said Howard, "it's — it's a big hobby of his."

"Right, and if I stay in Avaleer, I'm not going to learn anything more about them," Leon explained. "You yourself told me that when we last talked about this."

"Yeah, you're right," Howard agreed.

"I want to know what I'm supposed to do with the

cane," Leon continued. "Tim wanted me to do something with it, fix something he did, I think, but I don't know what that is yet.... You know, I owe it to him to figure it out, Howard."

Howard nodded understandingly.

"My boss would probably have some idea of where to begin," he said. "And I know he would love to get his hands on that cane, but what about your life here? Are you really sure you want to leave Avaleer? We're going somewhere far away, you know."

Leon reflected on those words, thinking about Vellenwood, Maria, and her parents. Even if they were not his real family, they had treated him lovingly like one of their own. They would be sad to see him leave, he was sure of that; however, he also knew he would never be happy leaving things as they were. Not after what Tim had done for them all.

"Mr. Treckle is the sort of man who would understand what I have to do right now," Leon explained to Howard with the same bright grin he wore when they fought in the alleyway. "I'm going with you."

Howard stayed silent at first, but then he smiled back at Leon.

"I'm not paying for your boat fare, Snail Boy," he jabbed, making Leon flustered.

"I wouldn't want you to!" Leon snapped. "I can pay for myself anyway."

"Boys," said Abel, walking back into the room, "I have a package and letter that need to go to Louis.

Master Dreming is too busy planning for a trip at the moment to see you two, but he thanks you and Louis for delivering some of his favorite wines."

"It was no problem at all," Howard said with a quick bow of his head. "Everything Mr. Dreming requested is in this crate. Would you like me to put it somewhere?"

"The table here is fine," said Abel, gesturing with his hand. "I am always impressed to see the bottles of Orange Fin."

"Are they rare?" Leon asked.

"Incredibly so," Abel replied, placing the letter and package into Leon's crate. "You would be hard-pressed to find a single bottle in this part of the world."

Leon was surprised to hear that. He knew Louis had plenty of Orange Fin hiding under the bar counter.

"I can't keep you both any longer," said Abel, "so let me walk you two to the door."

"Thank you, Mr. Clive," said Howard with another bow of the head. Abel lightly smiled and nodded back. He walked them out, and once the door closed, Leon and Howard hurried off down the stairs.

With the sun getting close to setting, Gorn's Cavern was gradually filling with artificial light. Howard and Leon raced through the city, stopping very briefly to pick up the cookies and bread on the list before dashing off to their final stop for the day: Quirbly's Repair Shop.

Leon and Howard stepped inside the familiar shop

and immediately heard Quirbly hammering away at something in the back.

"Is that you, Leon and Howard?" he called out to them.

"Yeah, it's us," Leon answered back.

"Good, good," said Quirbly. "I'm almost finished. I just need to add … there we go! Alright …"

Quirbly walked into the front, wiping his hands on an old rag.

"Sorry about that," he said, taking off his glasses next to wipe them clean of grime. "A lot of work piled up today. I have all the tools Maria needs to keep, um … has she picked out a name yet — ?"

"No," said Howard bluntly.

"Oh, well, I'm sure she'll think of a good one for him. He hasn't spoken again, has he?"

"I don't think so," said Leon, admiring an assortment of small wooden clocks sitting together on a shelf, all ticking in sync.

"Such a shame," Quirbly remarked. "I was so excited when he introduced himself to you, but then he shut down without another word. I guess I should be thankful I got him working at all after that. Anyway, I unfortunately still have a little more work to do, so here are the tools," Quirbly handed Howard a small crate full of bolts and tools. "Tell Maria to take good care of him."

"Sure," said Howard aloofly, plopping the crate on top of the one Leon was holding.

"Thank you, Mr. Quirbly," said Leon, trying not to look too annoyed with Howard and his poor behavior.

They followed Quirbly out, said their goodbyes, and then ran full speed back to the Sleeping Cheese. It wasn't far at all, so they reached the bar in only a matter of minutes, but upon arriving, Leon came to a stop, having noticed the lights weren't on inside.

Maybe Louis isn't feeling well, he thought, though Maria was still there to help run things if need be. The sight worried Leon, but Howard didn't seem to mind: He opened the door as usual and walked straight in. Leon followed closely behind, closing the door gently as if he didn't want to be heard. Then, all at once, the lights sprang on and Leon was greeted by a dozen or so faces he knew well, all shouting, "Happy Birthday!"

With paper decorations and a banner that said "Happy Birthday" in bright, colorful letters, the normally dim and quiet Sleeping Cheese was brimming with life tonight. Neighbors, friends, and patrons were crowded around the circular tables, enjoying wheels of cheese and beverages prepared by Louis.

"Happy Birthday, Leon!" Maria merrily repeated once more. Her hair had grown out a little too, still short but now beginning to brush against her shoulders. Instead of her favorite coat, she was wearing a long-sleeved red dress with black velvet slippers to match. She stood there holding Warren in her arms, excited to see Leon truly surprised by what she and their friends had planned.

"When — when did you all plan this?" Leon asked with an expression full of dismay and joy.

"A while ago," Maria giddily answered. "It was hard keeping it a secret. You almost caught us yesterday making decorations."

"Were you in on this too, Howard?"

"Yeah," Howard calmly replied as he took a seat. "It was my job to keep you busy all day so they could set everything up."

"Hello," a lady's voice was heard at the front door, "am I late?"

Maria moved forward and opened the door for an old friend of Tim's named Malinda Evans. She was a middle-aged woman with slightly long salt-and-pepper hair. She had a lovely face and a bright, sweet disposition that easily showed. As a tailor in love with her craft, she made it a point to always be dressed her best. For the party this evening, she had chosen a long dark blue skirt with a white blouse and matching ribbon tied into a bow around her collar. It all looked perfect on her.

If there was a notable fault to name about Malinda, it had to be her complete inability to keep track of time, and tonight, unfortunately, was no exception. She looked a little out of breath as she stepped inside, most likely from running straight to the shop. When she saw Leon standing there, staring back at her, she sighed in disappointment at herself.

"I was hoping to be on time ..." she said in a sad

tone. "Oh! I did get it done, though, Maria! I have it right here —"

"Shhhh!" said Maria nervously, shutting the door behind Malinda. "Not yet. I want it to be a surprise."

"Oh, you're right, you're right. But, how am I supposed to hide it?" Malinda asked, waving a fairly large wrapped package in her hands. "I can't hold it all night."

"Leon! Howard!" Maria suddenly barked. "Close your eyes."

"Huh — ?" Howard began to say.

"Close them!" Maria shouted.

Leon laughed and did as she said.

"There," said Howard, covering his face with his open book, "happy?"

Leon listened to Maria and Malinda whisper while walking about. Other guests, in the meantime, quietly giggled while watching this all unfold.

"Alright, you can open them," said Maria.

Leon quickly opened his eyes, looking for anything out of place, but Maria had done a good job of hiding whatever it was that Malinda had brought.

"Have a seat, have a seat, please," said Louis in his gentle voice, walking out from the back with a tray containing a steaming tea pot and several pale yellow teacups. As he poured Howard a cup first, he added, "Everything tonight is on the house, of course, so, everyone, please enjoy yourselves."

With that said, the room filled with cheers and the

party continued. Leon, Howard, and Maria all sat together at a table, sipping Brumstead tea as the adults talked amongst themselves. Several discussed work while others chatted about recent news or how their families were doing. It was nice, thought Leon, that everyone could take a night to stop and relax.

"I need to remember to thank Louis later for all this," he remarked.

"Yeah, you do," Howard replied.

"It was really no trouble at all," said Louis, taking a seat between Howard and Maria. "I always love to find an excuse to celebrate like this. It's so nice to see my home so lively ... are those the items from Mr. Quirbly's shop, Leon?"

"Wha — yeah, they are —"

"Let me see!" said Maria excitedly as she pawed at the crate on the table. "Pendle will be so happy to have these."

"*Pendle*?" Leon and Howard both questioned back in unison.

"Hmm?" replied Maria.

"Who is Pendle?" Howard asked.

"Oh! I'm talking about our horolock. I finally came up with a name for him when you two were out. He has a habit of rocking back and forth, so I named him that."

"What a fine name," Louis remarked as he sipped on a cup of tea.

"Yes," Howard sarcastically agreed.

"I'll be right back," said Maria, standing up. "I need to get something from the kitchen."

Once she was out of sight, Louis put his cup down and leaned forward, gesturing for Leon and Howard to do the same.

"You two will be heading out tomorrow morning," he whispered.

"Huh?" said Leon.

"My cousin has informed me that there is a ship going up north to Volgiev soon, something quite rare this time of year."

"Volgiev?" Leon repeated. "Aren't we going east to Pradow?"

"Yes, but you need to sail by Volgiev and make a slight arc to reach Pradow," Louis explained. "It's much easier than going straight across. You avoid terribly dangerous seas."

"That makes sense," said Leon, trying to imagine a map of these places in his mind.

"I think this is your best chance to leave, so I arranged for you two to be taken aboard that ship. While this may be a celebration for your birthday, Leon, I also thought we could have a farewell party for you both as well."

"What are you all whispering about?" said Maria, having just returned, and with Pendle in tow. The horolock was covered head to toe in heavy clothes, perfectly disguised so that none of the guests present had any idea he was a machine.

"Oh, it's not really a secret, I was just having some fun. we were discussing plans for when Howard and Leon should —"

"Louis!" Leon suddenly barked over him. "Th-that's a — um — a surprise!"

As Leon finished nervously speaking, Louis and Howard's eyes started to grow wide.

"You didn't tell her that you're included in all this?" said Louis worriedly.

"Leon," Howard spoke firmly, "you have to tell her, now."

"He's right," Louis said in agreement as his index finger anxiously tapped against the lip of his teacup. "She has a right to know."

"But —"

"What do they mean, Leon?" Maria asked. "What do you need to tell me?"

"I'm ..." Leon was struggling with his words, but he knew how painfully right Louis and Howard were, "I'm leaving with Howard tomorrow for Pradow."

What little color there was in Maria's face drained right out. She looked as startled as could be. Seconds seemed to crawl by for Leon and everyone else at the table before she finally responded to the news.

"Tomorrow?" she asked in a lifeless voice.

"Yes," said Louis, standing up as he tried desperately to diffuse the situation, "I know it is sudden, but this was the best opportunity I could find. Boats rarely go north, especially around this time of year. I never imagined you didn't know, though — Leon," he turned to give Leon a concerned look, "I still can't believe you didn't tell her! Traveling to Pradow is not a small matter you fail to tell your friends!"

"Oh," Malinda spoke up happily, holding a sloshing mug in hand, "Leon, if I'd known you were leaving, I would have made a coat for you!"

"I … I want …" Maria mumbled, the color slowly returning to her pale cheeks.

"Quickly, stand up, stand up for me," Malinda continued, pulling on Leon's arm. "It won't take long."

"This might not be the best time for that, Malinda," said Louis worriedly.

"It's fine —" Malinda pressed on without a care, tugging even harder.

"I want … to go …"

"— I'm just gonna measure his arms real quick to see if I have anything that might —"

"I WANT TO GO TOO!" Maria shouted over Malinda, looking at Leon defiantly. "You aren't leaving me behind again!"

Leon had expected her to tell him not to go, but he never imagined she would actually want to tag along with him.

"You can't!" he shouted back, standing up. "Your mom and dad are already worried sick about you as it is! What about your farm?"

"None of that matters," said Maria, shaking her head. "My parents will eventually understand. It's more important right now that we figure out what to do with Tim's cane. That's why you're going with Howard, right?"

"Y-yeah, it is, but … h-how do you know that?" Leon questioned, genuinely curious.

"I'm not dumb, Leon," said Maria, sounding very frustrated with him. "You've looked like you've had something on your mind ever since the night we left Gildfoil. You haven't told me what it is, but it's not hard to guess."

Leon nodded, looking a bit surprised to know she had been so observant.

"You're right," he admitted, "but it's not your fault Tim ended up in the factory, so you shouldn't feel responsible for what —"

"But I am! You all got caught up in that very mess when you found me at that office, remember? I want to help so we can go back home together someday. Besides, we need to find who built Pendle so he can go home too."

Leon shook his head. No matter how convincing Maria was, Leon was not going to risk something bad happening to her.

"I don't care what the reason is," he said sternly, "*you* are not going anywhere. It's too dangerous!"

"But —"

"Leon's right," Howard spoke up. "You don't have a real reason to go, and I am definitely not taking that *thing* with me."

Howard had no trouble showing his contempt for Pendle, no matter how docile the machine acted.

"I ... I want to go too," Maria's eyes were welling up with tears, but Leon would not budge on this.

"No, I won't let you," he said firmly.

Trying her best not to cry, Maria swiftly turned and stormed away. Pendle scratched his head while Malinda grabbed hold of Leon's arm.

"Let's, um, get you measured real quick," she said, doing her best to cut the awkward tension that had filled the room.

CHAPTER FOUR

THE HUNGRY FLOUNDER

E ver since Tim's cane had tried latching itself onto Leon's hands in Silas's office, Leon had been wary of holding it. Pendle had been the one to carry it back to Tawton, and now, as Leon sat on the edge of his bed, he stared at the mysterious spirit weapon leaning in the corner, untouched for months.

"Are you done packing?" Howard asked from the doorway, holding a leftover lemon cookie from yesterday's party. "We need to get going if we want to make it on time."

"Yeah," Leon replied.

"Good," said Howard, taking a bite of his cookie while stepping back into the hallway.

Leon got up and walked to the corner where the cane was waiting. He stopped right in front of it and for a moment, just stared tentatively before taking a long, deep breath to calm himself. He then reached out and lightly pressed his fingers against the cane's wooden body. He was ready for it to react to the slightest touch, but oddly ... nothing happened. That was certainly unexpected, thought Leon, to say the least. He gripped the cane harder, yet it still acted normal. As Leon then took it in both hands, he was almost a little disappointed.

"Come on, Snail Boy," Howard mockingly called out to him from the hallway. Leon groaned at that nickname, but hurried along after him.

Leon walked out of his room and down the hallway until he reached the door to Maria's bedroom right next to the top of the stairs. There he stopped and leaned on Tim's cane. Ever since their argument last night, Maria had locked herself in her room and had not said a word to anyone. Leon stared at the door with a sad expression, unsure of what to do.

"Maria," he eventually spoke in a soft, quiet voice, "I'm … I'm going now. I'm sorry, but I-I just can't let something bad happen to you."

There was no answer from the other side, but Leon imagined she could hear him.

"I'm —"

"Come on, Leon," Howard shouted from downstairs in the kitchen.

"Coming," Leon shouted back. He then spoke in a hurried whisper to the door, saying, "I have to go now, Maria, I'm sorry."

Leon then immediately darted down the stairs, afraid that Maria might now actually say something. He yanked his bag off the kitchen floor at the bottom of the steps and strode right past Howard and Louis, both of whom were standing next to each other while enjoying a cup of tea.

"Would you like some morning tea, Leon?" Louis asked.

"No, thank you," Leon replied from just outside the kitchen doorway.

"You ready?" Howard asked.

"Yeah, let's go," Leon answered.

"Alright," said Howard, putting his teacup down on the kitchen counter. "Louis, thank you for everything. Hopefully I can come visit you again someday."

"It was a pleasure to have you here, Mr. Wavern," said Louis, putting his cup down as well. "Look after Leon and Warren."

"Warren?" Howard questioned back.

"Yes, he will be going with you two, of course," said Louis, pointing behind Howard.

Howard turned and saw the cat was sleeping on top of his backpack, looking very comfortable.

"He will be very helpful," Louis assured him.

Howard sighed, but didn't voice any complaints. He put his bag on his shoulders (being as gentle as possible not to wake Warren) and then proceeded out of the kitchen to the front of the shop. There he found Leon standing beside Pendle, who had been sitting quietly at the bar counter all this time.

Leon saw Howard was ready to leave, so he turned and said, "Bye, Pendle," patting the horolock on the shoulder. Pendle turned his head, and, though it took him a moment, he slowly nodded.

Howard had no parting words to give the machine, choosing instead to go to the front door, open it wide, and wait outside.

"Goodbye, Louis," said Leon, to which Louis happily nodded.

"Have a safe journey, you three," he said.

"We will," Leon replied. "I'll try to write when I can."

"I look forward to hearing all about your journey."

Leon beamed hearing that. He waved goodbye with cane in hand and then stepped outside, closing the door behind him.

Once the door was shut closed, Louis nodded to himself.

"… So much to do," he remarked, turning around, "never a moment to rest."

He strolled to behind the bar and stopped in front of Pendle, who had remained quietly sitting this entire time.

"I would like to ask you a few questions, Pendle, if that is alright with you," said Louis, reaching for a balled up rag on the counter.

Pendle slowly nodded.

"Good," said Louis, unfolding the rag, "you still don't recall who had modified you, correct?"

Again, Pendle nodded.

"Right, and you don't know if it was someone working at the Wrivenworth factory, either, do you?"

Once more, Pendle nodded.

"Have … have you ever heard of someone by the name of *Tock* before?"

Though it took him a moment to respond, Pendle eventually shook his head slowly side to side.

Louis folded the rag into a neat, perfect square and then stared at Pendle, studying the horolock's glass eyes carefully.

"To be perfectly honest, I still don't trust you very much," he said, "but Maria seems to like you a great deal, and she believes you were responsible for saving her and her friends from the factory, so I'm going to trust her judgment for now and not worry. However," Louis's voice grew eerily heavier, "if you do anything to disappoint her, I'll make you pay. You understand?"

Pendle nodded.

"Good," said Louis, sounding more like his usual self as he reached under the counter. He then pulled Tim's sack of worldly goods out from under and placed it on the bar.

"Please look after this bag until I come back down," Louis instructed, to which Pendle nodded once more.

Louis then turned and walked through the kitchen and up the stairs, stopping right at the top in front of Maria's room. There he then stood in silence for a moment, staring at the grains in the door's wood. Eventually, he took a deep breath through his nose and then gently knocked on the door.

"Maria, may I come in?" he asked.

A few long seconds passed before Maria replied.

"... Y-yes," she sniffled.

Louis opened the door and found her lying in the dark, curled under the covers. She sat up, hugging a pillow while rubbing her tired red eyes. Her hair was a bit ruffled in places, and she was still wearing the dress from yesterday evening.

"I-I'm sorry," she said, but Louis shook his head.

"I understand that you just don't want to lose your precious friend," he said, plopping down on the end of the bed. "A long, long time ago, I knew a girl just like you who also wanted to help her friends. I worried something bad might happen if she did, and unfortunately, my fears came true."

Maria was saddened to hear him end his story like that, but Louis had a little more to say.

"However," he continued, patting her feet, "it was her choice to make. Everyone has their own journey in life they must take, you included."

Louis reached into his apron pocket and pulled out a tiny yellow vial. He then picked up the sleeve of Maria's coat hanging off the end of the bed, studying the moon and feather.

"In many ways, I was more shocked to meet you that day than I was to hear of Mr. Halvahn's passing," Louis remarked. "I doubt that foolish fellow told you a thing, but I know he has great expectations for you. After all, he wouldn't give such important treasures like these to just anyone."

Maria's eyes came to life as she realized Louis was not referring to Tim, but to the mysterious gentleman.

"Do — do you know him?" she asked. "The masked man?"

"Yes, I do, but I am bound by a promise not to talk

about him. I can only aid you with this small vial of ink. You see, if you wish with all your might to go somewhere, and draw your dream in the sky, you will get there in no time. Now, I've packed some of your things already, but you need to get dressed quickly, or you might miss your boat —"

Maria lunged forward and hugged Louis as hard as she could, crying into his chest.

"Thank you so much, Louis!" she wailed. "T-thank you!"

Louis patted her gently on the head as a small tear welled in his eye.

"You had better hurry," he said.

"Yeah," Maria answered him back with a giddy expression on her face.

"Do you have everything you need, Mr. Glint?" asked Owen.

They were back in the wasteland, though Glint looked much more refreshed than when he had first arrived to this barren place the day before. His bandaged body was protected from the wind by a new coat and his face wore a relaxed, calm expression. In his hand was his repaired lighter, looking as polished and pristine as could be. Flicking it open once to be sure, Glint watched a bright flame shoot out. He smiled at it, flicked the lighter closed, and then pulled a smooshed carton from his pants pocket. After picking out a cigarette, he lit it and took a drawn-out puff.

"Yeah, I think so," he said, doing his best to blow out a cloud of smoke without having a coughing fit. "I'll go find what Tock wanted from the next lab and activate the arch."

"Yes, and soon afterward we will get in contact with you about what to do next," said Owen.

"You sure I need those two with me?" Glint asked. "They kind of stick out."

He was referring to the two cloaked figures sitting in the front of the car, silently waiting.

"Of course," said Owen. "The horolocks will be very useful, I promise."

"Ha," Glint chuckled. "I guess I've got no reason to doubt you, so I won't complain. Let me ask, though, why do you keep calling those machines that name?"

"The horolocks?" said Owen.

"Yeah," Glint replied, pointing at Owen. "I've never heard Silas call them that. A recent idea of his?"

"That's just what they were originally named," said Owen, shrugging.

"Huh," said Glint, unsure of what to make of that answer. Instead of pressing that matter any further, he looked around and said, "You really don't need a ride? We are kind of in the middle of nowhere."

"You don't need to worry, Mr. Glint," Owen replied with a smile. "Seeing you act so kind towards me is out of character."

Glint let out a loud, wheezy laugh at hearing that.

"You know, you're right," he said with a wicked grin. Without another word, he walked to the car, waving goodbye. A moment later, the horolocks were driving him away to the east, back to Avaleer.

It took Leon and Howard most of their day to ride Gorn's Elevator down the mountain and then walk to the tiny port town of Dampshore where their boat was waiting. Once there, Leon found himself admiring the buildings, thinking they were just like the ones in the center of Vellenwood, but he also noted that the vast sea in the distance, the somewhat clearer sky, and the smell of salty air were all things far different from what he was used to experiencing in his swampy valley world. Eventually he and Howard reached the docks where many large vessels sat floating on the water as men loaded and unloaded cargo from them as fast as they could.

"Look for the name on the side of the boat," Howard instructed Leon as they walked between the boats. "The old men back there told us the *Hungry Flounder* should be somewhere up ahead."

"Louis didn't say what it looked like?" Leon asked.

"No, just the name," Howard replied.

There were boats of all kinds present. Some were more modern, being powered by steam and coal, while others still relied on wind to get them from place to place. Leon was excited to see which one would be taking them up north until he spotted a particularly old wooden ship sitting at the very end of the pier. He didn't want to believe it to be so, but as they drew closer, his heart sank further.

"Howard, I … I think it's that one," he said, half-heartedly pointing at the faded name *Hungry Flounder* painted on the wooden ship's worn hull. Howard, who was looking side to side at each vessel, looked forward and grew a disappointed look on his face as well.

"It could be worse, I suppose," he remarked somewhat sarcastically, and Leon nodded in agreement.

They walked up a thin, wobbly ramp to the deck of the ship, and there they found a handful of men preparing their vessel for its sea voyage.

"Who are you kids?" said a plump man with a fat red nose and wary-looking eyes. His hair was thinning, and the brown cap sitting slightly off-center on his head was doing a poor job of hiding it, though Leon imagined he didn't care much.

"Hello, sir," said Howard with a quick, polite nod. "Our friend Louis should have sent your captain —"

"I'm the captain," the man interjected quite gruffly. "Ernest. You two?"

"Oh, I'm Leon."

"And my name is Howard. It is good to meet you, Ernest. Louis should have sent you a letter —"

"He did," Ernest interrupted yet again.

Howard waited briefly to see if he had anything more to add before continuing.

"He should have sent you a letter about us coming. I have the payment —"

"I could have sworn he only mentioned one person," Ernest interrupted yet again. Leon could tell Howard was having a hard time remaining polite.

"No —"

"I can't just give rides to every single kid that wanders by —"

"Louis," Leon interrupted this time, placing his bag on the ground, "is so grateful for your help that he had us bring you gifts for your troubles."

"Gifts?" said Ernest.

Leon nodded. He then crouched down and pulled out a quarter of a wheel of cheese and a bottle of wine. Ernest's somewhat bored look brightened a great deal.

"I have a bottle of Purple Orchard," Leon explained (having memorized a few lines Louis had taught him to say to customers), "a rare vintage of apple wine from the oldest distiller in all of Sotshire."

"And the cheese?" Ernest asked eagerly, doing nothing to contain his excitement. "Is ... is that actually woolly goat cheese?"

"You are correct," said Leon with a smile.

It took Ernest a moment to stop gawking and collect some of his composure.

"It's-it's one thing after another today with that damn mouse," he said, shaking his finger at Leon and

Howard. "he's lucky I have such a big heart! Ralph," he shouted over his shoulder.

"Captain?" one of the crewmen shouted back from behind a tall crate.

"Show these two to their hammocks," Earnest commanded. "You two, we're departing in half an hour."

Ernest then walked past Leon and Howard. Leon smirked at Howard, feeling quite proud of himself for appeasing the grumpy captain of the ship.

"You two, follow me," said the voice belonging to whom Leon imagined must be Ralph. Leon and Howard turned their heads and saw an average-looking man with long, dark brown hair, slightly tanned skin, and a very pointed nose.

"You're Ralph, right?" Leon asked to be sure.

"That's right," said Ralph. "This way, follow me. Most of the cargo is down below," he pointed as he led them into the ship. "We all eat over there in the galley — don't eat the pickles if you can help it — Captain's room is farther up ahead, bunch of us sleep below, and your beds are down the stairs on the bottom floor. Make yourselves comfortable, I still need to help Norton get a few things ready before we leave."

And with that, Ralph's tour was abruptly over. He went right back to the deck, leaving Leon and Howard to show themselves the rest of the way around.

"Well, now that we've been overwhelmed with information ..." Howard dryly joked, taking the lead. Leon chuckled, agreeing with his sentiment.

They walked down two flights of creaking stairs and found themselves in the belly of the ship where the cargo was stored. It was cold, hard to see, and the air smelled a bit stale. Right next to the stairs were several shabby hammocks strung from beams in the low ceiling.

"Which one you want?" Leon asked, trying his best not to sound too disappointed in the accommodations.

"I don't care," Howard replied, plopping his backpack down. Warren hopped off and stretched his legs.

"I guess I'll take the closest one —"

"W-wait," a voice spoke up from amongst the cargo. A moment later, a tall man with horribly overgrown grayish brown hair and a long, wild beard stumbled out. He looked to Leon like he was wearing an expensive suit, except it was very wrinkled and covered in specks of dirt and dust. In his arms he was hugging a bucket like it were the most precious item in the world.

"Please, could-could I ..." he said, sounding almost winded, "could I please k-keep that one? It's got a few boxes by it, so it's perfect for my bucket."

"Um, s-sure," said Leon, not really understanding his point.

"Oh, thank you!" the man sighed with relief, sitting down on a crate. "It-it's nice to know I'll have company. My name is Charles. What's yours?"

"I'm Leon, and this is Howard."

"Well those are fine n-names ... do you by chance know if we are departing soon?"

"I think the captain said in about half an hour," said Leon.

"Half an hour ... well, we might as well relax until then," Charles remarked, reclining on the crates.

"Yeah," Leon agreed.

After putting his bag down, he pulled himself up onto a hammock (it took him a couple of tries), and then he reached down and grabbed Tim's cane leaning on a post. Holding the cane tightly in his hands, Leon was curious to know now why it was so well-behaved. All day on their way here he had been holding it, but the cane never once reacted in the slightest. Leon still didn't know much about spirits, but if one lived in the cane, he imagined then that perhaps he needed to do something special for it to act.

Hey, Howard," Leon called down to Howard who was sitting on his backpack, reading while petting Warren on his lap, "how do you make sparks come out of your daggers?"

"What makes you ask?" Howard questioned back.

"Just curious," Leon replied with a slight yawn.

"Well," Howard shut his book closed, "you need to concentrate hard. My boss taught me that you need to imagine you are speaking to the weapon with your mind."

"With my mind ...?" Leon repeated, finding that explanation a little too vague. Closing his eyes, he gave it a try anyway.

Wake up ... wake up ... he told the cane in his head.

Time to get up … hey, wake up, please … Over and over Leon kept trying for several minutes until finally he opened his eyes back up in frustration and said, "Nothing's happening."

"Let me see it," said Howard, standing up. "You probably aren't doing it right."

Leon rolled his eyes at the know-it-all.

"Here," he said, playfully poking Howard in the shoulder with the cane. Howard, not looking very amused, grabbed the cane and yanked it away. As he then took hold of it with both hands, Leon could see a slightly excited expression growing on his face. Howard briefly admired the cane, rolling it in his fingertips. He then closed his eyes. As his brow furrowed, it looked like he was concentrating hard. A minute or so went by before he finally opened his eyes back up.

"Well?" said Leon.

"Nothing," Howard replied, seeming a bit perplexed as he studied the cane more closely. "Normally I get some kind of reaction, but the cane feels completely empty."

"M-maybe it doesn't like you?" said Charles.

Both Leon and Howard were surprised to hear him join in on their conversation. They turned their heads and saw him sitting up, watching them.

"You know about spirit weapons?" Howard asked, sounding skeptical.

"Just a bit," said Charles. "Sometimes they get picky with how — y-you use them."

"I guess you aren't doing it right then, Howard," said Leon smugly.

Howard, rolling his eyes, shoved the cane back into Leon's hands.

"I'm going to go ask the captain something," he said, turning around.

"Ask him what?" said Leon.

"I'll tell you when I get back," said Howard, walking up the stairs. "Keep practicing."

Howard left, and now Leon was alone with Charles, who was staring into his bucket.

"Did I say something wrong?" Charles wondered. "He seemed mad."

"No, he's always like that," Leon replied, and then he closed his eyes. For a minute or so he called to the spirit in his mind like before, but eventually he grew bored and opened his eyes back up. He saw Charles still sitting there, staring wearily into space.

"Charles, can I ask you something?" said Leon.

"Sure," Charles gladly replied.

"You're Avalean, right?"

"Yes, I am."

"How do you know anything about spirits then?"

"Because there aren't any in — in Avaleer, right?" said Charles with a weak smile.

"Yeah," Leon answered.

"Well, I travel from t-time to time for work. Not too often, but enough that I — I get to see the world b-beyond our shores. Is this your first trip?"

"It is," said Leon. "Until recently, I'd never left my home before."

"Don't worry, y you get to see spirits and all kinds of other interesting things that — that don't exist where we live."

"Like clover kings?" said Leon.

Charles smiled.

"If you're lucky, y-you might," he said. "If you don't mind me ask — asking, where'd you get t-that cane? A weapon like that isn't common, especially here."

"A, um ... a friend gave it to me," Leon quietly answered him.

Charles nodded. For a brief moment neither said a word, both lost in thought, but then Charles suddenly groaned loudly.

"Nooooo!" he moaned, sounding miserable. "I — I thought we had more time!"

"Hmm?" said Leon. He then noticed the belly of the boat was slightly swaying. "Are we moving, Charles?"

"Y-yes," moaned Charles, his head deep in the bucket. "We're m-moving — ohhh.... G-go out — and have a look," Charles struggled to say. "T-the view — is — is nice."

Leon was more concerned at the moment, though, with Charles's health than what the boat was doing.

"Are you okay — ?" Leon began to ask, but Charles waved his hand back and forth to reassure Leon.

"Just — a bit motion sick," he awkwardly laughed. "I'll be better if I just close m-my eyes and sleep it off.

Go and take a look before we — we get too far from the coast."

"... Alright," Leon finally gave in.

He awkwardly climbed out of his hammock, took a brief moment to quickly stretch his back, and then turned to leave —

"Don't forget your cane," Charles spoke up.

Leon turned back around and saw Charles still had his head in his bucket, but his hand was pointing at the hammock where Tim's cane lay (Leon thought he could just leave it there for the time being).

"It was your friend's, w-wasn't it?" Charles spoke into his bucket, breathing a bit hard. "Take good care of it."

Leon realized then how bad it would be if something were to happen to the spirit weapon.

"You're right," he admitted, grabbing the cane. "I'll keep it with me."

Charles slightly nodded with his head still in the bucket.

"Hurry — along," he then groaned.

Leon smiled, doing his best not laugh.

With Warren bounding ahead, Leon walked up the stairs, enjoying the swaying feeling of the boat far more than Charles was. After reaching the top, he turned left and walked out onto the deck, where he was amazed to see nothing but open water all around the ship. The docks and boats that had surrounded them only a little while ago were now quickly shrinking from view. The crew didn't seem as enamored as Leon was, working tirelessly to make sure their departure went smoothly.

Howard was standing by himself against the railing of the deck, leaning on it as he watched the boat sail away. Leon walked up and stood next to him without saying anything.

"Taking a break?" Howard asked.

"Yeah," Leon replied as he leaned his head over the edge to get a better look. He had ridden on a few row boats in the past, but none of them traveled through the water as fast as this boat. The coast was growing more and more distant as they headed for deeper waters. At the same rate, Leon was realizing just how grand and vast the ocean really was.

"So," he eventually spoke up, "what did you ask the captain?"

"Just how long he thinks it will take to reach our destination," replied Howard.

"And?"

"A little under a week, Snail Boy."

"That doesn't seem too bad," Leon yawned.

"Yeah, I was expecting closer to ten days, so that was good news. We still need to find another boat when we stop in Volgiev that's going east. It might take us a while —"

"Hey, you two, time to eat."

Leon and Howard turned and saw a man who looked and sounded just like Ralph, but he was dressed differently, wore glasses on the tip of his nose, and was a few inches shorter.

"Are you Ralph's brother?" Leon asked.

"Yeah, we're twins. My name's Norton. What are your names?"

"I'm Leon."

"And I'm Howard."

"Glad to meet you two," said Norton, giving each of them a quick, firm handshake. "Food's almost ready, so follow me, I'll take you to the galley. Oh, but don't eat the pickles if you can help it, though."

Leon and Howard both smiled from hearing his warning, being reminded of his brother. They followed Norton inside, walking past the stairs.

"We actually have a couple new faces here today," said Norton as he led the way. "One or two of them should be joining us."

"Does that include Charles?" Leon asked. He was still a little worried about him.

"No," Norton shook his head. "I left him sleeping and moaning down below in his hammock. He's not gonna want to eat anything for a while."

"How come?" Howard asked.

"Seasick," said Norton.

"Oh," Howard slightly grimaced, "that's not good."

"Yeah, it's not, but hopefully he will get over it in a day or two. Most people do."

Just as they reached the door to the galley, a familiar voice was heard from the other side.

"... He likes wildowart tails a lot."

No, Leon told himself with a worried expression quickly growing on his face. *There's no way she —*

Norton swung the door open, and Leon and Howard both froze, stunned as could be to see Maria and Pendle sitting on a bench, talking to the boat's young cook.

"Smells great in here, Robby," said Norton.

"Yeah, it does," Maria agreed, turning her head to see who else had come to join them. It was then that she saw her two friends standing in the doorway, staring at her with shocked eyes. Letting an awkward smile slip, she bashfully waved at them.

"Hi, guys —"

"WHAT ARE YOU DOING HERE?!" Leon yelled so loudly that the entire boat heard him.

"Calm down —" Maria said nervously.

"Turn this boat around!" Leon howled. "She needs to go home!"

"Stop yelling, Leon!" shouted Maria, shooting up from her seat. "You don't get to tell me where I go!"

"But —"

"AND," Maria was cowing him now with a horrible glare, "you fools forgot to bring Tim's bag with you," she said, pointing at the sack sitting next to Pendle.

Leon and Howard both looked at the bag and then at each other nervously, knowing she was right.

"No more complaining," said Maria sternly, crossing her arms. "The boat has departed, so you both are stuck with me whether you like it or not! B-besides ... don't you want your gifts?"

Leon and Howard were both perplexed yet intrigued by what these *gifts* might be. They slowly sat down across from Maria, folded their hands, and waited for her to continue. Knowing now that she had finally pacified them, Maria sat back down and then leaned to the side.

I was going to give these yesterday," she explained, rummaging through her bag, "but ... anyway, let's start with this one for you, Leon."

Maria pulled from her bag a fairly large, square-shaped present wrapped in green paper and placed it on the table in front of Leon. Without saying a word, he slid the gift a little closer towards himself. Leon then briefly admired the gift, guessing in his head what it might be, before ripping the lovely wrapping apart and finding a wooden box hidden inside. Its lid was covered in beautiful carvings with the words "Whimsy & Co." engraved in the center. Leon knew they were a famous toy company, but the box didn't tell him much about what its contents were. He undid the metal latches on each side and lifted the lid, revealing a collection of shiny marbles sitting in little indentations. There were quite a few colors represented, though one side was mostly reds, yellows, and oranges while the other was greens, blues, and purples.

"There's more," Maria said excitedly, "pick up the tray."

"Okay," said Leon, still trying to look upset with her for sneaking aboard (though he was doing a poor job of it at this point). He followed her instructions, carefully picking up the tray of marbles and finding a folded board underneath. He then put the tray aside and pulled out the board.

"So, what am I looking at?" he asked as he unfolded it on the table.

"It's called *taw*," Maria explained as she picked up a large white marble from the tray. "It's a popular game people like to play in Tawton. Each color has its own rules for jumping around the board with the goal of capturing the taw piece to win. It looked like fun, so I thought you would like it."

"I do," said Leon warmly, smiling. "Thank you."

Maria smiled back, looking pleased.

"And for you, Howard," she then said, rummaging once again through her bag, "it's getting cold, and I know yours is thin and full of holes, so ..." Maria handed Howard the next present: a beautiful heavy coat. It was made of a smooth, chocolate brown suede leather, and its inside and collar were lined with matching dark fur.

Howard stood up and tried it on right away.

"It's so soft," he remarked, looking amazed. "I hope this didn't cost too much."

"Don't worry," Maria waved off his worries, "Malinda gave me a discount when I told her who it was for. I was going to give it to you yesterday since I didn't know if we'd get the chance to celebrate your birthday, but then … well —"

"Thank you, Maria," said Howard, wearing a rare bright smile on his face.

"It suits you well … Howard," said Pendle.

Leon, Howard, and Maria's eyes all immediately turned towards the horolock.

"Did you just talk, Pendle?" Maria asked, unsure but excited at the prospect.

"Yes," Pendle plainly answered.

"He's finally talking again!" said Leon, pointing excitedly at the horolock. "He even knows your name, Howard!"

"While I had been unable to communicate properly … with you all," Pendle explained, "I was still able to learn your names from … passing conversations each day. For instance …" he paused momentarily as if his mind was stalling, "the small feline sleeping next to Leon is named Warren."

"Oh, me next! What's my — ?"

"Alright, so you know everyone's names," Howard interrupted Maria. "Now explain why you saved us from the factory."

Pendle said nothing for almost half a minute. Leon didn't mind, and Maria was content staring giddily at her machine, but Howard's normally calm demeanor was crumbling fast. Leon could see him growing increasingly irritated as they listened to Robby hum while slowly stirring a large pot of soup.

"Well — ?"

"I believe ... I was asked to protect you all. I was told ... to keep you safe and ... help you learn the truth behind this world."

"Truth? What do you mean by *truth*?"

"I don't know ..."

"Who asked you to protect us then?" Howard's voice was growing louder and angrier with each question he asked.

"I ... don't know ..."

"Well that doesn't tell us much!" Howard shouted.

"Hey, stop yelling, you little crank," Maria snapped back in place of her slow-to-speak horolock. "If he doesn't know, then he doesn't know!"

"I am sorry that I ... can not be of more help, Howard. My maker must have known ... about you all somehow."

"Well, let's assume that's true for a moment," said Howard, still sounding quite angry. "It's probably because this maker was a friend of Tim's, but that doesn't do us much good since Tim was over 100 years old and had been everywhere imaginable. So we are looking for a mechanical genius that could be anywhere now. I'm sure someone like that will be easy to find in no time!"

"Calm down, Howard," said Maria. "We still have some of Tim's belongings as clues."

"Except we haven't been able to open the bag," said Leon.

CHAPTER FOUR

The cords around the neck of Tim's sack had been tied with an incredibly elaborate knot that no one had been able to undo. They thought about cutting it open to see what was inside, but no one wanted to damage one of the few items left behind by their lost friend.

"We'll think of something —" Maria began to say, but she stopped as they all heard a loud crash from below.

"What was that?" said Leon.

"Don't worry," said Robby, continuing to stir his pot, "crates tip over all the time at the start of a voyage. We're on a ship after all —"

Several more crashes were heard, followed by a man yelling.

"Well that doesn't sound good," Robby remarked, sounding a bit more worried now. "Norton, can you go — oh, he's not here. When did he leave?"

"No idea," said Maria.

"Yeah, I didn't see him leave either," said Leon. He and Maria then looked at Howard, but Howard just shrugged.

"He left ... right as Leon and Howard ... sat down," said Pendle.

"He must have forgotten to do something, I bet," said Robby. "Um, I'm a little busy here, so could one of you go see what's going on for me?"

"I'll go," Leon volunteered.

"I'm coming too," said Maria, standing up from her seat.

"It's not —" Leon was about to object, but Maria stared daggers at him, daring him to try and say *no*.

Another crash was heard and several men were now shouting.

"Fine," Leon sighed, standing up. He then turned and opened the door to the kitchen; immediately, he was hit by a dense wall of fog.

"What's happening?" he said, swiping at the fog.

"Oh," said Robby, "looks like we got some murhs on board."

"Murhs?" Leon and Maria both questioned back.

"They're fog spirits," Howard explained, studying the foggy hallway carefully. "You can find groups of them floating over the sea. They're harmless, but they make it hard for ships to navigate."

"I don't see any —" Leon fell silent as he caught sight of little blue orbs floating gently through the fog. They approached him, and Leon realized they were a pair of bright glowing eyes. They looked over him and then Maria before floating off back into the fog. Another crash was then heard below.

"We'd better go see what's happening," said Howard, walking straight into the fog without a care.

"Yeah," Leon mumbled in agreement, but he did not take a single step forward. He was too in shock from knowing he had just seen a spirit for the first time in his life. Even after witnessing firsthand the power of Tim's cane, he had still found it hard to put much credence in what Howard had often told him, that all kinds of spirits supposedly existed outside of Avaleer. But now, after seeing those eyes, his mind was overwhelmed with thoughts of just how many spirits there might actually be. How big or little could they grow? What colors do they come in? What do they eat? Were they nice or mean — ?

"Are you guys coming?" Howard called out from the fog.

"Y-yes," both Leon and Maria answered.

Having come back to his senses now with a smile, Leon glanced over his shoulder and saw Maria standing behind him like he were a shield, waiting for him to proceed. It still took Leon a few seconds more to find a bit of courage, but he soon enough stepped into the fog as well, and Maria followed right behind.

With Howard taking the lead, Leon in the middle, and Maria gripping the back of Leon's coat sleeve, the three of them slowly worked their way down the hall to the stairs of the ship. Every so often, a ghostly pair of blue eyes would float by, and Leon and his friends would stop to momentarily gawk at the spirit until it wandered off. Once they reached the stairs, they carefully walked down, and at the bottom they found Ralph and Norton in the hull holding up lanterns while two other crewmen inspected a pile of now shattered wooden crates.

"Did the murhs do this?" Leon asked, but Ralph shook his head.

"They are just wimpy puffs of air," he explained.

"They don't even have hands to move things. They're just annoying to sail through."

"But what did all this then?" said Howard, inspecting the pile too.

"A lot of this stuff we don't even ask what's inside," said Norton. "Captain prefers not to know."

"So there could be something alive down here?" said Maria worriedly.

"Maybe," said Norton. "It's not impossible, but it'd probably starve to death without us knowing about it. Wouldn't really make sense."

"If it doesn't eat us first," Maria fearfully remarked.

"Let me ask a few more questions," said Howard. As he then interviewed the members of the crew for more details, Leon walked up to the debris. He poked and prodded at the fragments with Tim's cane to see if there were any clues, but all he could find were pieces of the crate. He looked around, but the fog was far too thick to see a thing.

"So, you all just arrived like us, and didn't see anything out of the ordinary?" said Howard, and all the crew members nodded.

"We need to look around," said Ralph, speaking a little lower than normal as though he were afraid to be heard. "Norton, stay here with the girl while the rest of us spread out."

"Sure," Norton quietly replied with a nod.

Ralph nodded back and then turned to Howard and said, "Here, take this," handing his lantern to him.

"You boys head towards the back. If you see anything, yell."

"Alright," said Leon, already climbing over a box.

He and Howard proceeded deeper into the ship, navigating through a maze of cargo. It was night now, so no light shone through from outside, but Leon could see the murhs drifting all about, their bright blue eyes piercing through the darkness and fog.

"Wait here for me," said Howard once they reached the far end of the ship, "the space up ahead is too tight for two people."

"Okay," Leon replied, sitting down on a crate. Howard went ahead, leaving Leon to count the floating eyes. After half a minute or so, though, he started to quickly grow bored.

"Howard," he called out, "you done yet?"

"W-who's there," Charles groaned from somewhere close by.

Leon, surprised to hear his voice, had no idea Charles was still down here, let alone this deep in the hull.

"Charles," he called out to him. "Where are you? Did you see what happened?"

Charles didn't say anything back, worrying Leon. He climbed over a stack of crates and found Charles on the other side, hugging his bucket.

"Charles, did you see what happened?" Leon repeated, kneeling beside him.

Charles sluggishly nodded in response but then

quickly leaned his head into his wooden bucket. Fortunately, he only spat.

"L-look out," he groaned.

Leon's eyes widened as he heard an all-too-familiar sound of gears clicking behind him. Grabbing Charles by the arm, they both dodged just in time to avoid a horolock lunging at them. As a second one then crept out from between two tall boxes, the first redoubled its efforts, lunging yet again at Leon and Charles, but Leon used Tim's cane this time to bat it away; to his surprise, the machine's hand fractured with a single swing. The horolock staggered back, acting somewhat surprised too. Leon quickly followed up with another swing at the machine, putting a giant dent in its chest and sending it tumbling to the ground.

"Leon, are you alright?" Howard called out.

"Careful!" Leon shouted back to him as he kept his eyes on the remaining machine. "There are horolocks!"

"I'm well aware!" Howard yelled. Leon then heard the sound of electricity and metal clashing from Howard's direction.

"There were five," said Charles weakly.

"Five — ?!" Leon repeated.

Suddenly, a rifle went off near the stairs. Leon's mind immediately filled with anger and worry, fearing something bad may have happened.

The horolock, thinking Leon was distracted, tried to swipe at him, but Leon fiercely countered with a swing to its side, smashing the machine against one of the ship's posts. The post cracked, and the horolock collapsed.

"Wait here," Leon said to Charles as they heard the rifle fire again. Without waiting for a reply, he then darted between the boxes towards the source of the noise. Leon was sure the horolocks were after them, perhaps trying to steal Tim's cane. Even worse, they might be trying to silence him and his friends for good. How did the machines find them, though, Leon wondered. And more importantly, who was controlling them if Glint was dead?

Leon quickly reached the center of the hull and found Norton with a rifle, nervously reloading after having fired at the last of the horolocks. He had managed to hit it in the shoulder, but the machine was still hobbling forward, straight at him and Maria.

"Stop — !" Leon began to yell, but before he could even act, Pendle stepped forward through the thick fog near the stairs, grabbing the horolock's hand. As his fellow machine desperately tried to yank itself free, Pendle slowly raised his free hand and then thrust it under the horolock's chest plate.

"The weak point ... is the left gear," Pendle remarked, pushing his hand in deeper. Then, with one good tug, he ripped a single gear out and the machine completely stopped.

"I ... think that did it," he said, admiring the gear.

Leon, Maria, and Norton were all impressed by how easy Pendle had made that look.

"I-I took care of both of mine," said Howard, sounding exhausted.

Leon turned and saw him walking back to the center of the ship with poor Charles leaning limply on his shoulder.

"What's going on down here?!" Ernest roared. He and several other members of the crew had come storming down the stairs to see what all the commotion was about.

"We should be asking you that," Howard replied angrily. "What are you doing with these dangerous machines on board?!"

"Machines?" Earnest questioned back, having no idea what he meant.

"Those!" Howard barked, pointing at the one by Pendle's feet. "You had five of them on board!"

Earnest slowly walked up to the fallen horolock, marveling at it.

"Can ... can they move?" he asked.

Howard nodded.

"I-I've never seen these things before, I swear. They must have snuck aboard —"

"They came from the crates," Charles weakly spoke up as Howard helped him take a seat on the floor. "The ones in pieces. I-I was trying to sleep w-when all of a sudden they smashed out of the crates. There was — nothing else inside but them."

Ernest and much of his crew looked thunderstruck hearing all that.

"I-I … I had no idea we were carrying something like that," Ernest admitted.

"Who had you deliver them?" Howard asked next.

"Well, that, uh," Ernest quickly glanced at the broken crates, "if I recall correctly, a highly reliable customer who —"

"No!" Maria suddenly shouted, but she was too late: All the while Howard and Ernest had been speaking, she had been watching a murh drifting close to Norton. The spirit had at first innocently floated near his head, inspecting him carefully. It then drifted down until it came upon the lantern hanging from Norton's hand. As though the spirit had made a grand discovery, its eyes became entranced by the light in the glass container; and then, just as Maria shouted, the poor thing grew too bold and got too close to the flame, stinging one of its eyes against the hot glass.

The very next second, the murh cried out in pain, making a horribly high pitched shriek of a sound. Like a chain reaction, the other murhs then shrieked as well. Each shriek lasted for only a few seconds, but they were nonetheless grating on everyone's ears. As the cries of the spirits seemed to finally die down, the fog then rapidly started to gush out of the hull.

"WHAT IS HAPPENING ?!" Leon yelled.

"I don't know," Howard yelled back.

"Let's go up," Maria shouted. "It's hard to breathe down here like this."

"Good idea, miss," Ernest agreed, and he gladly led

the way up the stairs. However, upon reaching the exit to the deck of the ship, they were confronted by an unbelievably thick wall of fog blocking their path.

"I've never seen it this bad before," Ernest remarked, poking at it.

"Captain, that you?" a man shouted from the deck.

"Yeah," Ernest shouted back. "Is everyone alright?"

"I think so," a squeakier sounding man spoke up this time.

"L-let's go," Ernest nervously said, stepping into the fog.

Everyone followed behind him, moving as closely as possible together so as not to lose sight of each other. Eventually, they came upon several members of the crew crowded around the mast of the ship.

"Captain, what happened?" asked a small, little man with the squeaky voice.

"I'm not sure, Mick," Ernest replied.

"The murhs might be upset with us," Howard casually remarked.

"It's not our fault the thing burned itself," Ralph whined.

"Look!" Maria pointed.

Everyone watched in terror as the fog began to thicken even more in places, slowly molding into shapes. Large clawed hands grabbed hold of the edges of the boat while glowing bluish green eyes formed overhead, peering downward at the ship. Slowly, a face began to take shape next as the eyes leaned in closer, inspecting each person with a passing glance until they came upon Norton. Seeing the lantern in his hand, the eyes crinkled into a glare.

"I-I think it's mad at you," Howard nervously whispered at Norton, who slowly nodded back, frightened out of his wits.

One of the giant murh's hands slid to the center of the deck, scratching at the wood, peeling it off like bark on a tree.

"Please," Maria suddenly called out to it, stepping forward, "I'm sorry your friend is hurt, but it's not our fault."

The murh lowered its head, and Leon stepped forward, placing himself bravely between Maria and its giant eyes. The murh squinted hard at first, studying the two foolish humans carefully, but then its eyes widened a great deal. The next second, the fog, eyes and all, faded away, revealing a beautifully clear night's sky.

"W-we're ... we're alive?" Ernest mumbled, staring at his equally confused crew. "The fog spirit didn't eat us ... it didn't eat us ..."

"Howard, what was that thing?" said Leon quietly, terrified that the spirits might come back if he spoke too loudly.

"I'm not entirely sure, but I think it was a murh," said Howard.

"Wha — How?! Do they all get that big?!"

"No, it's an ancient murh to be exact. They are a

far more rare and dangerous spirit than the little ones."

"It apologized ..." Maria mumbled, looking a little troubled.

"Huh?" Leon questioned back. "What do you mean by — ?"

"WE'RE ALIIIIIIIVE!" Ernest shouted joyously over them all, hugging Howard and Norton. "This is a great sign, children! The spirits of the sea have given us safe passage! Tonight we celebrate! Ledo —"

"Leon," Howard quickly corrected him, trying to pull his head free.

"— Leon, bring out all that wonderful cheese you brought."

"But —" Leon still wanted to know what Maria meant.

"No buts!" Ernest happily roared. "Get the cheese this instant!"

"Alright," Leon laughed.

He turned to leave, but not without noticing the troubled look still on Maria's face.

CHAPTER FIVE
FROZEN PORT

The weather had gotten so cold lately. Leon and Maria had been excited at first to watch the snow pour down and the ocean's water slowly begin to turn into patches of ice, but, as the short days passed by, the snow's charm quickly faded, and the harsh winter winds left the Vellenwood pair constantly shivering. They no longer wanted to wander about or admire the wide ocean, preferring instead to stay inside where it was warm and cozy.

Leon and Howard spent many of their mornings like today sitting on the floor in Maria's spacious cabin, playing taw. Warren was asleep at the foot of the bed, and Pendle silently watched the two boys play.

"Howard, it's your turn," said Leon with a tinge of annoyance in his voice.

"I know," Howard calmly replied. "I'm thinking."

"Think faster."

"How many times have I won ..." Howard slowly moved a piece forward, "there, your move, Snail Boy."

Leon fell silent, wanting badly for once to beat Howard at this game.

With a loud creak, the door to the cabin swung open and in came Maria holding a loaf of stale bread in one arm.

"Breakfast!" she shouted with a gleeful smile on her face.

"You're in a good mood," Leon remarked as Maria handed him a piece of bread. She gave a piece to Howard as well and then had a seat on her bed.

"The captain told me we should reach port some time this afternoon," Maria informed her friends as she tore a piece of bread off for herself.

"Really?" said Leon excitedly.

"Yeah," Maria happily replied, taking a bite.

Without thinking, thanks to the news, Leon was about to place a marble in a bad spot, but Pendle grabbed his hand at the last second. Shaking his head side to side, Pendle slowly let go and continued to spectate.

"No helping ..." said Howard with a glare, knowing that move would have ended the game with another win for him. Leon nervously made a different move.

"Hey, Howard," Maria said between bites of her bread, "teach us about spirits today."

"What brought that on?" Howard questioned back, debating in his mind what move to make next. Leon was curious to know why too.

"I've been thinking about it for a while, ever since the murhs had appeared."

"You finally believe they're real?" said Howard.

"Yeah," Maria replied, flicking a few crumbs off her lap. "It was hard for me to imagine that they really existed until I saw the murhs. You've talked about spirits before, but I still don't really understand what they are."

Howard nodded, made his move, and then reclined with a slightly smug expression on his face, knowing Leon was going to have a hard time now.

"Well, I guess we can start with the basics then," he said. "Spirits are ethereal creatures that live throughout the world."

"What does *ethereal* mean?" Maria asked. "I've never heard of that word before."

"They don't have a normal body," Howard explained. "My boss likes to use that word."

"Can you be a little clearer, Howard?" said Leon as he finally made a move. "It's hard to understand what you mean."

Howard quickly made his next move, leaving Leon perplexed over what to do next.

"I told you this before, Leon," said Howard, studying the board briefly; he then turned his focus back towards Maria. "Normal animals are made of skin and bones, right?"

"Yeah," said Maria, nodding.

"Well, spirits don't have bodies like that," Howard explained. "Instead, they are made of things like fire and stone."

"Fire and stone," Maria repeated to herself.

"And water, wind, mud, sand — anything you could imagine throughout the world. The spirits grow from the elements around them and take on their properties. It's still a mystery how that works, but my boss is sure we'll find the answer someday."

"What about the ones from earlier in the week?" Maria asked.

"You mean the murhs?"

"Yeah, what are they made of?"

"Well, in their case, mostly fog. I think I mentioned it before when we saw them, but they are harmless fog spirits that drift over the ocean. They move in packs or herds or whatever you call it, and as we saw, sometimes an ancient murh travels with them, looking after its smaller friends. From what I've heard from my boss, the ancient ones have a mean personality and will attack ships that pass by."

"But the giant murh didn't do anything to us," Maria remarked as she rubbed Warren's head.

Howard nodded.

"I still don't know why, though," he said.

"Can they talk?" Maria asked next.

"The murhs?" said Howard.

"No, spirits."

"No, they can't," Howard answered.

"But all the murhs were screaming," Maria quickly replied.

"Yeah, and animals can hiss and cry, but that does not mean they can speak," Howard calmly rebutted.

"Oh," said Maria, looking a little sheepish as she reflected on what he said.

"Anyway, spirits have a sort of hierarchy to them,"

Howard pressed on in his lecture. "You can often find animals that exhibit power similar to that of spirits, but that doesn't mean they are spirits. Some people refer to them as fake spirits. An easy example I always liked was a lizard breathing fire. It's still a lizard, but it has some power that a fire spirit would possess. I guess they are somewhat like an animal version of a caretaker."

"And what is a caretaker?" Leon asked, still studying the board for any kind of move to save himself. "Tim mentioned that word once before."

"They are people who look after a spirit," said Howard. "Since spirits don't have normal bodies, you can house them inside objects, and those who look after such objects are called caretakers."

"Does that make you one then?"

"No, my daggers are only made from metal where a lot of spirits live."

"Wait," Maria spoke up, "what does that mean? How do spirits affect metal?"

"Good question," said Howard. "When spirits live in one place for a very long time, their bodies slowly saturate the land with their energy, altering the stones and metals to be more like the spirits around them."

Howard pulled one of his daggers out to show.

"The blade looks normal enough, but if you focus your mind and try to speak to it ..." Howard closed his eyes briefly and the dagger emitted sparks, "the metal will come to life just as it had done in the past."

Howard loosened his grip a bit and the dagger returned to normal.

"Really though, what I have is just a cheap imitation compared to what a caretaker's weapon is capable of. You have to make them really well, or they will break easily, and then you have to somehow convince a spirit to live in one of them. Those requirements are why caretakers are fairly rare."

Leon instinctively gripped the cane lying across his lap.

"Tim was a really good caretaker, wasn't he?" he asked as he finally made a move.

"Incredibly good," Howard nodded in agreement as he studied the board.

"What comes next after fake spirits?" said Maria with eager eyes. Howard's little lesson on spirits had become quite entertaining for her.

"Well, as I explained earlier," Howard continued, "spirits are normally ethereal in nature, so pure or real spirits fall into two categories. Most are a lesser, simpler type that match the place they come from. Despite their size and power, even ancient murhs fall under that category."

Howard moved a marble before making his next point.

"In any given place, there is usually one spirit of a higher quality with many powers. They are extremely rare and unique, and they make up the second category. If lots of different kinds of lesser spirits dwell throughout a volcano or a forest, there is usually a single greater spirit that rules over them all there. My boss knows of a few, and he's told me that they embody the very world itself."

No one spoke for a moment, thinking hard on everything Howard had said so far. Leon jumped one of his marbles over Howard's, to which Howard immediately made his next move.

"Howard, what is your boss's … line of work?" Pendle asked this time.

"Yeah," said Maria excitedly, liking this new line of questioning, "you keep talking about this boss of yours and how much he knows, but what does he do, Howard? And what do you do for him while we're at it?!"

"Um …" Howard for once was a little unsure of what to say. Leon started to smile. He knew how much Howard kept his personal life to himself, so this looked like a great opportunity to finally learn more about the secretive Mr. Wavern.

"I want to know too," Leon added, quickly making a move (and unknowingly a good one).

"Well …" Howard looked like he desperately wanted to avoid the topic, but Leon and Maria were both staring so eagerly at him for answers. Eventually he gave in and reluctantly said, "H-he makes spirit items."

Leon and Maria both remained silent but gazed at Howard with now starry eyes, begging for him to go on.

"I work for a small company that specializes in making all kinds of things out of materials from where spirits live. Part of my job, and my boss's hobby, is learning everything we can about spirits so that we can make better products."

"So that's why you were so interested in Avaleer," Leon remarked.

"What do you mean, Leon?" Maria asked.

"He told me and Tim once that he was looking for information on spirits, but Avaleer doesn't have any spirits. You were looking for something really rare, weren't you, Howard?"

"I guess," Howard mumbled, making a move.

"Leon won," Pendle plainly remarked.

"Huh?" said Howard, sounding a little annoyed with the horolock.

"He's right," Leon laughed, jumping a green marble forward. Howard eyed the board over carefully and realized his black crown piece was trapped.

"Well done," he spoke mockingly. "Even a blind squirrel finds a nut once in a while, huh?"

"What — ?" said Leon, genuinely confused from having never heard that crack before.

"Forget it," Howard quickly replied, standing up, "I'm going to go talk to Ernest for a minute. I'll be right back."

"He should still be in the kitchen," said Maria.

"Eating those awful pickles, I bet," Leon added (Maria giggled, knowing he was probably right).

Howard stepped out, and Leon decided to set the board back up for another game.

"Pendle, play against me," he said, to which Pendle nodded. After Leon made the first move, Pendle took a moment to think.

"Hey, Maria," said Leon, keeping his eyes on the board, "tell me what the spirit said."

Maria didn't readily reply, looking at him blankly.

"Huh?" she said.

"You said the murh apologized," Leon continued, briefly glancing at her, "remember?"

"N-no," Maria nervously answered, doing a poor job of feigning ignorance, "w-when did I say anything like that?"

"Right after all the fog vanished. That's why you asked Howard if they can talk, right?"

"Y-yes, I did, but ... but Howard said they can't speak," Maria timidly replied.

"He did," Leon yawned. "Maybe you're just crazy," he mockingly added with a sleepy smile.

"I just ... I was so sure I heard someone say 'I'm sorry' right as the murhs left. It wasn't loud, but it was clear to me. You didn't hear anything like that?"

"No," Leon answered, shaking his head.

The door to the cabin suddenly swung open and Howard poked his head in.

"Guys, come up to the deck," he said, sounding a little out of breath.

"Why?" Leon asked.

"Just come up and see," he urged them. Howard then quickly left.

"I guess we should go look if he's that excited," said Leon, standing up. "We can finish our game when we get back, Pendle."

"... Yes," Pendle replied, standing up too.

"Warren, you stay and guard this place," Maria jokingly instructed.

Warren briefly opened an eye at the mention of his name, but then went right back to sleep.

Leon, Pendle, and Maria all filed out of the cabin and walked out to the deck of the ship. It was snowing heavily outside today, but a lot of the crew and Howard didn't seem to mind as they all leaned on the left side of the ship's railing, watching something down below. Leon and Maria, both curious to know what had grabbed their attention, leaned over the railing as well and were surprised to see Ernest standing on a rowboat, talking to someone in the middle of the ocean. The other man standing across from him was in a heavy brown fur cloak, making it hard to see who he might be.

"Captain's chatting with a Volgian soldier," Ralph whispered to Leon and Maria as he passed by.

"What's a soldier doing in the middle of the ocean?" Maria asked him. "Is he lost?"

"No, no, no," Ralph laughed, "soldiers get stationed out here to keep an eye on what ships are coming or going towards their ports. Only those authorized to trade by the kingdom's rulers may enter, but lucky for us, the captain knows this guy pretty well."

The soldier and Ernest shook hands, and then Ernest turned to climb back onto the boat.

"Are we all clear, Captain?" Norton asked.

"Yeah, no problem at all," Ernest chuckled, giving the crew a big thumbs up. "Let's head straight to the docks."

The crew cheered and immediately got to work. As they scrambled, Leon and Maria walked up to Howard, who was still gazing out at the sea.

"Well, that was a little interesting," Leon remarked, having expected a bit more.

"That's not the best part," replied Howard, pointing straight ahead.

Leon and Maria peered into the distance where his hand was pointing, but all they could see was floating ice and water.

"What are we looking for?" Maria asked.

"You can't see the coast?" said Howard, sounding a little surprised.

"No —" Leon began to say.

"Oh!" Maria shouted over him. "I see them! They're huge!"

"I've heard they're like that all year," said Howard.

"Really?!"

Leon, feeling goaded by not knowing what they were talking about, squinted as hard as he could. It took him a moment, but eventually he realized what Howard meant: the tall chunks of ice in the distance were actually snowy cliffs looming over the ocean.

CHAPTER FIVE

"We can't see it yet, but we're close to the port town of Povask," Howard explained. "The port itself isn't that impressive, but it's one of the few along Volgiev's eastern coast, which makes it important for trade. We should make sure we're all packed and ready to go before we arrive."

"S-sure," Maria replied, her voice a bit jittery as her teeth chattered from a strong wind rushing by, "a-any-th-th-thing to get out of the c-cold."

Maria darted inside while Howard and Leon took their time. The two boys walked down to the hull and found poor Charles sitting on a crate, leaning over his bucket like usual. Leon worried if he had eaten anything since their departure.

"Hi, boys," Charles meekly waved at them.

"We're landing soon, Charles," Leon told him as he rummaged through his bag, making sure his clothes and provisions were all still there.

"We're c-close to Povask?" Charles asked with a little more energy in his voice for once.

"Yeah," Leon grinned back at him. "You need to get ready to go."

"I've never been more ready!" Charles exclaimed, standing tall on the crate. For a moment, it seemed like he was a new man, thought Leon, but a second later, Charles put his head in his bucket, groaning loudly.

"T-there's nothing left to heave," he moaned. "I should never have agreed to travel like this!"

Leon and Howard were soon all packed and ready

to go. With Charles leaning on their shoulders, the three of them walked back up to the deck. Pendle, who had remained outside the entire time, was covered in snow. Maria was beside him, trying to brush him off, while Warren's little face could be seen peeking out of her backpack.

"Guys," Maria shouted to Leon and Howard, "we're here!"

"Oh!" said Charles, pulling his dangling head up. Leon and Howard looked out and saw a town sitting in the mouth of a snowy bay. Quite a few boats were present, but the docks were nowhere near as busy as Gildfoil's, or even Dampshore's.

"You all had better wait here," said Ralph, directing them to the doorway of the ship. "Let the captain talk to the port authorities first before you try leaving. We don't want them bothering you with questions."

"Right," Howard replied. He then dropped his backpack down by the doorway and had a seat on it, pulling out a book to read. Following his example, everyone else sat down on the ground and waited patiently. The boat soon docked and Ernest quickly chatted with the guards waiting on the pier.

"Please hurry," Charles groaned, sitting between Leon and Pendle. "I want to get off this damn thing."

"Just hang in there," Leon comforted him.

Leon kept himself distracted by admiring the buildings of the town. They looked to him like cruder versions of what he might see built in Vellenwood. The walls were made of stone and the roofs were made of wooden shingles, and it all looked rough, like it lacked a craftsman's finishing touch. However, much of these faults were hidden by the constant downpour of snow. The white blanket hid their blemishes and gave the town some charm.

"Alright, men," shouted Ernest, now back on the deck of his ship, "start unloading!"

"We can leave now?" Charles asked, pulling himself up to his feet.

"Yeah —"

Before Ernest could finish answering, Charles bolted past him. Everyone else on board watched in confusion as he flew across the deck and then slid down the ramp connecting the boat to the pier, looking awfully close to slipping off once or twice. The second his feet reached the bottom, he dashed straight into town without a single parting word.

"Well ... I guess he's feeling better," Leon remarked, grinning a little.

"Yeah," Howard agreed, seeming a bit bemused too.

"Let's go, guys," said Maria, pushing Leon and Howard forward.

"Don't shove us," Howard growled, but Maria just rolled her eyes and pushed harder.

With Pendle strolling along in the rear, Leon and his friends walked down the ramp behind Ralph and Norton, who were already carrying boxes off the boat.

"Gonna miss you guys," said Norton cheerily, patting Leon on the back.

"It was a fun trip," replied Leon with a smile.

"Do you guys know anyone we could speak to here about boats leaving for Pradow today?" Howard asked, but Ralph and Norton both shook their heads.

"No one's getting through for a month or two," said Ralph.

"... Huh?" said Howard, taking his eyes off his book.

"No one told you guys?" said Norton. "The ice's way too thick this time of year for ships to get through."

Howard froze in place.

"Howard?" said Leon. "You alright?"

Howard answered him back with a troubled look on his face. Leon raised an eyebrow.

"What's the matter?" he asked.

"Don't you get it?" said Howard. "We're stuck here!"

It took Leon a moment, but the color slowly drained from his face as well.

"What do we do then?!" he shouted.

"I don't know, Snail Boy!"

"Get out of the way," Ernest barked as he stomped past them, carrying a crate on his shoulder.

Leon and Howard politely moved themselves to the side of the pier while stewing over what to do.

"We're going to need to stay somewhere," Leon anxiously whispered.

"That could cost a lot," Howard whispered back,

"especially for foreigners like us. Volgiev doesn't make it a secret like Avaleer that they don't like outsiders."

"What are you two guys whispering about?" Maria asked. She had been leisurely trailing behind them, having no idea about the terrible predicament they were now in. Leon dragged her over, explained what they had learned, and watched as the problem slowly sank into her mind.

"W-what do we do?!" she hissed in Leon's ear.

"I don't know — !"

"YOU'RE THE ONE!" Ernest suddenly yelled.

Leon, Maria, and Howard all turned their heads to the side to see Ernest glaring at some shivering man twice his size wearing a green scarf around his mouth.

"Y-you don't need to yell," the man whined back, but Ernest slammed his crate down hard on the pier in frustration.

"Those contraptions nearly killed my crew, you idiot!" he yelled, clenching his fist. "You fools didn't tell me those things were in there, and alive to boot! What is wrong with you all at that damn company?!"

"Shhhhh!" the man begged. "I'm just here to collect them —"

"Enough! You tell Wrivenworth that it's going to cost triple if you want those scraps back!"

"Triple?! I don't have that kind of money on me!"

"Wrivenworth," Maria repeated in a whisper.

"Yeah," Leon whispered back. *"He must work for the Wrivenworths."*

"I'd thought the horolocks were after us," said Howard, *"but maybe not actually. It seems like that guy is here to pick up the machines, but why is the Wrivenworth Company bringing those things up here — ?"*

"Oh! Howard, is that you?" asked someone behind them.

Leon, Maria, and Howard all turned to find a young man with short hair similar in color to Howard's, but a much more pleasant expression on his handsome face.

"J-Jean?!" Howard blurted out, looking shocked yet a little annoyed. "Why are you here?"

"Boss was worried about you," Jean replied with a grin. "It looks like you made some friends, though."

Jean turned towards Leon, Maria, and Pendle.

"My name is Jean Ellecton," he introduced himself. "I work with Howard in the Felix Spiritcraft Company. It's a pleasure to meet you all."

Jean then politely bowed, making Howard frown even harder.

CHAPTER SIX

ROYAL PROCESSION

J ean ..." growled Howard, "why are you really here?"
"To pick you up —"

"The truth, Jean!" Howard shouted.

"Why's he so mad?" Maria whispered to Leon.

"No idea," Leon whispered back with a smile, trying not to laugh.

"Boss," said Jean, nervously gesturing for Howard to calm down, "sent me to Volgiev to meet with a couple of clients and make sure you get home in one piece. He's worried since you've never gone off on your own before."

"I'm fine," said Howard, sounding a little calmer. "I made the delivery just like he asked."

"Oh, that's wonderful," said Jean with a gentle smile. "Good job."

"How did you know to find me here, anyway?" Howard asked.

"Well ..." Jean fished through his pocket and pulled out a folded piece of paper. He unfolded it, cleared his throat, and then began to read: "'Dear Mr. Ellecton, I must be brief today, but I wanted to let you know that a ship by the name of the Hungry Flounder will depart from Avaleer tomorrow. I plan to have Howard and Leon ride aboard it before the weather grows too cold to travel. The ship should arrive in Povask towards the end of the week, so keep an eye out for the boys. Stay warm, Louis.'

"Louis has been keeping in touch with me and Boss, filling us in on what you've been up to," Jean explained while folding the letter back up. "I heard you'd be landing today with your friend Leon, but the letter didn't mention anything about two more."

"His name is Pendle," said Maria, pointing with her thumb behind herself at Pendle, "and I'm Maria."

"Pendle is an interesting name," Jean remarked.

Pendle did a slight bow.

"It is ... a pleasure to meet ... you," he slowly said.

"Thank you, "Jean replied. "It's nice to meet more of Howard's friends. So, have you all found a place to stay at yet?"

"Er," Howard was taken off guard by that question, "um —"

"No, we haven't," Leon bluntly answered. Howard turned his head and glared at him, but Leon just shrugged.

"Good, that makes things simpler," said Jean.

"Huh?" said Howard. "How?"

"Well, because I already have a place for us all to stay."

"Really?" said Leon excitedly, knowing that his reaction would probably annoy Howard to no end (it did).

"Yeah, it's a little ways out of town, but my friend has plenty of room for guests. He's actually expecting you all. I just finished up here with a client, so we can leave right away."

"Who?" asked Howard.

"My friend?" said Jean.

"No — well, yes, him too, but who was the client you just met?"

"My friend is a surprise," said Jean sweetly, "and I'd rather not talk about clients in the middle of the street. So, shall we go?"

Leon could see Howard's eye twitch a little, looking like he badly wanted to raise some kind of objection. Instead of trying to argue, though, he breathed deeply through his nose and exhaled a loud sigh for them all to hear.

"Lead the way," he then said, opening a book up.

"Alright, everyone," said Jean in an upbeat voice, "follow me — !"

"Wait," Maria suddenly spoke up, "what about that guy Ernest was yelling at?"

"I almost forgot!" said Leon, quickly turning his head, but neither Ernest nor the large Wrivenworth employee were anywhere to be seen.

"What's the matter?" Jean asked. "Did you forget to say goodbye to someone?"

Leon then began to realize it might not be wise to talk about the Wrivenworths right now in the open, especially after what had happened on the ship.

"No, it — it's nothing important," he replied, looking at Maria and Howard to be sure. "Right?"

Howard and Maria both nodded back, seeming to have realized the same thing.

"Y-yeah — yeah, you're right," said Maria.

"You sure?" Jean asked. "We can wait."

"No, it really isn't important," Maria replied, waving her hand in the air.

"Jean, weren't you going to show us where to go?" said Howard in an attempt to change the subject.

"Yeah, we should get going before it gets late," Leon added in hopes of helping Howard.

For a moment it seemed from Jean's curious expression that he might want to know what they were talking about earlier, but then he nodded.

"You're right," he agreed, pointing forward. "follow me this way."

Leon and his friends were relieved he left it at that.

With Jean in the lead, everyone stepped off the docks and walked into town. Leon noticed fairly quickly that Povask was a sizable place, yet very few people were out and about at this time of day. There were no stands selling goods, and almost none of the shops looked open for business. It was chilly out, thought Leon, so maybe everyone was just home keeping warm, but still … he imagined a little more activity than this.

"Hey, guys," said Maria, stopping to point, "what is that?"

Everyone looked down the thin alleyway she was pointing towards and saw a dirty little clump of a thing rolling through the trash. At first, Leon thought it was just a cat or dog, but he quickly realized its body was too round.

"I think it's a snezy," Jean answered.

"Snezy?" Maria repeated.

"Yeah, it's a snow spirit. They are living snowballs with no feet and stubby arms. Pretty docile creatures, though you never see them in towns."

"It doesn't really look like snow, though," Maria remarked, and Leon nodded in agreement. Rather than white snow, the spirit's body looked more like it consisted of dirt and ash.

"It's just filthy from being in the streets here," Jean explained. "Once back in the forest, the dirt and grime will come off it."

As if it knew it was the subject of their conversation, the snezy hopped around and stared back at its admirers. Leon was surprised to see such bright, beautiful glowing blue eyes. In its mitten-like hands it was holding a red rag. The spirit stared blankly at them all for a few seconds before turning and then pushing itself up into the air with its hand, sort of hopping away.

"We'd better not follow after it," said Jean. "The townspeople will be really excited if they find a spirit wandering here."

"Yeah," Howard agreed, "even a common one like that is special to them. We'll be stuck bowing to it all day or something."

"Hey, Jean," Leon spoke up, "where are all the people here?"

"The townsfolk?" said Jean.

"Yeah, there's barely anyone here."

"Now that you mention it, It is kind of empty," Maria agreed.

"Well, it's to be expected with everything going on in the kingdom lately," said Jean.

"What do you mean?" said Leon. "Was there a blizzard or something?"

Jean briefly peeked over his shoulder at Leon with a confused look on his face and then asked, "Do any of you three from Avaleer know about the recent political turmoil here?"

Leon and Maria both shook their heads, while Pendle remained silent.

"We never really hear anything about Volgiev," said Leon. "Everyone back home always said there was just snow and mountains this far up north."

"Yeah," said Maria, nodding in agreement.

Jean smiled.

"Let me try to explain what I meant," he said. "To start with, unlike Avaleer, Volgiev doesn't have a large amount of technology at its disposal. That, in turn, means you see less trade and activity than in a city like Tawton. Put simply, the people here are poorer than what you are used to seeing."

"Oh," said Leon, somewhat saddened to hear that. "What does that have to do with turmoil, though?"

"Well, lately, some people here want Volgiev to be more like their southern neighbor."

Leon nodded.

"Is that a bad thing?" he asked.

"Um —"

"To some it is," Howard interjected.

"Why?" Leon questioned back, not seeing how.

"They revere spirits and believe Avaleer's love of technology is why spirits no longer live there," Howard explained. "They fear Adrok will punish them if they follow your country's example."

"What's Adrok?" Maria asked.

"Good question," said Jean. "Adrok is said to be an ancient ice spirit that rules this land. I don't know if it really exists, but many of the people here believe it does. Their beliefs directly conflict with modernization, creating the turmoil I mentioned earlier. You have people who want something new, and you have people who want to keep the old. It has gotten so out of hand lately that some people are revolting against the kingdom in protest. Citizens are more wary of walking about these days because of it all."

Leon and Maria both grew nervous looks on their faces from hearing all this.

"You two don't need to worry that much," Jean assured them, trying not to laugh. "Most conflict is far to the west away from here. Povask was never that lively to begin with, but we should see a little more life up ahead."

CHAPTER SIX

As Jean finished speaking, they exited a small side street and found themselves on a far larger road that ran adjacent to an enormous river. There were plenty of people walking about, giving Leon some hope that Povask was not completely dead.

"Leon, look at that!" said Maria, shaking his shoulder as she pointed excitedly down the road. "Isn't it pretty?!"

"Hmm?" Leon sleepily replied, slowly turning his head. "What is it ... whoa ...!"

As the southern end of the road curled towards the river, it connected to a bridge made of pure ice. It was a sculpted marvel as wide as the road, and it stretched across the river, disappearing into the snowy distance.

"That's the King's Bridge," said Howard, looking just as awestruck as his friends. "I read it had been crafted by powerful caretakers centuries ago."

"Let's get a closer look," said Leon, to which Howard nodded in agreement. Just as they were about to cross the road, though, Jean grabbed them both by the collar and gently yanked them back.

"Hold up, you two," he said.

"What are you pulling us for?" Howard growled, but he quickly calmed down as he and Leon realized something was amiss: The bustling crowds of people had grown eerily quiet all of a sudden. Leon watched as they all stopped and turned to face the road. Then, in one long wave, the citizens of the town lowered their heads and remained perfectly still.

"Jean, what's going on?" Maria whispered.

"Watch," said Jean.

The distant sound of hooves pounding against the stone road was coming towards them. Leon and his friends looked over the crowd of bowed heads and watched as four pairs of massive horses came into view next. They were magnificent, black creatures that moved in an orderly, straight line, and each of them had a stern-looking rider wearing a fur cloak, just like the soldier patrolling the ocean. A fifth pair of horses pulled a beautifully charming carriage behind them. The windows of the carriage were curtained so that no one could peer in, but Leon imagined someone very important had to be inside. Two more pairs of riders followed behind the carriage, keeping watch for the rest. The horses never once paused as they passed by, moving swiftly down the road towards the bridge.

Once the sound of the hooves had completely faded away, all the people along the road raised their heads and went on as if nothing had happened.

"Hey, Jean," Leon spoke up, "w-what was that?"

"A royal procession," Jean calmly answered.

"Royalty?!" shouted Maria, looking as thrilled as could be to know such people exist.

"That's right," Jean nodded, leading them across the road, "Volgiev has been ruled by the Medov family for centuries. Many noble branch families exist with different names today, but they are all connected to the Medovs. Judging by the looks of the carriage and the number of guards, it was probably a member of the royal family inside."

He pointed out across the river.

"If you keep heading down that bridge, you will reach the capital city in no time. That's part of why it's called the King's Bridge."

"Yeah, and because only the King and his family get to use it," a man remarked as he passed by. "That'll change soon enough!"

"Don't say something so stupid!" the woman beside him hissed. "You want to get in trouble?!"

"It's fine, they're foreigners, not guards —"

"That just makes it worse! The spirits will curse you!"

"Don't be silly, the spirits don't care who I talk to."

"Only a fool would say that!"

"Right, *I'm* the fool. *I'm* the one who believes in every single superstition he hears. *'We'll be cursed by an evil spirit just like the village of Tem,'*" the man mocked in a high-pitched voice. "The only thing haunting that place are the dead too bitter to forget what the King did to them."

"I should report you!"

"Go ahead," the man goaded with a laugh.

As the two continued down the road, arguing with one another, Leon was a little curious to know what the man meant by *evil spirit*. Leon also finally began noticing the wary stares from other townspeople as they walked by.

"Where are we going, Jean?" said Howard, not caring to be the center of attention.

"Well," said Jean, "first we need to get out of this town and head northwest."

"And what is northwest?" said Howard.

"That's a surprise," Jean replied with a grin.

"Howard scowled, but remained silent.

It didn't take them long to reach the edge of Povask where tall, thin pine trees took the place of the town's buildings, and the stone road shrunk in width and turned to dirt. Leon could still see the frozen bridge to the capital even from this far away, a real testament, he thought, to the work it must have taken to make it.

"Louis told us a little about you guys," said Jean out of the blue.

Leon looked forward and saw Howard had gone up ahead while Maria lagged behind, helping Pendle walk steadily, so it was just him and Jean left to chat.

"Y-yeah?" Leon awkwardly replied. "What did he say?"

"Not a whole lot," said Jean. "But he did mention you needed help with a spirit weapon. My boss and I thought it was a good idea for you to come visit. Is it that cane you're holding?"

"Um, yeah," Leon nodded. "My friend gave this to me, but I'm not sure what to do with it. I can't even get it to work."

"May I hold it for a moment?" Jean asked politely.

"Sure," said Leon, holding out the cane without a

second thought. Jean quickly took off his gloves and grabbed hold of it. He then brought the cane closer to his face, eying every inch of it over carefully.

"I don't see any signature ..." he remarked, "and it doesn't feel that sturdy ..."

He handed the cane back to Leon.

"I don't recognize the maker," he said, slipping his gloves back on. "Your friend didn't mention how he got this weapon, did he?"

"No, I don't think so," said Leon, feeling a little disappointed to have to say that.

"My boss will probably know more," said Jean. "It's his job to know everything about spirit weapons."

"Howard said something like that too," said Leon.

"He did?" said Jean with a smile growing on his face. Then, in a slightly quieter voice, he asked, "How did you guys meet Howard anyway? He isn't exactly the most personable fellow in the world."

"That's one way to put it," laughed Leon, grinning hard knowing exactly what he meant.

"Jean," Howard called out from up ahead, "which way do we go here?"

Leon saw that they had reached an intersection in the road.

"I'm pretty sure we go left," Jean quickly shouted back.

"Alright," said Howard.

"So, Leon," Jean spoke in a quiet voice again, "what made you laugh a moment ago?"

Leon then told him the story of how he and Tim had met Howard in Tawton.

The road they were walking on gradually narrowed while growing increasingly steep. With snow and ice everywhere, they had to be careful not to slip and fall. Pendle especially took his time hobbling along, struggling to keep upright. Eventually they reached a wider pass between two tall mountainous walls.

"So you two were working in the kitchen the whole time?" asked Maria, who was now listening to Leon's stories as he helped her support Pendle.

"Yeah, Howard hated it a lot," said Leon.

"Probably because he couldn't read his books," said Jean, to which Leon and Maria both laughed.

"Jean, how much farther to your friend's place?" Howard shouted from up ahead.

"He must have finished his book," Leon whispered to Maria, making her snicker.

"We still —" Jean began to shout back, but then he fell silent all of a sudden, stopping dead in his tracks.

"What did you say?" Howard shouted.

"Quiet!" Jean shouted.

Leon, Maria, and Pendle all came to a halt as well, wondering what had him so worried.

"What — ?"

"Just be quiet, Howard!" Jean yelled over him, looking quite on edge. Leon finally noticed then that the gorge was gradually filling with the sounds of howling.

CHAPTER SEVEN

YOWLING PASS

One by one, furry white beasts shaped somewhat like humans crawled out from holes throughout the icy stone walls of the gorge. They then clung to walls and studied the travelers foolish enough to pass through their territory. They all looked very, very angry, thought Leon. Some were scowling, others gnashed their teeth, and many of them constantly belted out an awful, feral cry.

"There are so many of them!" Maria gasped. "Leon, what are they?"

"I don't know," said Leon worriedly.

"Jean," Howard hissed, "didn't you say this was the right way? It's filled with apes!"

"Um," Jean's serious expression diminished as he awkwardly smiled and said, "we might have taken a wrong turn."

Howard looked so disappointed to hear him say that.

More and more apes continued to pour into the gorge. Several had climbed down to the cavern floor and were circling Leon and his friends, who had huddled together in fear. Up close, most of these creatures were only half the height of a human, but the few older ones were nearly as tall as Leon.

CHAPTER SEVEN

"We need to run," Howard whispered. "Now."

"Yowlers are too quick, especially in the snow," Jean retorted.

"Well we can't fight them."

"We might have to," said Jean, slowly putting his hand in his coat.

"You can't be serious —"

A long, shrill, squeaking sound suddenly blared out from behind Leon and his friends, silencing the entire gorge passageway. A moment passed without a sound before Leon heard several musical notes slowly flow out next. The yowlers calmed down at once as they looked to be listening quite attentively to the soft melody. Leon and his friends turned their heads to see what was making such a sound; to their utter and complete surprise, Pendle was sitting on top of Tim's old sack, playing the fiddle.

"What in the world ...?" Howard mumbled.

"I think they like it," said Maria, letting a smile slip out.

"I heard a rumor once that yowlers like music," Jean remarked with a slight grin.

"Couldn't you have told us that earlier?!" Howard growled at him.

"Sorry, I forgot."

"Forgot?!"

"Please stop bickering," Leon quietly begged. He was terrified that the yowlers might get upset with them if they disturbed Pendle's performance.

For several minutes, the horolock continued playing and the yowlers happily listened. Once the song
came to an end, Pendle lowered the bow of the fiddle
and sat perfectly still, staring out as if he were waiting
to see how his captivated audience of apes would
react.

At first, the yowlers responded with cold silence,
worrying Leon that Pendle needed to play more, but
then several of the apes started to hop up and down
excitedly. More and more did the same, hooting in a
silly manner at one another. A few walked up close to
Pendle, who didn't seem to mind in the slightest, and
poked at the fiddle.

"Excuse me," Pendle politely spoke to a small yowler crouched by his knees, "could you ... help us find
our way ... out?"

The yowler hooted and nodded, tugging on Pendle's
coat sleeve. Everyone was amazed to see how easily
the horolock had befriended these creatures.

"We'd better follow him," said Jean as Pendle stood
up and slung Tim's sack on his shoulder. Leon and his
friends walked over to Pendle; as they approached
him, the yowlers standing around the horolock's feet
looked up at the humans apprehensively.

"They are my ... friends," Pendle assured the yowlers, patting one on the head. The yowlers seemed to
understand as their tense expressions relaxed. They
then turned and pulled Pendle along who obediently
followed.

"Pendle," said Leon quietly as he, Maria, Howard, and Jean huddled behind their mechanical hero, "how did you know to play a song? I didn't even know you could play music."

"I ... believe my maker taught me," Pendle replied.

"Taught you?" said Leon.

"Yes, the apes of Yowling Pass ... I remembered that they communicate with sound, and ... they adore soothing melodies."

"Where'd you get the fiddle, though?" Maria asked, crouching down to pick up Warren as he cowered between her legs. "None of us were carrying one."

"That's Tim's, isn't it?" Leon answered, eying the instrument over carefully now. "He played it for me once when I first met him."

"I remembered seeing it in this sack ... so I borrowed it," Pendle explained. "Was ... that wrong of me to do?"

"N-no," Leon quickly replied, "but none of us have been able to undo the knot on the sack."

"That ... is not a problem," said Pendle, stopping. He lowered the sack to the ground and then raised the fiddle and its bow towards Leon.

"Hold these ... Leon, please," said Pendle.

"Sure," Leon replied, taking the instrument in hand. Pendle then knelt and pulled at the cords of the sack, tugging like mad in places while his fingers worked tirelessly to undo the complicated knot.

"You must pull here and here ... at the same time,"

Pendle explained as everyone watched the cords slowly come undone. "Then, pull the knot ... to the right once as you press it with your thumb, and ... that should do it."

The sack opened and everyone leaned over Pendle, curious to see what in the world was inside. It all seemed normal enough, though: stacks of old books, clothes, a scrunched hat, two rolled-up newspapers, and other typical items Leon imagined Tim would have had on him. Frankly, it was a little disappointing to learn the truth.

Pendle pushed several shirts aside and pulled out from under them a wooden box. He then placed it on top of the sack.

"Leon ... the fiddle, please," said Pendle, opening the box.

"Oh, here," said Leon, handing it over.

Pendle carefully placed the fiddle and bow inside the box, closed it shut, and then slid it back down into the belly of the sack.

"Is there anything else you ... would like to see?" Pendle asked, but everyone shook their heads. "Alright then," and he immediately closed the bag and got to work redoing the knot.

"Everyone," Jean finally spoke up, having no real idea what was going on, "we need to get going if we want to make it by dark."

"He's right," Howard agreed. "It's getting too cold to be out here at night."

"Exactly ... so ..." Jean was too nervous to hurry Pendle along, afraid that he might upset the yowlers.

"There ... we go," said Pendle, having finished tying the knot. He stood back up, slung the sack over his shoulder, and then followed the yowlers who had waited patiently for him.

"Don't ... fall behind," he warned, hobbling awkwardly along through the snow.

Keith sneezed hard.

"Need a handkerchief?" asked Zeke.

The pair of them were sitting together on a long crate outside a large tent.

"No," Keith tersely snorted.

"No need to be mad at me," Zeke calmly replied. "Not my fault we're stuck here."

Keith glared at him.

"This was my grandfather's idea," he said, "not mine."

"Yes, it was his idea," Zeke agreed. "He wanted you to help your older sister here and learn more about the company. Get some real experience in what it's really like to run the business. So here we are in Volgiev, sitting out in the cold —"

"I don't need to sit in there," Keith growled, "and listen to her go on and on all day about machines and gears. I hear enough of it already at home."

"So what should she be talking about then?" Zeke asked. "The Wrivenworth Company is built on those machines and gears. They pay for the nice clothes you are wearing. And for the nice guards who make sure you don't slip and fall off icy docks."

"Are you ever going to let that go?" Keith whined, rubbing his head.

"Eventually," said Zeke. "Is your head still bothering you?"

"No, not really. I just ... I thought I could do more while I'm here," said Keith, sounding a little frustrated. "Evelyn is making all the decisions and I can't go anywhere."

"Yeah, we can't really have you wandering around. The camp is safe, but much of this country is ready to fall apart with the right push. It's best to be careful. Besides," Zeke added with a smug look, "we're here to work, not play."

"I guess," Keith sighed.

Zeke pulled a lighter and cigarette out from inside his coat.

"You sure you don't want to sit in there and listen?" he asked, lighting the cigarette.

"No," Keith tersely replied, trying not to sneeze.

"Hey, you two," said Orval, running towards Keith and Zeke. "I-is the missy still having a meeting?"

"I can barely hear you," Zeke replied. "Take off that scarf."

Orval was wearing a large, green scarf around his

head to keep warm. He pulled it down, allowing Keith to see the panicked look on his face.

"We got big problems," said Orval.

"What kind?" Keith asked, curious to know.

"I-I should really wait and tell the missy first," said Orval, looking side to side.

Keith couldn't help growing a bit annoyed from hearing him say that.

"What do you mean — ?"

"Tell me what, Orval?"

"Oh, uh, um, m-ma'am, um ..." Orval stuttered as he, Keith, and Zeke all turned their heads and saw Evelyn Wrivenworth standing beside them.

Evelyn was a tall and slender girl with long hair as dark as Keith's. It had a slight frizz to it and was pulled back into a ponytail. She had a smattering of freckles on her lovely face, though the growing black lines under her tired, dark brown eyes and the somewhat cold, indifferent expression she often wore made it hard for others to see her beauty. She wore a long brown coat and what Keith would describe as shabby workman's clothes underneath.

"Miss Wrivenworth," said an elderly man who followed Evelyn out from the tent, " It really was a pleasure to meet you. We shall meet again soon with the rest of the eastern leaders to discuss how your company may aid us."

"I look forward to it," she said with a nod.

The man nodded back and then strolled away.

"Orval," Evelyn turned her attention once more towards him, "what do you need to tell me?"

"Um," Orval was so nervous that he was struggling to speak.

"Spit it out, Orval," said Evelyn firmly. "It's getting dark very soon, and I still want to run several more tests today on my grandfather's prototypes to see how they perform in this frigid environment. I also want to do an inventory to be sure that we have enough machines in stock so that our clients will have faith in us that we can come through, so tell me what is the matter, Orval —"

"The machines are broken!" Orval blurted out.

"Huh?" said Keith.

Evelyn remained silent, but they could all see the startled look on her face.

"I-I went to pick up the shipment your father sent up," Orval nervously explained, "but when I got there, the captain said they were all broken — h-he said they attacked his ... his crew ..."

Keith felt a little giddy yet nervous to see Evelyn's short temper boiling fast as Orval spoke.

"Did you at least bring what's left of them here?" she asked in a low voice.

Orval grew a terrified look on his face.

"I-I tried, b-but the captain — h-he wanted triple the cost for them because of what they did, and I didn't have enough —"

"MONJI!" Evelyn screamed.

"There is no need for you to raise your voice, Miss Wrivenworth," said a man standing behind Orval, making Orval jump in fright.

Monji was well dressed, wearing a suit with a dark gray overcoat and a brimmed hat on his bald head to match. He wore shaded spectacles and had a calm yet somewhat cold expression.

"Take this fool," said Evelyn, pointing furiously at Orval, "and get those machines here right now. Pay them what they want and double it to keep them quiet about what they saw. Then, tell Vadim's men at the docks to keep an eye on them. We cannot afford any mistakes this far along!"

Keith had trouble not recoiling at her foul attitude. Zeke was only a little taken aback, while Orval looked ready to die.

"I'll have it done at once, Miss Wrivenworth," Monji obediently complied, acting almost indifferent to her anger. "Come along, Orval."

"O-okay," said Orval, sheepishly following behind him.

"I'd better go see if they need my help too," Zeke quietly told Keith, looking for any excuse to not be around Evelyn right now. Once he was out of sight, Keith was left alone with his sister.

Evelyn turned to go off somewhere as well, but Keith decided to finally speak up.

"Evelyn, you didn't have to yell at him," he said with a snicker. "You sounded crazy."

"Better than looking dumb and lazy," she retorted. "Why not make yourself useful for once?"

"And do what?" said Keith, rolling his eyes. "Sit around all day with your mechanics and tinker?"

Evelyn raised an eyebrow at him, looking almost confused.

"Yes, tinker," she said. "You may have forgotten, but the main factory for producing grandfather's prototypes burned down, remember?"

"Yes, I remember —" Keith answered.

"So you must be well aware then," Evelyn spoke over him, "of the fact that we don't have an unlimited supply of those machines at our disposal."

For a second she paused, making Keith wonder if what she had just said was meant to be another question for him, but then Evelyn pressed on.

"Without enough of Grandfather's machines," she continued, "I can't convince the revolutionaries that we'll be of any help to them in their war. And if that isn't bad enough, Keith," Evelyn's voice was slowly growing angrier, "what few new models we had left in stock may be too damaged now thanks to what I imagine was some dumb mistake on a boat! Those models were more durable and were going to be tested right away in this cold climate!"

Evelyn finally paused again. While taking a brief moment to rub her tired eyes out of frustration, she breathed deeply through her nose before continuing in a slightly calmer voice.

"We're behind schedule as it is, so I need to start improving the machines we have left. When you get bored of brooding, Keith, you can help me *tinker*."

With that said, Evelyn turned and strolled off.

Keith glared hard at her until a strong wind rushed by, making him shiver. He then bitterly wondered to himself how much longer he would be stuck here with her.

"Is she gone?" Zeke suddenly asked.

Keith turned his head and saw Zeke hiding behind a stack of crates with a cigarette in his mouth.

"Yes, she's gone now, you big coward," Keith mockingly answered.

"Can you blame me?" said Zeke, stepping out from his hiding place.

"No," Keith defeatedly chuckled.

"We finally made it," said Jean.

It had taken Leon and his friends several hours to make their way through Yowling Pass, but they had finally reached where Jean's friend lived. With the sun close to setting in the distance, they all peered down a steep hill and saw an open valley surrounded by pine forests. In the center was a small frozen lake. On the far side of the valley near the lake's edge sat a two-story house made entirely out of logs. The shingles, shutters, stairs, and front door were all crafted from wood as well. The only exception was the chimney made of stone.

"This is kind of out of the way," Howard remarked as they walked down the hill.

"The people of Volgiev are not just afraid of machines," said Jean.

Leon was about to ask him to explain better what he meant, but Leon's question was quickly answered as the front door to the log house swung open. Just like when he had lowered his menu during his first visit to the Sleeping Cheese, Leon was shocked to see a new furry creature, only this time, it was a weasel instead of a mouse. The creature was far taller and thinner than Louis, and it had a pure white coat of fur. It didn't wear any clothes, just a pair of glasses.

"Took you bunch long enough," it shouted from the door. "Hurry them inside, Jean."

CHAPTER EIGHT
THE WHITTLER

H e sounds a bit mean," Jean explained nervously, "but he can sometimes be really nice if you —"

"Today, Jean!" the weasel shouted from his doorstep, tapping his foot very impatiently.

Jean sighed a little and then started to run. Everyone followed his lead and hurried to the house.

"Make sure you stomp your feet before you come inside," their host ordered as they got close. "I don't want snow on my floors. The water will ruin them."

Everyone in turn kicked their feet on the steps leading up to the door before entering the house. Leon was the last in line, and once he was inside, the weasel closed the door and then scurried on all fours to another room.

Right away, Leon could feel how much warmer it was inside. As he pulled his gloves off, the weasel's head suddenly poked out from around the corner.

"Jean," he barked, "give them the tour."

"Sure, Heath," Jean replied, "I can do that."

"Good," the weasel gruffly said, and then he scurried off again.

"Take your stuff off here, everyone," said Jean as he knelt down to untie the laces on his boots.

CHAPTER EIGHT

"His name is Heath?" Leon asked, having a seat on the floor.

"Yes, it is," said Jean. "I stayed here for a while when I last visited Volgiev."

"He seems to like you a lot," Howard remarked sarcastically. Jean weakly grinned in response.

As Leon worked on undoing his own laces, his eyes wandered. Somewhat like the house's exterior, everything from the furniture to the floors inside was made of wood. Even more notable, the carpentry was outstanding. Every table leg, every finish Leon could spot was carved full of beautifully intricate detail. There weren't many walls to divide up the rooms, but that made the house appear all the more spacious. As far as Leon could tell, there were no electric lights to keep the house bright at night. The only source of light and heat was coming from the large fireplace at the far end of the house.

Once everyone finished taking off their coats and boots, Jean led them around with a lit lamp in hand.

"The staircase right in front of us goes upstairs to the bedrooms," he explained, pointing. "To the left is the dining room, which you need to walk through to get to the kitchen."

The dining table was a polished, sturdy piece of furniture that easily fit ten chairs around it, and at its center sat a large, oval-shaped wicker mat. Leon was impressed by the table's length and thought what a pain it would be to ever have to move it. He also started to notice that there weren't really any pictures or decorations adorning the house. He didn't think that was necessarily a detraction, though, but it was still odd to him.

Jean headed right and everyone followed.

"This is the living room," he said, walking around a long leather sofa with a matching armchair on each side and a short rectangle table in the middle. The armchairs in particular reminded Leon a great deal of the ones he'd seen in Tim's home, making him wonder if the same person had made both pairs.

Jean stopped at the fireplace to warm his hands.

"We'll probably be spending a lot of time in here," he remarked. "The sofa is pretty comfortable to take a nap on."

"You're right," said Maria contentedly, sinking into the sofa's large cushions and pillows.

Leon had a seat as well beside her and immediately reclined, finding himself very comfortable. Looking to his side, he saw Warren had already made himself at home in one of the armchairs, while Pendle stood behind the cat's seat, staring blankly at the fire. Howard chose instead to sit on the hearth (probably for better lighting while he reads, Leon imagine with a smile).

"Hey, Heath," Jean shouted, "can we go in the workshop?"

"Just don't break anything," Heath shouted back from the kitchen. "And don't burn it down either," he quickly added.

Jean chuckled a little at hearing that. He then turned and headed for a door off to the side.

"Let's take a peek," he said, opening it wide. He then went inside and everyone sluggishly stood up and trailed after him. The freezing trek through the mountain pass followed by the cozy living room setting had nearly put the trio to sleep, but upon entering, Leon, Howard, and Maria were all quickly roused awake by how amazed they were to find an incredibly sophisticated carpenter's workshop hiding on the other side.

It was a long room with a few tall windows along the exterior wall and a set of large double doors at the far end leading to the outside. The walls were covered with shelves packed full of pieces of wood, hanging carpentry tools of every kind, and a few tall cabinets with lots of small drawers. Much of the floor space was taken up by several very thick-looking workbenches. A pile of sawdust sat in one corner, and a stack of wood in another. Part of a tree trunk split in half lay across two benches while a third bench had an unfinished musical instrument of some kind lying on top of it.

"Louis might know everything there is to know about wines and cheese, but Heath can make just about anything out of wood," Jean explained.

As everyone admired the workshop, Leon walked up to a particularly odd sight that had caught his eye: Near the far end of the workshop, a small tree sat against the exterior wall. It was dead, having no leaves, but otherwise looked to be remarkably intact.

Its roots were all lying on the floor above ground. Leon tried to pull on one, but it was petrified, feeling more like stone than wood. He pressed his hand on the trunk next, and it felt the same.

A larger branch to the left had been cut and sanded into a shelf with a few books sitting on it. Underneath the branch beside the tree was a wide stump with a carved backrest protruding from it. With the window behind the strange seat, Leon imagined Heath would sit here from time to time and read.

"Must have been hard to get this in here," Howard remarked, marveling at the tree as well now.

"Yeah," Leon agreed.

"Tea's ready," Heath shouted from the kitchen.

"Coming," Jean shouted back. He then gestured with his head and said, "come on, it's best to not keep him waiting."

Everyone filed out and walked across the house to the dining room. Several candles, in the meantime, had been lit and placed on the dining table, making it much easier to see. Leon and his friends sat down around the long table, and a moment later, Heath walked out from the kitchen, holding a stack of bowls and utensils all made of wood.

"Pass these around," he instructed as he plopped them on the table before hurrying back to the kitchen.

"Do you need any help?" Maria offered, passing a bowl to Leon.

"No, I'm fine," Heath answered. He soon came in

holding a steaming kettle in one hand and a tray of wooden teacups in the other.

"Pass these out," he said to Jean, handing him the tray.

"Sure," replied Jean, taking a cup and then passing the rest to Howard.

As the tray made its way around the table, Heath quickly and clumsily poured hot water into each cup. Once finished, he scampered back to the kitchen, and then returned right away with a basket; it was filled with plump red berries. He placed the basket in the middle of the table and then had a seat at the end.

Leon and Maria were confused, unsure if they were supposed to drink the hot water as is. They watched Howard and Jean each reach for a berry from the basket and drop them into their cups. Leon, and then Maria, quickly did the same.

"Let them sit for a minute before you drink," Heath instructed, preparing his cup as well. "An old ermine like me doesn't have much up here like in that fancy bar of Louis's, but krassberries aren't too bad."

"Krassberries ..." Maria repeated, "is that what they're called?"

"That's right. I imagine you all are hungry, but the food will still be a little bit longer, so tea will have to do for now." Heath took a small sip from his cup before continuing. "I heard from Louis that Tim died."

Leon, Maria, and Howard were all startled to hear him say something so grave out of the blue.

"Can you tell me how it happened?" he asked. "Louis didn't go into much detail in his letter, but I'd like to know ... he was my friend too."

Leon could see that as Heath finished speaking, his expression grew a little saddened. Deep down, it must have been difficult for him to talk about this terrible matter too.

"Um," Leon spoke up, feeling the need to be the one to answer, "he died protecting us."

"Yes, but *how*?" said Heath. "This was not just any man that died. It's hard for me to imagine anything could kill him."

"Did Louis explain anything about the factory in his letter?" Leon asked.

"Yes," said Heath. "How you got there and what you found them making inside. You tried to rescue Tim when the horolocks attacked you."

"Yes, they'd knocked me and Maria down and were about to stab me, but Tim s-stood in the way and got stabbed in the back instead," Leon explained, doing his best to remain composed as he spoke. "Then a man named Glint somehow shot fire out in a big wave, but Tim shielded us all from getting hit — h-he was burned so badly that I —"

"That's enough," said Heath softly. "I don't need every detail. Good grief ... not a kind way to go...." he remarked, rubbing his head. "Could any of you tell if that Glint guy was a caretaker?"

"I don't think so," Howard spoke up as he gently

tugged on the stem of the berry floating in his cup. "He had a strong spirit weapon, but I don't think a spirit lived inside it."

Heath nodded understandingly and then took another sip.

"Heath," Jean spoke up this time, "we will probably need some lamps to use while we're staying here. We can't see well in the dark like you can."

"Right, right," Heath agreed, "It's been some time since I last had human guests."

"Someone besides me?" Jean asked.

"Yes," said Heath, rolling his eyes, "you aren't my only guest ever. I'm not a hermit. I should have a few lamps stored away somewhere upstairs. We can find them later when we're getting the blankets and everything else ready for bed."

Heath sniffed hard and let a toothy grin show.

"Food's ready," he said gleefully, standing up. "I'll be right back."

"Need any help?" Jean asked.

"Just stay put," Heath replied.

He then scurried to the kitchen, and Leon decided to try the strange tea while the ermine was away. He took a sip and immediately grimaced, finding it so tart that it almost stung. Maria, not daunted by Leon's reaction, took a sip too and also grimaced.

"It took me a while to get used to the flavor," Jean whispered from across the table with an awkward smile. "Howard oddly seems to like it, though."

Looking over at Howard, Leon saw him casually enjoying his tea. Both Leon and Maria did their best to hide their distaste as Heath came back in, carrying a very large pot in his hands.

"It's not every day that I make my favorite stew," he explained, sliding the basket aside as he placed the pot onto the middle of the table. Heath then removed the lid and stirred the contents once to be sure it was mixed well. Leon breathed in through his nose and was delighted by the smell.

"What is it?" Maria asked, looking quite eager to try a bite.

"Turkey," Heath answered enthusiastically, pouring stew into Maria's bowl first.

"Turkey?" Leon questioned back. "I've never heard of it."

"Me neither," said Maria. "Is it some kind of fish?"

Heath shook his head in disappointment.

"You two don't get out enough, do you?" he remarked (Leon and Maria could only blush from hearing him say that). "They're big, round birds that make silly sounds, and they taste great. Try some."

Heath poured a big ladleful of stew into Leon's bowl, and Leon quickly took a spoonful, blew on it twice, and then tried a bite.

"It's so good!" he laughed. Not only did the turkey taste absolutely wonderful to him, but Leon could also taste a mix of vegetables and some sort of fruit that turned the broth into a feast.

CHAPTER EIGHT

"This is great!" Maria giddily spoke with her mouth full of stew.

Leon happily nodded in agreement. Howard and Jean both ate a spoonful next, and then they happily nodded too (Pendle just blankly stared at his own bowl, unsure of what to do in this sort of situation).

"I'm glad you all like it," said Heath, sitting back down. "Turkeys are a little expensive, and they take a while to cook, but the taste is worth it, especially when you have potatoes with them. I should have asked earlier, but let me see if I can guess all your names from reading Louis's letters. The girl here is obviously Maria, right?"

"Yeah," Maria said between bites.

"Howard has to be the one with the glasses," Heath guessed next. "He kind of looks like you, Jean."

"Really?" Jean chuckled.

Leon could see Howard was a little annoyed to hear that, but Howard didn't say anything, choosing to quietly sip some broth from his spoon instead.

"So then, you must be Leon," said Heath, pointing his fork at Leon. "Louis tells me that you plan to take Tim's place."

"Doing what?" Jean asked. Leon was also unsure of what Heath meant.

"None of your business," Heath replied. "Anyway, while you are all here under my care, I can't have you laze about. Rest tonight, but tomorrow I will have work for you all to do. You included, Jean."

Jean sighed.

"I wouldn't expect anything less from you, Master Heath," he said.

"What kind of work?" Maria asked with a curious look on her face.

"The real busy kind," he answered vaguely. "Don't worry about it too much for now. More importantly ... he's a horolock, isn't he?"

Heath pointed down the table at Pendle, who had not said a word all evening. Leon, Maria, and Howard were all surprised he could tell.

"H-he is," Maria admitted, unsure if she should really say or not.

"I thought I heard gears ..." Heath remarked, "why is such a thing here in my house?"

"How do you know what they sound like?" Howard asked.

"Because I've heard them before," Heath calmly replied with a spoonful of stew in his mouth.

Howard, Leon, and Maria were all shocked to learn that. They'd all assumed from the earlier conversation that he had only just learned of the machines recently from Louis's letter. As far as they had known, only Tim and people connected to the Wrivenworths were aware of the horolock's existence.

"How?" Howard asked.

"That's my business," said Heath, looking sternly at Howard to make clear that the matter was closed.

"Is something wrong with Pendle?" Jean spoke up,

not enjoying being kept out of the loop any longer. "He seems like a nice guy to me."

"You can be so smart and yet so dense sometimes," Heath sighed. "Jean, that thing sitting down there isn't human."

It took Jean a few seconds to even understand what Heath had said.

"Huh?" he bluntly replied.

"Hey, you, uh — what was its name?"

"Pendle," Howard quickly answered.

"Pendle, take off your hat."

Pendle obediently did as he was commanded, removing his hat and revealing his metal head and glass eyes. Jean, for once today, grew a shocked look on his face.

"H-h-he's a ma-machine!" he stammered, shaking Howard's shoulder excitedly. "A machine — he's actually a machine, right?!"

"Yes, it is," Howard answered.

"But he talks and everything, that's incredible!"

"There's nothing great about a horolock," Heath growled, glaring at Pendle as Maria put his hat back on for him. "I want it out of here immediately."

"No," Maria spoke up.

"No?" Heath repeated, glaring at her, not looking pleased.

"Yes, no. Stop treating him like he did something wrong! Pendle has saved us several times before. He's our friend, and — and we have to find his home."

"You think I care ..." Heath's glare slowly softened as Maria defiantly stared back at him. Eventually, a bright smile grew on his face.

"Louis was right about you, young lady," he chuckled, standing up.

"Huh — ?" said Maria.

"Fine, I'll pretend for now like that thing is nothing to worry about. Why don't you help me clear some of the dishes while I get dessert? Or do you want to argue about that too?"

"No, I'll help," Maria replied, looking happy that she had won her little bout over her pet machine.

Heath went to the kitchen while Maria began collecting and stacking some of the bowls and utensils.

"So," Jean whispered excitedly, not wanting to be heard by a certain ermine, *"Pendle is a machine called a horolook —"*

"Lock," Howard quickly corrected him as he handed his bowl to Maria.

"Horolock," Jean repeated. *"How did you all find such a machine? Boss is going to be astounded when he sees him!"*

"The Wrivenworth Company's been building them in secret," Howard explained. "This one we have malfunctioned and acts nice, but they normally are violent and heartless."

Jean's giddy expression faded quite a bit hearing that.

"Are they meant to be a weapon?" he worried.

"We don't really know, but I think so. Our friend Tim seemed to know a lot about them, and he didn't like them much."

Jean nodded and then said, "If they're supposed to be a secret, though, how does Heath and your friend know so much about them?"

"I have no idea," Howard admitted, shrugging in defeat. "Tim never really liked to talk about them, and Heath doesn't seem to either."

"Yeah," Leon agreed, finishing what was left of his stew before adding his bowl to the growing stack.

"Maybe they both knew the Wrivenworths somehow," Maria suggested on her way to the kitchen with the pot.

"Tim I could imagine," said Leon, "but not Heath, for a lot of reasons."

"Can you tell me more about this Tim guy?" Jean asked next. "Everyone here keeps talking about him tonight, but I have no idea who he is."

"You never stop prying, do you?" said Heath, holding a large green fruit under his arm while Maria stood behind him, carrying a stack of small wooden plates. "Worry about all that later and cut this up for me."

"Yes, sir," Jean groaned, reaching behind his lower back. Heath put the fruit on the table as Jean pulled out a small dagger. Then, with one quick stab, Jean cleanly split the fruit into five even pieces, revealing a fleshy white pulp inside.

"Getting better at that," Heath remarked as he

picked up a slice. "Everyone, take your share of frost melon and eat up."

Leon followed Heath's example and picked up a slice. He took a bite and found it to be much sweeter than the krassberries.

"Did you grow these?" Jean asked between bites, but Heath quickly shook his head.

"Of course not," he said, sounding annoyed. "Stop asking dumb questions."

Jean laughed and took another bite.

A little squeak of a meow was heard between Leon and Maria all of a sudden. They both looked down and saw Warren was awake for once, staring back at them.

"Did you sleep well?" Maria asked happily, picking Warren up.

"Heath, I had no idea you had a cat," said Jean. "Are you finally getting lonely out here?"

"Warren!" said Heath excitedly, ignoring Jean's jab as he got up and walked over to Maria. "It's been so long since I last saw you."

Heath gently rubbed Warren on the head.

"He was Tim's cat," Howard explained to Jean.

"Oh," replied Jean, taking another bite of melon.

"There should be some stew left, I think," said Heath, quickly dashing to the kitchen. A moment later he came back with a bowl and placed it on the table. Warren, as if he knew it was for him, jumped up off Maria's lap and started lapping the stew.

"I'm glad he likes it," Heath remarked proudly. "Let

me get rid of these rinds. Maria, bring that stack of bowls to the kitchen. Leon, get that cane out. I want to check something before you go to sleep."

"Al-alright," Leon replied, a little surprised to hear Heath make such a request.

Leon walked to the front of the house and grabbed the cane leaning in the corner by the front door. He then walked back to the dining room just as Heath and Maria finished clearing the table.

"Can you get it to do anything?" Heath asked as he held out his furry hands.

"No," said Leon, handing him the cane. Heath then studied it, though not with the same discerning eye that Jean had used. Heath looked more emotional, thought Leon, as he rolled the wood in his hands.

"Looks to be in one piece, so that's good," he said, handing the cane back to Leon. "Take good care of it."

"I will," said Leon. "Um … can you tell me more about what you meant when you said I was taking Tim's place? Does it have something to do with being Elm? I'm still not really sure what that means."

Heath seemed confused by Leon's question, looking unsure what to say.

"That's … that's not a simple matter," he said. "Let's talk about that another time. For now," Heath spoke up to be sure everyone heard him clearly, "all of you grab your stuff and head upstairs — the horolock stays down here, though. It's not like the thing needs to sleep anyway."

Leon could see Maria getting annoyed, but Pendle patted her on the head.

"Do not worry," he assured her.

"Come on," Heath barked. "You all need to be up bright and early tomorrow!"

CHAPTER NINE

THE MEDOV FAMILY

I t had been nearly half a year since Lily had left her home in Ledy, the capital of Volgiev, to travel abroad, but now, she had finally returned. Ever since her carriage had reached the city a little while ago, Lily kept staring out the side window. It was getting late in the day, so it was getting harder to see, but she easily recognized many of the homes and shops she passed by. Sadly, though, few of them had lights on, and some of the shops were boarded up in the time she had been gone.

The driver knocked on the carriage's front window and Lily opened it to see what he needed.

"We will arrive in about twenty minutes, Princess," said the driver.

"Thank you —"

"Stop!" one of the cloaked guards riding up ahead suddenly commanded, and the carriage came to an abrupt halt.

"What is going on?" Lily asked.

"I don't know, Princess," said the driver, "but I am going to ask right now. I'll be back in just a moment."

He jumped down from his seat and hurried off, but Lily was a little too impatient to wait. She peeked her head out the side door and saw all the guards huddled together, looking at something on the ground. Even more curious now, Lily stepped out of the carriage.

"Princess?!" said a guard worriedly from beside the carriage. "You shouldn't be outside."

"I'm fine," Lily replied, walking forward. As she approached the guards, she could start to hear a low growl from where they were standing.

"It could take an hour for this thing to cross," one guard remarked.

"We could try picking it up —" suggested another.

"Are you stupid?" a loud guard snapped. "Our hands will burn off doing that."

"What is going on?" Lily asked, having just reached them.

"Princess!" several guards nervously replied as they immediately turned and bowed their heads in respect.

"I would like to see, please," said Lily calmly.

"Don't do anything foolish," said an old guard with a long, gray beard. "You can look, but I don't want you to get hurt."

"Yes, Kirill," Lily nodded, and with that said, Kirill stepped aside, revealing that a large polar turtle was sitting in the road. Its reddish brown shell was caked with slush. Its legs were tucked in, but the turtle's head was sticking out, growling at its onlookers.

"We've been trying to poke it along for the last half hour, Y-Your Highness," a city watchman explained, "but the thing won't budge."

"You don't think rebels put this here to distract us, do you?" another watchman worried.

"No," Kirill replied. "Miro already said it: you will burn your hands if you move them. The very top of their shells is fine, but touching anywhere else would be like holding a burning hot pan."

"We only stopped because most of our horses refused to go anywhere near it for some reason," said Miro. "Probably afraid to get burned or something."

"It's getting late," said Kirill. "I'd rather not kill it, but we can't leave a nuisance in the street."

"I don't think we have a better option," another guard agreed.

"Right," said Kirill. "Princess, let's go back to the carriage. I'd rather you not watch this."

"Wait," said Lily, actually taking a step closer to the turtle instead. She had been admiring the creature carefully this whole time and just now noticed something strange about its shell.

"Princess, you are too kind," said Kirill, "but we can't sit here all night —"

"No, that's not it," said Lily in a low voice, pointing at the turtle. "We can't touch this creature."

"W-why?" Kirill asked with a confused look on his face.

"Polar turtles' shells are warm enough to melt ice and snow, but this one's is frozen."

"Yes, but it could just be old and confused. That's probably why it wandered into the city —"

"No, that's not it either," said Lily firmly.

She quickly took off a mitten and slipped on a ring. She focused hard and ice slowly oozed from the ring until her hand was gloved in a layer of frost. She then brushed the shell very gently.

"I think ..." Lily stepped back and opened her hand wide, "it is carrying a spirit on its back."

All of the guards' eyes grew wide with shock to see a tiny ice spirit sitting in her hand. It looked like a frail creature made of twigs wearing a cloak of snow over its body. One eye was closed, but its other eye was open, staring up at Lily.

"I-it's so small," a young guard nervously remarked as he lowered his head to see better.

"Please be careful," Lily warned. "Frozen creepers are small but dangerous."

"Why's that, Princess?" another guard asked.

"Because," Kirill spoke up, "their bodies can freeze anything they touch in almost an instant." (Several of the curious guards leaned back in fear as he said this.) "I've never seen one in person, though. What is it doing on a polar turtle?"

"I think the turtle is ferrying it across the city," Lily explained as she carefully placed the spirit back onto the shell. "Most ice spirits loathe heat, but there are some like frozen creepers who enjoy the feeling. The shell is almost soothing to it. More importantly, a polar turtle is one of the only creatures that can carry such a spirit without freezing to death."

Lily turned and looked at her guards with a serious expression.

"The carriage will wait for the turtle to pass," she commanded. "Watchmen, I want you two to make sure this creature safely crosses the city."

"Yes, Your Highness!" the two watchman shouted and bowed.

"We probably should send someone ahead while we wait," Kirill suggested.

"I can still make it in time for dinner," said Lily, walking past the guards.

"And how will you do that … oh …" said Kirill as Lily smiled while pointing at one of the horses.

"We don't have a lot of time," she said.

Kirill rubbed his forehead hard and said, "And you want me to take you, don't you?"

"That's right," Lily happily replied.

Kirill breathed deeply through his nose.

"Fine," he groaned. "Men," he then shouted, "the princess and I will be going on ahead!"

"Yes, sir!" his subordinates shouted back.

"Princess," Kirill spoke more quietly as they walked up to his horse, "I hope your father doesn't get too mad if I let you ride with me."

"I think he'll understand," Lily replied.

With no more worries to voice, Kirill knelt down and put his hands together to make a foothold.

"Place your foot here and then grab the saddle, Princess," he instructed, and Lily did as he said, pulling herself up. Once she was seated, Kirill hopped up and sat behind her. He then wrapped his heavy cloak around them both.

"Are you ready?" he asked.

"Yes," Lily happily replied, having trouble holding in her excitement.

"Alright, let's go!" he shouted, and the horse began to move. It trotted for a few steps first before quickly breaking out into a full gallop down the road. Citizens marveled seeing the magnificent steed dashing by, but Lily's attention was solely on the palace coming into view.

It was a beautifully imposing structure to say the least. The architecture was remarkably symmetrical and ornate, having columns, ledges, balconies, and molding throughout the exterior's facade. The roof was black slate, but everything else was built of solid white stone, yet at this time of day, the candlelights inside made the palace's many windows glow, giving the outside walls an almost gold sheen. The surrounding palace grounds was covered in a blanket of snow and dotted with fluffy pine trees, and beyond the grounds was an expansive stone wall with heavy iron gates that protected Lily's home. Yes, thought Lily proudly with a smile, this was her home.

"Princess, I still can't believe you knew a spirit was hiding on that turtle's back," said Kirill. "I wouldn't have been able to live with myself if I had harmed it. Thank you."

"You don't need to thank me," replied Lily.

"I'll need to carry krassberries with me now for the rest of my life," Kirill chuckled.

"Why is that?" Lily asked.

"Oh, you've never heard? Polar turtles love them. Especially when cooked. If you roast a pile of berries in the nearby forests, the turtles will crawl out from everywhere to eat them."

"Really?" said Lily a bit excitedly.

"Yes, it's true. They love the smell."

"I had no idea."

As they drew closer to the front gate, Kirill had his horse slow its pace to a trot, not wanting to alarm the pair of guards keeping watch.

"Open the gates," Kirill shouted.

"Is that you, Kirill?" one of them shouted back.

"Yes, it's me."

"Where's the carriage?"

Kirill stopped in front of the gate.

"It's back in the middle of town," he explained. "A turtle got in our way. Open the gate."

"Huh?" the guard replied. "A turtle?"

Lily poked her head out from Kirill's cloak, shocking the guards.

"Please open the gate," she politely said. "I don't want to miss everyone at dinner."

"P-P-Princess?!" the other guard stuttered. "Uh, um — y-yes, at once!"

The pair of guards fumbled for a moment with the

locks, and then together they pushed the gate doors wide open.

"Thank you," said Lily as she and Kirill passed through. Kirill continued to guide his horse around the palace to a side entrance.

"Kirill?" said a guard standing watch by the door. "Where's the carriage?"

"No time for that," he said, jumping off his horse and revealing Lily. The guard was as shocked as the ones at the gate to see her.

"Princess — ?!"

"Yes, yes, it's her," Kirill gruffly answered as he helped Lily down. "Open the door. She's late enough as it is."

"Yes, sir," the guard obediently replied.

"Thank you," said Lily, shaking Kirill's hand.

"Hurry along," Kirill warmly replied. "Your father is excited to see you again."

Lily nodded and went inside. After walking up a short flight of stairs, she proceeded down a wide, open, and much warmer ornate hallway. While noting to herself along the way that a new landscape painting had been hung, she acted very casual, as if her return would go unnoticed, but each servant or maid she passed grew wide-eyed as he or she realized the princess had finally returned.

"Oh, Princess Lily!" a heavy, gray-haired woman shouted from atop a ladder as she fixed a set of long curtains. "Is that you?!"

"Yes, it is, Nonna," Lily answered somewhat bashfully with a smile. "I'm home."

"Oh thank goodness," Nonna breathed hard as she stomped down the ladder, "Inna has been so worried about you. She only came back a few days ahead of you, but you know how she is."

"I know, but I need to go see my family first," said Lily. "They should still be eating in dining room."

"You're right," Nonna agreed, and she gestured for two younger maids to come over. "Let's get you out of that cloak first so you look your best."

As Lily quickly pulled her mittens off and handed them to one maid, the other removed her cloak for her.

"They will take your things to your room," said Nonna. "Next, please tilt your head down for me."

Lily obliged, and Nonna took a moment to tug on the bow wrapped around Lily's hair, pulling it tightly to be sure it looked presentable.

"There ... well, hurry along."

"Alright," Lily giggled.

She walked down the long hall, turned right, and continued until she came to a set of doors guarded by a pair of armed stewards. Without her having to say a word, they pushed open the doors and she stepped inside. To her absolute delight, she found her mother, father, little sister, and little brother all seated together around the large dining table.

Her father, Ilya, sat at the head. He was a somewhat tall man with dark brown hair, a thick beard, and a mustache that curled ever so slightly. His most striking feature was his exceptionally blue eyes that Lily alone had inherited from him. Much of how Lily looked, though, was inherited from her mother, Maya, who sat to the right. She was a beautifully slender woman with long hair tied into a braided bun. Instead of eating, she was patiently listening to what her husband had on his mind this evening.

"My aunt is still not sure if she wants to come to this year's celebration," Ilya explained to her. "Maya, what should I say to convince her?"

Ilya then glanced to the side to see who had entered the room. To his surprise, his eldest child was standing there, smiling.

"Liliana — ?"

"Lily!" Lily's sister, Renata, shouted. She hopped out of her chair and ran up to Lily, hugging her waist as tightly as she could. Renata's hair was shorter, but it was the same color brown as that of her mother and sister. For a moment, Lily found herself admiring the dress Renata wore. It was colored crimson red and embroidered with gold thread.

"Lily," said her mother, standing up, "when did you arrive? We were not expecting you until tomorrow."

"It was a surprise," said Lily, watching her father and brother stand up as well. "Uncle will be coming later tonight too."

"Uncle Nikolai too?" said Lily's brother, Rolan, who hurried around the table to join his sisters.

"Yes, he wanted to visit Father," Lily explained. It really hadn't been that long since she had last seen Rolan, but Lily couldn't help thinking as her brother walked up to her how much more grown up he looked now. He was a few inches taller (though still not much taller than Renata), and his hair had been cut short. Lily easily imagined their father looked just like him when he was younger.

Maya was the next to stop in front of Lily, and she gently smiled at her two lovely daughters. She then ran her long fingers through Lily's hair.

"We've missed you so much," she said in a clear yet soft voice. Lily smiled brightly back, hugging her.

"We need to celebrate," said Ilya. "Bring her food at once."

A servant standing by a side door bowed his head and stepped out. Ilya then gestured with his hand, imploring his wife and children to have a seat.

"How was your trip?" Renata asked as she and Lily walked to the table.

"It was wonderful," Lily answered with a big smile, taking her seat next to her little sister. "Uncle's castle was beautiful. His library was much bigger than ours, and he owned all sorts of heirlooms from famous lords and caretakers. The snow outside often grew so high that the trees would get buried, but when it was better, Uncle showed me several kinds of spirits that lived nearby."

"Did you see any rime whales?" Rolan asked.

"No, Uncle told me they live even farther north, so it's very difficult to find them. Oh, but I did get to meet two caretakers who lived near the castle. They were such talented men."

"It sounds like you really enjoyed yourself," her father remarked happily.

A servant stepped into the dining room, moving with a real sense of urgency. He walked straight to the king's side and whispered in his ear.

"… Are you sure?" Lily overheard her father ask, to which the servant nodded. The king then sighed as he stood up.

"I have to speak to one of the generals," Ilya explained to his family.

"Did something bad happen?" Rolan asked, standing up as well.

"It's nothing grave," said Ilya. "I just need to speak to him now so that he and his men can depart for Kholsk before a blizzard picks up. I won't be long, but you should finish dinner without me."

"… Alright," said Rolan sitting back down.

Ilya left, and Lily's food soon arrived, but none of the children had much of an appetite now without their father present, Lily included.

"Do you think it has to do with the rebels?" Rolan eventually wondered aloud as he picked at his mashed potatoes.

"Maybe," Lily replied, putting her fork down. "That city is far to the west where rebels are more prevalent, so it would make sense to increase our army's presence there."

"It could also be that criminal Vadim again. He and his men are everywhere lately. I did hear, though, that the city watch almost caught him one night while —"

"None of these topics are something we should be discussing during a meal," said their mother as she sipped on a cup of tea. "But you all shouldn't worry too much. Your father and uncle are doing everything they can to resolve these matters."

All of the children nodded in agreement with that. They and their mother finished eating and then went to their rooms for the evening. Lily, though, took a roundabout path, wanting to see how everything was inside the palace. She strolled through the hallways at a leisurely pace, greeting stewards and servants who were all pleased to see she had returned. Eventually, she stopped at a window facing the heart of the palace where its courtyard lay.

"Tesha," Lily called out to a young maid with short hair nearby, "can you please go get my cloak."

"Yes, Your Highness," Tesha replied with a bow before hurrying off.

Lily, in the meantime, continued to stare out the window. It was too dark outside to see well, but she could easily imagine the scenery.

"Princess Liliana," a somewhat young palace steward called out to Lily from down the hallway all of a sudden, "a moment of your time, please."

"Yes?" said Lily, turning to face him.

The steward walked up to her, immediately bowed, and then raised his head.

"The Palace Commander sent me to inform Your Highness that he has ordered two more guards to aid in ensuring that the, um, p-polar turtle safely crosses the city this evening."

The steward seemed confused by this message, but Lily fully understood and was happy to hear it.

"Please thank Kirill for informing me," Lily instructed with a gentle smile.

The steward couldn't help slightly blushing at her pleasant expression.

"Yes, right away, Your Highness!" he replied in a loud, clear voice, bowing his head low. He then immediately turned and left. At the same time, Tesha returned with the cloak in hand. Without needing to be asked, she wrapped it over Lily's shoulders.

"Shall I accompany you?" she asked while buttoning the front next, but Lily shook her head.

"I'd like to go by myself," she said.

"Of course," Tesha replied with a nod. "I'll be here if you need anything."

"Thank you."

Once Tesha was finished, Lily walked around the corner and went outside into the courtyard. It was a peaceful place full of snow that very few people traveled through (not wanting to step into the cold if they could help it). Several large, barren trees covered in ice dotted the grounds. Their bark was beautifully pure white, and they had grown so tall over the years that their branches now easily touched the slanted roof of the palace.

Lily toured around one of the trees, admiring it, and then she walked to a stone bench in the center of the courtyard. Just as she had finished brushing off some of the snow and had a seat, she heard footsteps coming towards her.

"There you are, Lily!" a woman called out from the east entrance to the courtyard. "I just found out that you had arrived this evening! I-I would have greeted you in person if I had known!"

Lily bashfully waved as her one and only personal attendant, Inna Novotin, rushed across the courtyard towards her. She was tall, youthful, and lovely, yet her eyes had terrible dark bags under them (Lily could easily imagine why). Her braided golden brown hair rested on her shoulder, slightly bobbing up and down as she awkwardly stomped through the snow. Once she reached Lily, Inna dropped to her knees and stared hard at Lily. Her mouth trembled a great deal as her eyes nervously checked to be sure every hair on Lily's head was still in place.

"I was so worried about you!" Inna then moaned. "One minute you were with me, and the next you had disappeared! I couldn't find you anywhere! If your uncle hadn't said anything, I don't know what I would have told your father!"

"I'm fine," Lily assured her. "Everything went fine."

"Everything certainly did not!" Inna shot back angrily. "You witnessed a murder!"

Lily was a bit surprised to hear that she knew of that incident. Her uncle must have found out and told her, she thought.

" If ... if a-anything had happened to you, I-I ..."

Inna started to tear up, but she did her best to avoid completely breaking down. She continued once she had collected herself.

"A-anyway ..." she said, standing back up onto her feet, "you have a very busy schedule for tomorrow. We must resume your lessons, including meeting with your new dancing instructor, who I'm sure ... are you listening? Lily?"

Lily's attention was completely elsewhere. With her head tilted to the side, she giddily watched her Uncle Nikolai stroll through the courtyard towards them. Every time Lily saw him, she couldn't help thinking how much her uncle looked just like her father. He was a bit taller than his younger brother, and his hair had gotten far grayer, but his eyes were that same shade of blue. Instead of royal garb, he preferred to wear much more modest suits and coats.

"Liliana!" Inna shouted, trying to get Lily's attention. "It is very rude to ignore someone when they are speaking to you —!"

"I thought I would find you two here," said Nikolai as he got closer.

"Lord Nikolai!" said Inna nervously, immediately turning around and bowing her head in respect. "I-I had no idea you were here."

"Please, Inna, you don't need to be so formal with me," said Nikolai in a soft voice. "I just arrived a little bit ago."

"Does the King know you are here?" Inna asked.

Nikolai shook his head before letting out a silly grin.

"Not yet," he said.

"B-but, we need to prepare a bed, and heat a bath — have you even eaten yet?!"

"Stop worrying so much, Inna," said Nikolai, casually waving off her concerns, but saying that made her look all the more neurotic.

"I-I'm terribly sorry, L-Lord Nikolai!" she cried, bowing her head.

Nikolai, sighing to himself, looked a little disappointed to see her act so apologetic.

"You never change, do you?" he said.

" I-I'm sorry!"

"There's no need for you to apologize for that too," Nikolai chuckled. "Please, raise your head," to which Inna reluctantly did so. "Good. Now, if it will make you feel better, then please take care of everything for me while I speak to my niece for a moment."

"Of course, My Lord!" she happily replied, bowing her head once more before proceeding out of the courtyard. Once she was gone, Nikolai grew a smile and turned to Lily, who jumped up and gave him a big hug.

"Ohohoho," Nikolai laughed, "what's this for?"

"Thank you for helping me, Uncle," said Lily.

"I didn't do much, though," said Nikolai.

"That's not true," Lily replied with her face buried in her uncle's coat. "Father wouldn't have let me travel anywhere without your help."

"And as far as your father is concerned, you only came to visit my home. I would never hear the end of it if he knew what I let you do…. I'm glad you came back safely," he added softly.

Nikolai sat down on the stone bench, and Lily joined him. Her uncle then asked in an excited whisper, *"So, what was Avaleer like?"*

"It was incredible!" Lily exclaimed. "There were cars and people everywhere in Gildfoil, and the buildings were so tall."

"Were they now?" Nikolai happily asked.

"Yes, and all the buildings in the capital had electric lights too. They shined so brightly at night."

"That must have been quite the sight, I imagine. Sometimes I wonder if I should have gone with you to see the lights as well. Maybe learn something…. Did you know Vasily loved to read about Avaleer?"

"Really?"

"Yes, your cousin would always ask me for more books about it. He especially liked the ones written by a man named Hugo Welson. I found them to be far too wordy, but Vasily liked them, so I kept getting them for him whenever I had the chance. He never mentioned it, but I'm sure he would have loved to have seen those lights like you did."

"Yes, it really was incredible ..." Lily grew quiet, thinking more deeply on her recent trip.

"What's the matter?" Nikolai asked, patting her on the head. "I hope all my talk of Vasily didn't make you sad."

"No," Lily shook her head, "I'd never think that. I love when you tell me stories about Vasily. I was just thinking ... w-why can't our kingdom be more like that place, Uncle? It glowed so brightly, and the people there were far wealthier and happier than our own citizens here."

Nikolai nodded understandingly.

"Your father is just trying to do what's best for our people, Lily. You must have seen it there, that Avaleer purged the spirits from its land long ago."

"Yes, I could tell, but ... they didn't seem any worse off for it, though. It doesn't make sense to me."

"That is the reason why," said Nikolai, standing up, "our kingdom is in such turmoil right now. We have always been taught to honor the spirits and be wary of anything technological, and we have done so, yet it is the Avaleans who continue to prosper. Their homes are warmer, their food is better, and their medicine is stronger. It just doesn't seem fair, does it?"

"No, it doesn't," Lily answered, shaking her head.

"Yet that is the reality and the problem," Nikolai continued, pacing very slowly in front of the bench.

"Perhaps a day will come when the people of Avaleer are finally punished for what they have done to the spirits of their land, but many of our people no longer think that will happen, nor do they care. They've reached a point now where they will gladly risk the ire of Adrok if it means not having to live another day in complete stagnation."

Lily had been staring at the snowy ground around her feet while she quietly listened.

"I'm not sure what my father should do," she said, looking up at her uncle.

"I'm not really sure either," Nikolai admitted with a shrug. "If he gives in to change, Adrok may very well destroy the kingdom one day, but if things continue as they are, the people will get angrier, and the rebellions will increase. My only advice I've given to him before is to try and talk these things out, maybe make a few small concessions, but you know how your father is once his mind is set."

Lily nodded in frustration at that, knowing exactly what he meant.

"Like your grandfather, your father reveres the spirits greatly."

"Maybe we can find some kind of middle ground if we ask Adrok," Lily suggested absentmindedly.

"Oh," said Nikolai with a smirk, "are you going to talk to him for us? Maybe make him your spirit?"

"No," Lily quickly replied, blushing a little. Nikolai chuckled hard.

"It would be nice to have a caretaker in the family again, though," he said. "It would certainly help with all the negotiating I've had to do lately. Just imagine if I had Adrok right there beside me, nodding along as I spoke. I'm sure even your father would listen. Unfortunately, though, only the first king and Elm have ever met the Great Spirit."

Nikolai raised his arms out wide.

"It's said that Elm made these trees the day the three met," he exclaimed as he gazed upward. "They were a parting gift to ward off evil spirits and keep our family safe."

"And he's never come back since," said Lily flatly.

"True," Nikolai replied, lowering his arms. "It's possible he may never have even existed, but I like to believe he did."

"We need to do something before everything gets out of hand, Uncle," said Lily. "We can't wait for someone like Elm to stop the rebels for us."

Nikolai nodded, looking to have taken her point to heart.

Lily suddenly let out a mousy squeak of a sneeze.

"That'll happen when you sit out here for too long," Nikolai laughed.

"You're right," Lily sniffed.

"Come on," said Nikolai, offering her a hand, "let's go inside. We can worry more tomorrow."

CHAPTER TEN
THE SEA OF FEAR

M aria had only just fallen asleep when she heard an eerie whistling. It was rhythmic, slow, and somber in nature, and it sounded as if it were close to her ear. Maria imagined that it was probably just Warren curled by her head, snoring.

She did her best to ignore the noise at first, hoping it would eventually stop, but when it got to be too grating, she opened her tired eyes a crack, somewhat glaring. She then searched for the culprit, but all the while her eyes darted about, Maria slowly came to a startling realization: Heath's home had completely vanished. The wooden walls, snowy window, and her warm bed were nowhere to be found. Instead, Maria was lying alone under a dreary gray fog.

As she sat up tall to get her bearings, Maria finally began to notice the ground underneath her was gently swaying. She pressed her fingers down and could tell right away from the rough texture that she was on something wooden. The fog then cleared a little around her, enough so that Maria could see that she was drifting on a rowboat of sorts.

"Awake at last?"

Maria looked up and saw through the fog an individual sitting in front of her at the end of the boat. His back was to her, but she easily recognized the voice of the mysterious gentleman. His clothes were different, though: There were far fewer layers than before. He only had a blue and white diamond-patterned sleeveless robe covering him. Underneath, he wore a long-sleeved black shirt to hide his arms (the sleeves seemed a tad too long). His hands were gloved, and an incredible wild mane of white hair was draped over his shoulders, reaching the center of his back.

"Do you like fishing?" said the gentleman, turning his head and revealing a new mask. It had a similar lifelike nature to it like the one Maria had seen the night she left Vellenwood, but now the ears were gone and the white face was slightly rounder. The mane grew from the mask (explaining the sudden full head of hair), and the face's outline and features were painted black and blue.

Maria tilted her head, looking annoyed.

"What do you want this time?" she said in a surly tone.

"Nothing in particular," he readily replied in a quiet voice.

Maria was starting to feel upset with him for answering so easily. She could not understand why he still haunted her.

"Where are we — ?" she began to ask next, but, as the fog drifted away from them for a moment, Maria fell silent as her eyes widened with disbelief. She and the gentleman were completely surrounded by water.

She looked every which way, but there was no end in sight. The only exception she could spot was a single, massive rock jutting out of the water farther ahead of them. Maria then started to wonder if this was just another dream like before, or if perhaps the gentleman had somehow kidnapped her in the dead of night.

Suddenly, a fin as tall as a door cut through the water, sailing right past their tiny vessel. Maria's heart raced as she silently watched it disappear into the fog.

"Guess he didn't want to bite," the man calmly remarked, holding a fishing rod in hand. "So what's bothering you tonight?"

"Bothering me?" Maria mumbled. "Nothing except for you —"

"Something has to be," said the gentleman firmly. "Everyone has worries and fears ... something bothering them ..."

Another fin came sailing by, slightly larger than the last.

"Why am I here?!" Maria cried out, trying her hardest not to tear up.

"No idea ... nothing wants to bite tonight," the gentleman remarked. His tone was far more reserved and emotionless than what Maria was used to.

"You have to know, y-you brought me here."

"I did bring you here, but I have no idea why you are here."

Yet another fin appeared, and Maria shuddered as this one passed by so close that it nearly grazed the boat's edge. Once it was gone, Maria crumpled onto her side, wishing very much that this horrid nightmare would end. She then noticed the gentleman's round paper lantern lying on the floor, slightly rolling with the movements of the boat, tumbling back and forth. It had no flame to make it glow orange, looking gray and dull instead like the rest of this world.

Are you tired of this place too? Maria wondered as she rested her head on her arms.

For the next few minutes, she continued to stare at the lantern, mindlessly watching it to pass the time. Then, she heard that same eerie whistling from earlier. Maria crooked her head up and saw that the boat had gotten closer to the rock in the water … only, it wasn't a rock, she realized. Sitting up tall, Maria was certain now that with small, pointed protrusions, uniform grooves, and a somewhat smooth body, the rock was actually a massive, grayish white spiral seashell. From somewhere deep within it, the whistling sound could be heard.

"I wonder if that would look good in my office?" the gentleman asked himself, wiggling his fishing rod. "Maybe in the corner."

"You don't make any sense at all," Maria jabbed at him.

"You're the one who doesn't make sense," the gentleman jabbed back. "There must be something you are worried about."

"I don't think so —"

"Maybe something to do with that boy. You did find your missing boyfriend, right?"

Maria's face turned bright red.

"W-we're just friends," she nervously shouted.

"Hmm ..." the gentleman turned his head towards her for a moment, staring blankly, "alright, but something about him is bothering you for sure. I can tell."

"I really don't know ..." said Maria.

As they drifted in silence, Maria thought about her life and anything bad or troublesome that had happened to her lately.

"Leon and my new friend, Howard," she began to speak her thoughts aloud, "tried to leave the country without me. They were going to go across the sea and not take me with them."

"And why do you think they would do that?" the gentleman asked.

"Because ... I'd be in the way?" Maria suggested.

"Were you?"

"No, I ... I don't think so."

"You don't sound too sure ... why are they traveling so far away?"

"They had a friend who passed away recently, so now they're trying to learn more about him and the cane he owned."

"Cane?"

"Yes, I don't really understand it that well yet, but a spirit supposedly lives inside it. Leon and Howard are trying to figure out what to do with it."

"I see. Finding an ambition is a wonderful thing, especially for someone without one, but ambition also demands you take a path that others may not be able to follow. Friends part ways, destined to never see each other again. Quite tragic, really ... so perhaps what's bothering you is your fear that your friends are getting ahead of you ... that they are going to a place out of your reach."

It hurt Maria to hear him say such things, but ... she couldn't outright deny what he said.

"... I-I don't want that," she whimpered, "but I don't know what to do. I want to stay with them ..."

As Maria fell prey to her negative thoughts, the line on the gentleman's fishing rod tugged hard.

"Finally!" he cheered, standing up tall. "We got a bite — it's a real monster, I bet!"

He sounded much more like his old jolly self, thought Maria, putting a slight smile on her face. That smile didn't last long at all, though, because the next second she saw a giant fin cut right through the fog towards them. Maria feared at first that the monster below was going to ram the tiny boat, but the creature stopped just shy of hitting, and then Maria watched its fin begin to squirm wildly in place.

"He's fighting hard," the gentleman groaned, stepping up onto the very edge of the boat as he reeled harder.

"Do you need any help?" Maria asked worriedly.

"I'm perfectly fine —"

The next moment, the gentleman tipped straight forward off the bow. The color completely drained from Maria's face as she watched it happen.

"No!" she cried out, scurrying to the boat's edge. She was terrified that the gentleman had finally gone too far. As she looked over the edge, though, she was shocked to find him sitting in the water, staring back at her.

"What's the matter?" the gentleman asked, sounding truly confused. "Oh, I guess maybe I should have taken my shoes off before falling in. That's no reason to cry, though."

"H-how ...?" Maria couldn't understand what was happening.

The gentleman let out a howling laugh next, somewhat akin to that of the yowling apes. He then rolled to his knees, dipped his hands into the water, and fumbled around for a moment.

"You ... are not getting away ... from me!" he pulled until he dragged his catch up and raised it over his head. As water poured over the gentleman, Maria was shocked to see that the *monsters* that had frightened her so much this evening were delicate fish with enormous yet incredibly flat bodies. The one the gentleman caught wriggled helplessly on the palms of his hands.

"Fear is an illusion," he explained. "It is as vast as this sea, but as thin as paper. If you can bring yourself to confront it head on, fear will have no power over you."

His words had a powerful effect on Maria, but a tinge of doubt crossed her mind.

"H-how am I going to keep up with them, though?" she asked. "What am I supposed to do?!"

A bright smile grew on the gentleman's mask.

"Don't worry yourself," he said gently. "I won't let you fall behind your friends."

With that said, Maria couldn't help smiling back. She didn't know why, but she finally felt confident that everything would somehow turn out alright for her.

"It looks like it is time for us to part," said the gentleman, throwing his catch back into the sea.

"What do you mean?" said Maria.

"Your fears are no longer weighing the water down," the gentleman explained. "The Sea of Fear is free to flow once more. Rather a moody place, if you ask me."

As he spoke, Maria noticed that the water around his feet was rising.

"Get in," she urged the gentleman, but he shook his head.

"No need," he cheerily replied, reaching into the boat and grabbing hold of his lantern. He tied it to the end of his fishing rod, and then poked the lantern once with his finger and said, "Wake up."

The lantern in response flickered to life with a faint glow.

"Good, off we go then," said the gentleman, falling backwards into the water. The sea began to churn, and the gentleman started to drift off.

"It's not safe!" Maria shouted, but the gentleman simply waved the lantern in the air.

"Until we meet again," he said.

The boat swayed hard all of a sudden making Maria lose her balance. She stumbled to her knees. As the water rose, Maria gripped the edge of the boat as best as she could. With each second that passed, it seemed the sea was growing all the wilder. The boat, being helplessly carried by the sea's waves, rocked back and forth. Then, with one good smack against the tiny vessel, the water finally knocked the boat over and sent Maria flying into the air. Terrified, she closed her eyes tightly and braced herself for the sea's frigid embrace. A moment passed, but she didn't hit the water like she imagined. Instead, she heard a little meow in her ear. Nervously opening an eye, she saw Warren staring at her. Maria quickly sat up, realizing she was back in bed, hugging her covers tightly.

CHAPTER ELEVEN
BUSY HANDS

I t was the next morning, and Leon and his friends were all seated around Heath's dining room table once more. Leon found it very hard to keep awake, struggling over and over not to yawn or close his eyes. Across from him was Howard who seemed well rested as he thumbed through a book, keeping it turned so that Jean couldn't read it over his shoulder. Pendle was seated at the end of the table, petting Warren as he slept soundly in his arms. Maria was seated between the horolock and Leon, and she oddly looked groggy for once, something Leon wasn't used to seeing.

"Glad to see you all up bright and early," said Heath as he stepped in from the kitchen and took a seat at the far end of the table. He then proceeded to write on a few sheets of paper he had brought with him.

"Give me a moment," he said.

As everyone else then waited in silence for Heath to finish what he was doing, Maria stared down sleepily at her coat sleeve. Without her knowing how or when, a new charm had joined her moon and feather this morning. It was a copper-colored piece of paper folded many times into a flat fish. With its long dorsal fin, Maria imagined it had to be a tiny version of the ones she had seen last night.

Eventually, she grew bored of staring at her new trinket and decided to speak up.

"Heath, w-what ..." she had to stop herself to yawn. "Sorry. Um, what are we doing today? You told us you had work for us to do, I think."

"That's right," said Heath. "I can't have you all just rot here in my home all winter. Louis is a nice mouse, but he doesn't know when to get tough. Howard — Howard, put that book down."

Howard tilted his book down and gave Heath his attention.

"You have a good head on your shoulders," Heath continued, "but I can tell your stamina is pathetic."

"My stamina?" Howard repeated, sounding a little perturbed to hear Heath say that. "What's wrong with my stamina?"

"Not enough of it — Leon," Heath pressed on, "if you want that cane to be of any use, we are going to need you to do more than just stare at it. I don't need to explain much since Jean will look after you both, but put simply, I'm going to have you, Howard, go fishing, and you, Leon, collect ingredients in the forest —"

"What about me?" Maria spoke up, pointing at herself. "What will I do?"

"Um, w-we can talk about that in a little bit," Heath quickly replied. "Anyway, both of you boys look at these lists I've been working on to see what I'm talking about."

With that said, Heath slid one sheet of paper to

Howard and then another to Leon. Leon picked up his sheet and began to read it over to see what Heath meant by *ingredients*:

LEON

~ *150 whistle cones from the high branches of their trees. They are very delicate, so be careful not to break them.*

~ *30 frost melons. You're going to need to dig around in the snow to find them.*

~ *10 sackfuls of firebulbs. It's the wrong season, but bushes just past the north side of the forest should still have some.*

~ *75 velvet roots. They grow all around the hillside towards Yowling Pass.*

~ *20 dozen pepper leaves. You usually can find the vines growing all over the abandoned sleigh northeast of the house.*

~ *15 logs of petrified black hazel bark ...*

"Um ... H-Heath," said Leon as he continued reading through the list, "I don't know what any of these look like."

"That is part of the challenge," Heath replied. "More importantly, have you ever been trained before in how to use a spirit weapon?"

"Um, yeah, a little bit," Leon nervously answered back, unsure if his failed attempts on the Hungry Flounder really counted. Heath didn't look too amused to hear him answer so tentatively.

CHAPTER ELEVEN

"Good enough," he barked, standing tall. "Jean, take them to the lake to get started. I'll be right back."

"Alright," Jean answered, and Heath darted to his workshop. Howard looked slightly annoyed to have this sudden pile of work to do, and Leon could easily tell Maria was peeved for not getting a chore list of her own. As he glanced once more at his own list, Leon personally felt overwhelmed more than anything by Heath's tasks.

"Don't look so worried, Leon," said Jean, standing up from his seat. "I can probably help you with anything you aren't sure about."

Leon was relieved to hear him say that.

"Thank you," he said.

"Come on, you two," said Jean, "let's put on our heavy clothes while we wait."

"Alright," Leon replied, standing up as well. Howard made a small groan for a response, taking his time getting out of his chair, while Maria remained seated with her arms crossed, still looking very peeved for not being included (Leon thought it wise to not say a word about it right now and risk incurring her wrath).

The three boys all walked to the front of the house and put on their boots and coats. Soon afterward, Heath returned, carrying a fishing rod.

"Here," he said, handing the rod to Jean, "I don't expect you two to finish much of what's on your lists today, but we've got plenty of weeks for you both to do it all."

"Weeks?!" Leon and Howard both shouted together in shock.

"Of course," Heath slyly grinned as he pushed the front door wide open, letting a freezing gust of air blow against their faces, "don't stay out past dark."

"This is going to be fun," said Jean happily, pulling poor Leon and Howard along.

Once they were gone, Heath shut the door closed. He then returned to the dining room where he found Maria sitting at the table with her head resting on her folded arms, sulking.

"What's the matter with you?" Heath asked as he had a seat.

"Nothing," Maria glumly answered. "Should I go clean the kitchen or something."

"Why?" Heath chuckled, organizing his papers.

"Well ... I can't just do nothing."

"Of course you can't. Nim would haunt me every night if I didn't train you properly."

"Nim?"

"Yes, the spirit who kept you awake half the night."

Maria looked up at Heath with a startled expression on her face.

"H-how — how did you know that — w-wait," she shouted, "his name's Nim?!"

"That's right," Heath answered, looking a little confused by her question. "He didn't tell you?"

Maria shook her head and Heath groaned hard.

"Why does he always have to be so damn confusing

with everything?!" he moaned. "Well, too late now! His name is Nim, and he's the spirit who's taken a liking to you, whether you knew it or not yet!"

"Nim …" Maria repeated quietly. "So, he's a spirit?"

"Yes, and I am going to train you in how to invoke his power, but I couldn't say much until that nosy Jean and your two friends were out of the house. I'd rather they not pry. I would have thought Louis would have said something … maybe he didn't have permission either …"

As Heath spoke, Maria couldn't help growing giddy. She still had so many questions, but they could wait for now, she thought. Knowing that the gentleman was a spirit came as a pleasant surprise (and explained a lot in her mind), but what really made her smile was knowing that she also had a real purpose for being with Leon and Howard on their journey. Maria's smile faded slightly, though, as Heath slid a sheet of paper and a pencil towards her.

"Draw this cup," he said, holding a wooden teacup in his hand; Maria responded with a blank stare.

"Huh?" she eventually answered back.

"Draw —" Heath wiggled the cup right in front of Maria's face, "— this cup. I want you to draw it on that piece of paper."

"A-alright," Maria nervously said, reluctantly putting pencil to paper.

She had only made a quick circle of the rim of the cup when Heath suddenly yanked the paper back.

"Poor attention to detail ..." he remarked, shaking his head in disappointment.

"B-but, I'm not finished —"

"We are going to have to beat the basics into that noggin of yours!" shouted Heath, getting up from his chair. He then darted to the kitchen, and a moment later, he was back with a tall stack of paper. He dropped it down in front of Maria and calmly said, "draw a circle."

"Jean," said Howard, trudging ahead through the snow, "what exactly am I doing?"

"I thought Heath explained already," replied Jean. "You'll be fishing."

"Yeah, but why?" said Howard, sounding annoyed. "What does fishing have to do with my stamina? And why do I even need more anyway? I can run for miles already."

"I'll explain in a minute," said Jean. "First, let's get settled near the lake."

"Fine," Howard answered tersely, flipping a book open to read.

Leon, lagging slightly behind Howard and Jean, was lost in thought over what Heath had told them earlier. Somehow collecting all kinds of strange ingredients from throughout the forest was going to make him better at using Tim's cane; but Leon couldn't see how though, or why it even mattered if he could use the spirit weapon. He wasn't planning to fight with it like Tim did, or turn into a wooden monster.

"This is a good spot," said Jean, stopping by a large rock near the lake's edge. "Sit here, Howard, and take this fishing rod."

"What about bait?" Howard asked, yanking the rod from Jean.

"You won't need it," Jean replied, crouching down beside him. "The rod works just like your daggers. Focus on it and see."

Howard looked a little skeptical, but closed his eyes. Leon watched and saw tiny sparks begin to leak from the hook of the rod as Howard concentrated.

"Good," said Jean, "you've gotten much faster. You must have practiced like Boss told you to."

"How does this help me fish?" Howard asked, opening his eyes; the sparks immediately ceased. "Am I going to electrocute the whole lake?"

"Don't be silly," Jean chuckled, standing up. "Your list should have a bunch of fish on it, telling you how many you need and about how much voltage each requires."

"Voltage?" Howard questioned back, checking his list again. "Is that what those numbers are?"

"Correct," said Jean. "The fish in this lake are attracted to electricity, so, if you apply the right amount of power to the rod, you can catch each one."

"Sounds simple enough," Howard replied. Without

another word, he closed his eyes, brought the rod back to life, and then flung the hook into the water.

"So, Leon," said Jean, turning to talk to Leon next, "Heath has you gathering nuts and fruits from the forest, right?"

"Yeah," replied Leon.

"He made me do that a few times too when I was last here," said Jean. "Let me see your list. I should be able to help."

"Sure," said Leon, eagerly handing him the sheet of paper. Leon thought he could use all the help he could get, but it worried him a little when Jean started reading and his normally jovial face grew a concerned look on it.

"This is quite the challenge," he remarked, handing the sheet back.

"Really?" Leon nervously asked.

"Yeah, there's a lot on there," said Jean, "and some of the items listed are really rare, like velvet roots and slush berries. I've never even seen a black hazel tree before."

"What should I do then, Jean?" said Leon. This list was starting to look like an impossible task to him.

"For starters, let's get that cane of yours working," Jean calmly replied. "I imagine it will be helpful somehow or Heath wouldn't have bothered talking about it. You said you had a little practice using it, right?"

"Um, I once tried with Howard teaching me," Leon sheepishly answered.

"Do as he instructed then," Jean urged him. "Give it a try right now."

Leon nodded and closed his eyes. Holding the cane out with both hands, he started trying to talk to it again like he had done on the Hungry Flounder.

Hey, wake up —

"Leon, you should probably take your gloves off," Jean interrupted, pointing at his own hand. "It's a lot harder to work with a spirit weapon without physical contact."

"Oh, t-that makes sense," Leon replied. He quickly pulled his gloves off and tried once more.

You there, Mr. Spirit? Time to wake up ... I need you to wake up, please ... hello ...? For several minutes, he tried this same tactic over and over, kindly asking the cane to wake up, but it didn't seem to react in the slightest. Slowly, Leon grew dejected.

"It's not working," he eventually spoke up, opening his eyes. "It's not doing anything like when Tim used it."

"That's no good," said Jean a little worriedly. "What are you saying to it?"

"Just things like 'hello' and 'wake up,'" Leon replied, scratching his head in frustration. "I just keep asking it nicely over and over to wake up."

Jean nodded and then paced for a moment in silence, staring at the still lake waters as he thought on what to do. Leon in the meantime feared this was all hopeless for him. The cane had not done a thing to anyone since the night Tim had passed away, and now Leon was beginning to recall what Charles had said, that perhaps the spirit just didn't like him.

"Try again," Jean suddenly spoke up, walking back to Leon, "just like Howard taught you, but I want you to pour some emotion in this time. You are trying to call out the spirit, not whisper to it. My boss told me something like that before when I had trouble, and it worked well."

"Alright," Leon nodded and sat down. He gripped the cane tightly with both hands and closed his eyes.

... Wake up ... he said to the cane in his mind. *I need your help. Tim didn't really tell me anything about you, but I think with your help I can understand a little better what he meant that night. I need to understand ... or his death would have been pointless.... Please, please help me!* He pleaded. *I don't know what else to do —* !

"Leon!" Jean shouted excitedly.

"What?" said Leon, cracking an eye open. "I'm trying to focus —"

"It's sprouting!" said Jean.

Leon looked down and saw that several leaves had sprouted from the tip of the cane.

"It worked!" Leon gleefully shouted. "Jean, it actually worked!"

"Well done," said Jean happily, patting him on the back. "It looks like the spirit is finally awake. Now, try asking it to do something."

CHAPTER ELEVEN

"Like what?" Leon asked, unsure of what Jean really meant.

"Well, what did your friend Tim do with the cane?" said Jean. "Anything special, like growing some plants or maybe even some trees?"

"I've seen him grow a tree, it was a really big one too," said Leon, recalling what Tim had done when he had fought against the keeper in Moss Hill. "He also made moss move, and he turned the cane into bark like armor all over himself."

"Okay, it's a fairly strong forest spirit then if it can do all of those things," said Jean. "Why not ... try telling it to turn the cane into something like gloves," he suggested, pointing at the gloves by Leon's feet. "That should be easy enough for you to start with."

"Alright," Leon nodded.

With a serious expression, he closed his eyes, focused once more on the cane in hand, and asked in his head, *Hey, can you turn into gloves?*

The cane immediately started to twitch in response to Leon's question. Its wooden body began to unravel like threads, growing and warping in shape at a remarkable pace as it swallowed Leon's hands. Leon was very nervous that the cane might be trying to attack him again like it had done in Silas's office, but despite his worries, he kept his hands firmly stretched out. He anxiously watched as the wood gently enveloped his palms and fingers until both of his hands were encased in a perfect pair of wooden gloves.

"It worked!" Jean spoke in a quiet yet delighted voice. "I've never actually gotten to see a wooden spirit weapon in action before! They are so rare to find. Try moving your fingers," he instructed as he crouched down, staring hard at Leon's hands.

"Sure," Leon replied. He slowly closed his fingers, and like cloth, the wood bent with them. Leon was surprised at how easy it was to do, expecting the wood to have cracked a bit. He flexed his fingers open and closed several more times to be sure while Jean quietly marveled.

"How does it feel?" Jean wondered aloud.

"Really smooth," Leon answered as he grabbed a handful of snow. "I thought it'd be a lot more uncomfortable than this."

"It doesn't itch or hurt?" Jean asked.

"No," replied Leon, grinning a little now, "it feels like I'm wearing gloves. Hey, Howard, look —"

Sitting very hunched, Howard was scowling and breathing hard while holding the fishing rod tightly with both hands. He looked miserably tired, thought Leon.

"*Is — is he alright?*" Leon whispered to Jean, but Jean just smiled.

"*Let's leave him alone for a bit,*" he whispered back. "*I think it's about time you got started on your own list.*"

"O-okay," said Leon reluctantly, still not entirely convinced they should just leave Howard like this, but Jean really didn't seem worried.

CHAPTER ELEVEN

They walked a little ways away from the lake to where the edge of the forest began. As they got closer, Leon began to hear slight whistling coming from somewhere deep in the woods.

"I wonder what kind of bird that is?" he said.

"Those aren't birds," said Jean.

"Well, what are they then?" Leon asked.

"I'll answer that question in a moment," Jean replied, suddenly kneeling down, "but first, help me dig around the ground here. Keep away from the tree roots."

"What are we looking for?" said Leon, dropping to his hands and knees.

"Frost melons," Jean answered.

"Like the one we ate last night?"

"Yeah, they grow all over deep in the forest, but if you are lucky, you can find a few along the edge of the forest too. You have to find a spot, though, where tree roots aren't in the way. The melons don't like to compete with them."

Jean and Leon dug around in the snow for a minute or so, but they didn't have much luck finding anything. Eventually, Jean sat back and sighed.

"Well, at least you already know what it looks like," he said. "Shall we move on to the next item?"

"Sure," said Leon, standing up and patting snow off himself. He then offered a hand to Jean to help him up.

"Thank you," said Jean, pulling himself up to his

feet. Once standing, though, he didn't immediately let go of Leon's hand. Instead, he studied the wooden glove while squeezing it a bit.

"It's so flexible ... like skin," he remarked, looking almost entranced. "Does it feel heavy?"

"No, not at all," Leon answered.

Jean finally released his hand.

"Sorry," he said with a silly grin, waving his hands defensively, "I couldn't help myself."

"It's alright," Leon smiled back.

"So, you see the big cones lying around the trees?"

"Yeah."

"Those are whistle cones."

"Oh ... OOOOOH! Are they making that whistling sound?!"

"That's right," said Jean, picking up a cone. "The forest and trees here all get their name from these cones. Wind blows through them, making the sound we keep hearing."

Jean took a deep breath and blew against the cone in his hands, making a whistling sound.

"Unfortunately," he then continued, holding the cone up for Leon to see better, "the ones on the forest floor almost never have seeds because animals get to them first. You are going to have to climb up the trees to find some good ones."

Leon looked upward at the tall trees with thin branches, slowly realizing the challenge in acquiring whistle cones.

"I guess I should get started then," he said, not sounding too enthused any longer.

"I'm going to go back and check on Howard," said Jean. "Hopefully he hasn't snapped the rod in two yet out of frustration."

Leon grinned and nodded.

"I'll see you later then," said Jean, turning to leave. "Good luck."

"Yeah," Leon replied, waving goodbye.

Once Jean was gone, Leon walked up to a tree and studied it.

"Alright," he told himself, grabbing hold of a low branch. As he pulled on it, though, the branch easily began to crack. Leon stopped and stared at it for a moment before trying another one. Unfortunately, it gave out too.

How am I supposed to climb this tree? Leon asked himself as he searched for a branch that might be a little sturdier. He tried two more times, but the branches were just too thin. In no mood to be deterred, he turned and walked to another tree. Once more, he grabbed a branch, and once more, it easily gave out from his weight before he could pull himself up. Leon pressed his fingers hard against the trunk of the tree.

"I need those whistle cones," he told himself in a frustrated voice.

After a moment of sulking, he was ready to try another branch, but as he pulled his hands back, his wooden gloves stuck to the bark of the tree like glue, keeping his hands firmly in place. It took a few hard tugs, but eventually the gloves came loose. Leon then looked them and the tree over, trying to guess why they suddenly misbehaved like that, but slowly, an idea crossed his mind.

Reaching up high, he smacked his hands hard against the bark, and just like he imagined, the gloves stuck to the tree. A smile grew on Leon's face, and he carefully placed a foot on the base of a fragile branch. Pulling himself up with the gloves, Leon finally began climbing.

CHAPTER TWELVE
PURPOSE

Lily stared at Inna with a very bored expression on her face. For the last hour or so, her handmaid had happily watched her move about the empty ballroom of the palace, dancing by herself. There was no music, only the sound of an elderly instructor named Miss Gorsky clapping her hands in rhythm.

"Princess Liliana, you mustn't move so quickly," said Miss Gorsky suddenly. She stopped her clapping and walked straight over to Lily. Once in reach, she quickly moved Lily's elbow up an inch, straightened her back, and then took hold of her hand.

"A lady must move with grace and ease when dancing during the Spirit Ball," Miss Gorsky continued, leading Lily along in dance. "Everyone will be watching, judging your every move to learn what kind of woman you are. Do you want to be perceived as clumsy and rash?"

"No," Lily answered in a monotone voice. Miss Gorsky stopped.

"Try not to be so glum about it all," she said, patting Lily on the hand. "There is still plenty of time until the ball, so we can stop here today. Think about what we practiced. Inna, a word, please."

"Y-yes, of course," said Inna, stepping forward.

CHAPTER TWELVE

As the two of them talked, Lily did not wait for them to finish. Feigning an interest in what she had just learned, she danced her way across the ballroom and out of the corner of Inna's eye. Lily glided to the main doorway leading into the ballroom, passed through it unnoticed, and then scurried away.

As Lily walked briskly through the palace, she wondered how long it would take until Inna noticed she was gone. Lily had spent all morning and afternoon following a schedule without pause, waiting for a chance like this to slink off. She knew she would need to apologize to Inna later, but Lily desperately wanted to take part in a different sort of lesson today than the ones her handmaid had planned.

After walking all the way to the northwestern corner of the palace, Lily flew down a short flight of spiral stairs. Once she reached the bottom, she spun left and continued down a thin, empty passageway that ended at a door. She burst right through it and oddly found her little sister seated on the floor, waiting patiently by herself on the other side.

"You're late," said Renata with a smile.

Out of breath, Lily looked up and down the short hallway for any handmaids.

"W-why are you by yourself?" Lily asked.

"I said I was going to take a nap," Renata answered, standing up. "They won't notice for a while."

"That doesn't really answer my question, though. Your nannies will get worried if you're missing —"

"You'll need this, won't you?" said Renata, offering Lily her cloak.

Lily looked at the cloak and then at Renata with a slight smile, noticing Renata was wearing a little cloak of her own.

"You're only going to watch, alright?" said Lily, grabbing the cloak.

"Yes," Renata happily replied.

Lily threw on her cloak, and then together the sisters stealthy walked down the hallway, being careful not to be spotted by anyone. At the end was a short flight of steps that led to a large, old wooden exterior door. The pair hurried down the steps, Lily pulled the door open wide, and then Renata stepped through to the outside. Lily quickly followed, pulling the door closed behind them, and then the sisters remained standing where they were for a moment, watching with glee as the palace guards practiced in their training grounds.

Each royal guard was skilled in the use of spirit weapons, honing his abilities daily here in order to protect the royal family without failure. At the moment, two men were dueling with blunt ice spears while the rest watched, cheering them on.

"Men," Kirill suddenly spoke up over the crowd, "turn and bow to your princesses."

Everyone present, duelists and all, immediately stopped whatever it was they were doing, turned towards the princesses, and deeply bowed their heads.

"As you were," Kirill commanded next, and the guards once more raised their heads. As they then went back to training, Kirill walked up to Lily and Renata with a smile growing on his face.

"I didn't expect you to come running down here so soon," he said happily. "You seem eager to pick up where we left off last, but did you practice while you were gone?"

"I did," said Lily, smiling confidently back.

"Good," replied Kirill. "Princess Renata, I assume you've come to watch, so please have a seat on the bench over there."

"Alright," Renata replied.

"Now, Princess Lily," said Kirill, turning his attention once more towards Lily, "Let's start with the basics as usual. Mold a ball of ice."

"Yes," said Lily, raising her hand up so he could see. Calling out in her mind to the ring on her finger, the ring glowed and ice quickly began to gather in her palm.

"You are getting much quicker," Kirill proudly remarked as the ice condensed into a ball. After a moment, the ring stopped glowing, and Lily clenched the ball to prove it was solid.

"What's next?" she said eagerly.

"Let's try something a little harder for fun. Yefim, come here," Kirill shouted over his shoulder.

One of the young guards training nearby immediately stopped mid-swing and ran straight to Kirill.

"Sir?" said Yefim, seeming nervous as he tried to not look at Lily directly.

"Stand still right there," said Kirill. "Now, Princess, I want you to freeze him in place."

Lily looked a little worried to hear him say that.

"I'm not telling you to kill him, just snare his feet," said Kirill, pointing at the ground. "Focus on his feet and freeze them in place."

"That shouldn't be too difficult then," Lily replied, kneeling down. She placed her palm flat on the snowy ground, and as the ring glowed, the snow around her hand slowly hardened. The snow she froze then expanded and traveled straight to Yefim's feet, encasing his boots in a layer of ice.

"That should do it," Kirill eventually said.

Lily nodded and her ring stopped; the ice grew still.

"Yefim, try moving," Kirill ordered next.

Yefim wiggled his legs, but his feet wouldn't budge.

"I'm stuck," he remarked happily as he tried yanking his feet free.

"Perfect," said Kirill. "Break yourself free now and get back to practicing."

"Yes, sir," Yefim replied.

"I want to do something harder," said Lily.

"Harder?" Kirill questioned back.

"Yes, like what he's doing," said Lily, pointing at a group of guards. They were standing in a small circle, carefully observing one of their peers as he molded ice around himself into a sort of dome.

"Ah, that's not really too difficult to learn," Kirill remarked, "but it is very taxing on you to do it right. Are you sure you want to give it a try?"

"Yes!" Lily answered loudly like she were one of Kirill's trainees.

"Very well then," Kirill chuckled, "use the ground as the base and have ice grow up and around you into a solid shell."

Lily nodded and closed her eyes.

"Keep them open, Princess," said Kirill. "It might help you focus, but an enemy could easily hurt you while you do that. There's no point in learning our kingdom's techniques if you can't defend yourself while using them."

"Yes," Lily obediently replied.

She commanded her ring to grow the ice around her, and it did so, but, as the ice rose, she could feel her energy being sapped.

Suddenly, the door to the palace burst open and Inna stumbled through.

"Princess!" she shouted between breaths. "I knew — I'd find you here. What were you — thinking running off without a word? I was worried to death — Renata, you're here too — ?!"

"Please," Kirill spoke up, "let her focus."

"But, isn't this a bit much?" Inna asked Kirill, tugging on his coat sleeve.

"I'm alright," said Lily, breathing hard.

"Keep going," Kirill encouraged her. "You've got the

ice growing, now just mold the shape. Use the tips of your fingers to make it easier."

"Right!" Lily shouted back.

Doing as instructed, she pressed the tips of her fingers against the ice and gently brushed it along. She guided it upward until, at last, the ice came together to form a perfect dome. Collapsing to her knees, almost wheezing, Lily gawked at her creation. The dome was thin enough that she could see Kirill, Renata, and Inna standing on the other side, admiring her work too.

"How do we get her out?" Lily heard Inna ask.

"Like this," Kirill answered, placing his hand on the dome. The next second, the entire thing shattered into a flurry of snow. Lily was impressed as usual by his level of skill, though it saddened her to see how easily he destroyed her work. Kirill walked up to Lily and plopped down onto the ground in front of her.

"Good work," he said with a big grin, putting a bright smile on Lily's face. "You very well might be the first royal caretaker the kingdom has had in a while."

"Stop encouraging this behavior," Inna admonished Kirill. "She is a lady of the Medovs, not a soldier who —"

"The day might come when she rules over us all," Kirill spoke over her. "I would feel like a failure if I allowed our queen to not be proficient in how to fight alongside the spirits."

His words held so much weight behind them that Inna couldn't bring herself to object.

CHAPTER TWELVE

"If by some chance our princess could become a caretaker," Kirill continued, "it might even help quell the people's worries."

"B-but caretakers are rare," Inna finally challenged him. "Only a handful exist throughout the kingdom, and each of them inherited their spirit. There hasn't been a powerful spirit willing to serve the royal family for some time now —"

Inna stopped herself, looking nervous that she had said too much.

"I'm so sorry —"

"It's alright," said Lily, standing up. "Father and Uncle often tell me that it is our own fault that we are not caretakers. We spend too much time on the kingdom, making the spirits jealous."

"The Medovs are always looking out for us," said a young guard.

Lily turned and saw all the guards throughout the training grounds had gathered.

"My village would have starved without them!" another guard said emphatically.

"King Ilya treats us great!" a third shouted.

"Yeah, there is no better king!"

"Exactly!"

Lily was moved to see so much support for her family in these troubling times.

"Thank you all for your very kind words," Inna spoke up over the crowd, "but the princesses must be going now."

The guards grumbled hearing that, but Inna shook her head.

"Princess Liliana is late for her next lesson," she said sternly. "Or are one of you brave enough to tell the King that it's fine to miss it?"

Every single guard answered her with a silent, cowed expression.

"Good," said Inna, "let's go you two."

"Fine," Lily sighed. "Goodbye, everyone. I'll see you tomorrow afternoon."

"No you won't!" Inna whined in her ear. "You are still far too behind in your lessons as it is — stand still a moment."

Lily paused and Inna straightened the bow on her head.

"Much better," said Inna. "You never know who you will meet."

Lily rolled her eyes and pushed the door to the palace open.

"L-let me get the doors!" Inna fussed, following after Lily and Renata as they hurried inside.

"Keep that hand of yours moving, Maria," said Heath sternly.

He and Maria had moved from the dining room and were now seated across from one another at a workbench in his workshop. While Heath carefully carved an intricate design into an oval-shaped plank of wood, Maria was busy drawing circles on a sheet of paper.

"Let me have a look," said Heath, blowing on the wood.

Maria sluggishly slid the paper to him and then looked at her left hand. She had drawn so many circles over the last couple of hours that the side of her hand was turning black from lead. Rubbing her skin with her thumb, she waited for Heath to offer his opinion on her drawings.

"Hmmm … not bad," Heath remarked, rotating the sheet in the air. "Better attention to detail … almost no flaws …"

Maria grew a little excited, thinking she had finally drawn a perfect circle. However, her happy expression faded fast as Heath took the sheet and placed it to the side on top of a tall stack of sheets riddled with her failures from throughout the day.

"What was wrong with them?!" she asked, sounding a bit irked. "Those were perfect."

"No they weren't," Heath quickly replied. "Some were good, but I could still see carelessness in their design, especially the ones near the bottom. Those were starting to look more like squares than circles, so you need to continue practicing the basics —"

"The basics of what, though?" Maria interrupted him. "What am I learning the basics of?"

She had grown tired of doodling on sheets for hours now without any reason as to why.

Heath's eyes turned downward as he sat for a moment in silence, thinking. Maria slowly began to worry if maybe her little outburst had upset him.

"Hand me a sheet, please," Heath eventually spoke up in a calm voice.

"S-sure," replied Maria, picking up a piece of blank paper from a stack sitting on her side of the workbench. She handed it to Heath and he quietly thanked her.

"Also the pencil," he quickly added.

"Oh, right, here," said Maria, handing her pencil to Heath.

"Thank you," he quietly thanked her again. He then began to draw. With a single, crisp hand stroke, he made a perfect circle on the sheet. Maria was amazed and a little frustrated at how easily he had done that.

"The basics are the foundation upon which you must build," Heath lectured, holding up the sheet so Maria could see, "otherwise your work will be sloppy and full of mistakes."

Maria nodded, and then Heath put the paper down and began to draw more.

"Nim is a strange and carefree spirit, but his power is not something easy to control. I've seen firsthand what happens to those who do not take this matter seriously. I need you to get better at a lot of things, including drawing, if you want to be his caretaker."

"What kind of power does he have?" Maria asked,

watching Heath's pencil move as he continued to draw. "I keep ending up in strange worlds with him, but that's about it."

"Which worlds?" Heath asked.

"Um, one was really dark and full of candles —"

"The Lost Thought Office," Heath nodded.

"Yeah, that's what the creature in there called it," said Maria. "I can't remember the second time well at all, but last night it was a giant sea with paper fish."

"That would have to be the Sea of Fear," Heath nodded with a slight smile now. "I'm glad I've never been there. Not sure if anyone I know besides my friend Patrick has seen it."

"How do you know all those places?" Maria asked. "I still don't understand how you know Nim and what his power is."

"It's not my place to talk about all that ..." said Heath, "sorry. I really wish I could say more."

"It's alright," said Maria, feeling a little bad now for pressing the matter.

"Finished," said Heath, putting his pencil down. He then held up the sheet, and Maria grew a bewildered look on her face: In the short time they had chatted, Heath had drawn a sketch of Maria.

"You're so good!" she said, leaning forward to get a better look.

"I know plenty of others who are much better than me at drawing," said Heath modestly, "but I know enough to help you learn the basics. Once we have you drawing shapes well enough, I'll teach you something much more interesting."

"Alright," Maria nodded with a slight smile. She still couldn't entirely understand the point of all this drawing, but she had a little more faith now in Heath's tutelage.

"Heath, you home?" Jean shouted from inside the house. "We're back."

"I'm in the workshop," Heath shouted back. Then, in a much quieter voice, he whispered to Maria, "We can call it a day for now. Don't tell anyone what I have you doing or Nim might get mad at me, alright?"

"No problem," Maria happily whispered back.

She and Heath stepped out of the workshop and found Jean, Howard, and Pendle all by the fireplace. While Jean worked on getting a fire going, Howard sat slumped on the hearth, looking completely exhausted. Pendle had spent the day in a chair there, petting Warren as he napped on the horolock's lap.

"Howard, what happened to you?" Maria asked.

Howard looked up at her for a moment, and then responded with a groan and tilted his head back down again, closing his eyes.

"Don't mind him," said Jean. "The fishing took a lot out of him."

"How many did he catch?" Heath asked.

"Um," Jean spoke a little sheepishly, "not a lot."

"What is *not a lot*?" Heath replied, sounding a little annoyed. "Seven? Nine?"

"I put them in the kitchen," said Jean. "Go take a look while I finish up here."

"Fine," said Heath.

Maria followed behind him into the kitchen. She had been inside it once before, but she still found it charming how everything, from the cabinets to the plates, were made of wood like the rest of the house, keeping true to the theme.

"Pathetic," Heath growled.

Maria looked past him and saw four puny fish lying on the counter. They looked about big enough for Leon to have as a snack.

Heath turned hard and stuck his whole head out the doorway.

"Only four measly fish?" he yelled. "You're a lot weaker than I thought, boy."

Maria wasn't sure, but she thought she heard Howard weakly groan in response.

"Where's Leon?" Heath asked next, walking back into the dining room. "He didn't get lost, did he?"

"No, he should be here any second," said Jean. "Leon was just finishing up one last tree."

"Oh?" said Heath, sounding interested. "Is he getting better with that cane?"

Jean actually smiled at that question, but before he could answer, the front door suddenly swung open and Leon came stumbling in. He was out of breath and dragging a small sack with him.

"Leon, are you alright?" Maria asked worriedly as

he shut the door and then immediately plopped right down onto the floor.

"I-I'm fine," he said between breaths.

"Looks like you had a busy day too," said Heath. "You fare any better?"

"Well enough that I needed to get him a bag from the house for his haul," said Jean.

"These were all I could collect," said Leon, dragging the sack forward. He opened it and revealed that it was filled with whistle cones. Heath actually smiled, looking a bit impressed.

"Well done," he laughed. "You managed to get quite a few today."

"Yeah," Leon wearily answered.

"It's a good start, but be careful not to go too deep into the forest, especially as it gets late."

"How come?"

"Well, for starters, you might get lost and freeze to death. Kind of obvious, right?"

Leon nodded.

"There's also a really mean spirit named Sosnog lurking deep in the forest, so you want to avoid that too. Are those good enough reasons for you?"

"Yes," Leon tiredly chuckled.

"Now, where did you put your cane? You better not have lost ... it ..."

A surprised look grew on Heath's face as Leon grinned while wiggling his hands gloved in wood.

"Right here," he said. "It helped me climb the trees.

At first it was hard, but I thought about Howard and Jean's advice and kept asking the cane to let go or stick to the tree when I needed it to."

"Mori has taken a liking to you, it seems," said Heath, picking up the bag of cones. "I didn't think it was going to be so easy."

"Who's Mori?" Maria asked as she pulled on Leon's arm to help him up.

"Tim mentioned that name once before, I think," said Leon.

"It's the name of the spirit he looked after," Heath explained. "The one you are looking after now."

"Mori," Leon repeated, closing his eyes.

"You alright — ?" Maria began to ask, but she grew quiet as Leon raised his hands a little. The wooden gloves began to ripple and then warp. Slowly, the wood bonded together and stretched out until it was once again a single cane lying in Leon's hands. Maria was in awe.

"Well done," Heath said with a slight bit of pride in his voice.

"Mori is a pretty good listener," Leon remarked, admiring the cane.

Heath lowered his head a bit to look Leon in the eyes.

"You asked me yesterday if I could tell you more about what *Elm* means," he said. "Truthfully, like you, I don't know a lot about it either, but I do know it is a title given to each person who has looked after Mori.

The fact that Mori is helping you means that the spirit has acknowledged you as its next caretaker. You will need to travel a lot more to get a better answer, but for now, I want you to train here like you did today and get better at using the cane."

As Heath spoke, Leon could see in his soft yet serious expression how important a matter this was to him. Leon imagined he must have spent quite a bit of time mulling over what to say.

"Any questions?" Heath asked.

"No, I can't think of any," Leon replied with a light smile. He was happy for now with Heath's answer.

Heath nodded with a slight smile of his own and then turned around.

"Jean," he said loudly, walking towards the dining room, "I'm going to have to get creative with dinner tonight since your haul of fish was so pitiful. I want you and Howard to toast some of these whistle cones. You still remember how, right?"

"Yes, I haven't forgotten, Master Heath," said Jean. "Wake up, Howard. I'm going to need some help."

Howard replied with a long groan.

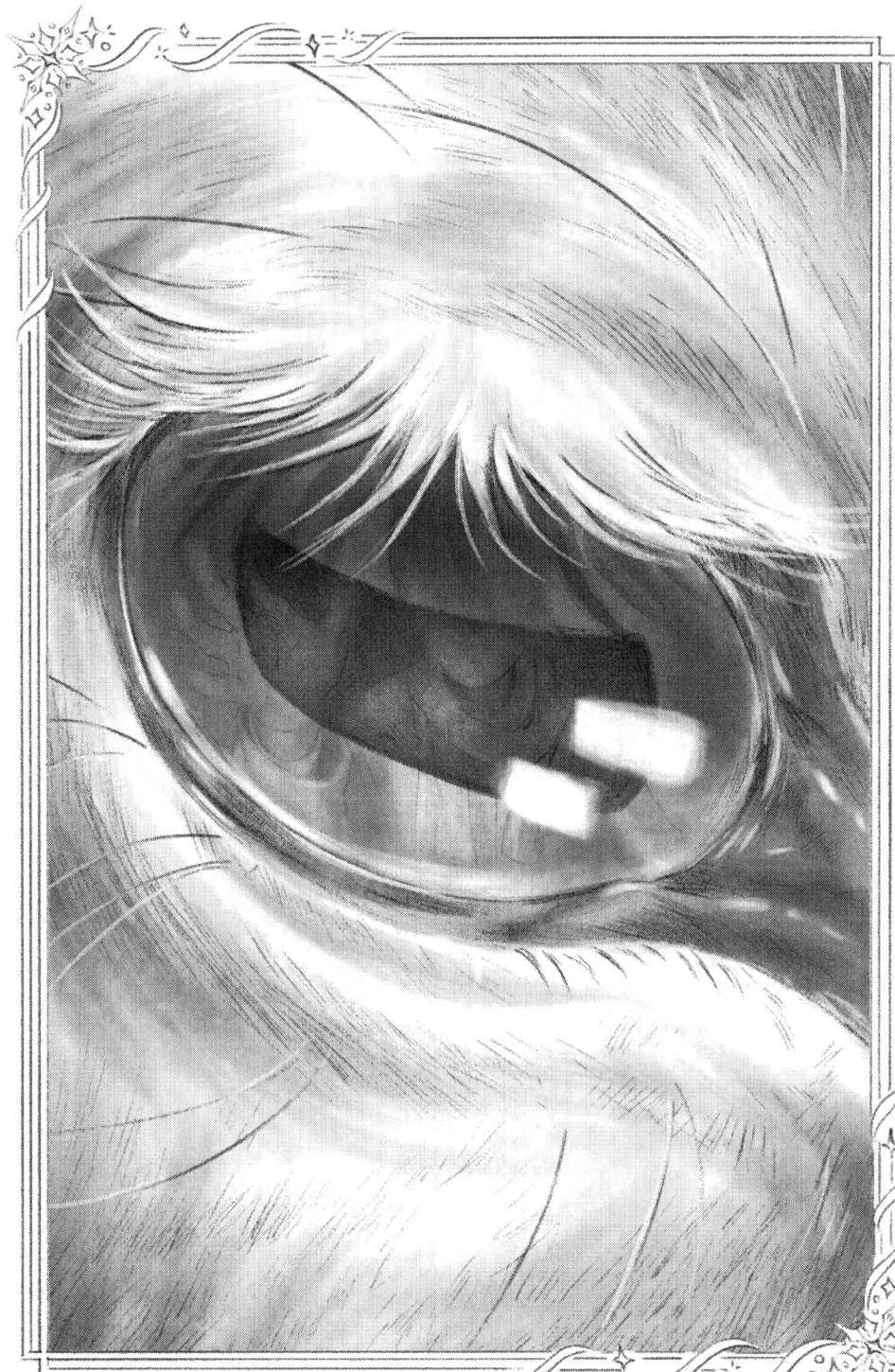

CHAPTER THIRTEEN
HIDDEN FRUIT

With the days growing shorter and the snow ever present, the year came to an end and a new one began. For Maria, this morning was not much different from the others lately. She woke up, got dressed, and walked downstairs to find Pendle and Warren patiently waiting for her at the dining table.

"Are Leon and Howard out?" she asked, leaning on the back of a chair while stretching her shoulders. Pendle slowly nodded in response. Maria yawned and nodded back before strolling into the kitchen. For the last several weeks, Leon and Howard had taken it upon themselves to get up at the crack of dawn to work through their respective lists of chores. Maria let a smile slip from her drowsy expression as she thought about them, finding their effort admirable.

Maria made herself a small bowl of crushed whistle seeds, milk, and dried fruit, and then she returned to the dining table and had a seat across from Pendle. As she then began to eat her breakfast, she thought of questions for her horolock.

"Are all your joints alright?" she asked first, and he silently nodded.

"Is Heath in his workshop?" she asked next, and again Pendle nodded without a word.

"Do you remember anything about the person who made you?" she then asked between bites.

"I might," Pendle answered.

At first, Maria didn't react at all, thinking he would say "no" like he had always done. When it finally sank in, though, her head shot up, looking very excited.

"R-r-really?!" she stammered. "W-what do you remember? Tell me!"

Pendle did not reply for a good half-minute or so, but Maria waited patiently, knowing he was simply putting his thoughts together.

"He ... was thin," Pendle eventually said. "He was a thin man with a ... ridged frame. I believe he was tall. His nose was ... pointed with a pair of glasses ... sitting at the very tip. He seemed ... happy. His hands moved tirelessly as he worked ... on something. He sometimes ... would hum."

Maria listened attentively, trying to paint a picture in her mind of who this man might be.

"Do you remember anything else?" she asked. "Like where he was or something he said?"

"No," Pendle shook his head, "I am ... sorry, but that is all I ... can recall."

"That's alright," Maria consoled him. "It's a start."

"Yes, it is," Pendle nodded back. "You had better hurry ... to the workshop, or Master Heath will ... get upset."

"Yeah," Maria replied, standing up.

She quickly put her empty bowl in the kitchen and

then walked through the house to the workshop in the back. There she found Heath working diligently in silence.

"Have a seat," he said. "I'll be with you in a little bit."

"Okay," said Maria, gently closing the door behind herself. Then, as she walked to the workbench and had a seat across from Heath, she asked, "Am I doing more hexagons today?"

"Yes, work on what you practiced yesterday for now," Heath quickly replied as he got up to grab a tool. "I'm a little busy today."

"Does it have anything to do with the instrument?" Maria asked, grabbing a sheet of paper.

"What makes you think it's an instrument?" Heath replied, carefully eying a piece of wood for what Maria imagined were imperfections.

"Well, it looks sort of like one," she answered as she began to draw. "You've been working on it for weeks, putting a lot of time into it."

"Quite observant of you," Heath mocked a little. "I'm making a violin. You do know what a violin is, right?"

"Yes," Maria curtly replied, rolling her eyes at his question, "we usually call them fiddles."

"Right," said Heath. "I need to have this one finished in a week for a very, very important person."

"Who is it?" Maria asked, curious to know.

"Someone you will be very shocked to meet," Heath

answered with a slight smirk, "but for now, I won't say any more."

"Well, is there something I could do to help you finish on time?" Maria asked next.

"Not with angles that crooked," said Heath, tapping his finger on Maria's sheet of paper. "You don't have time to help me."

Miffed to hear him say that, Maria sank back in her chair and continued to mindlessly draw in silence.

Though it had taken her some time, she had eventually been permitted to move on from circles. Heath would draw shapes each day and she would have to practice copying them over and over until she got them right. Maria found this sort of work rather boring, but after several weeks, she had somewhat gotten used to the drudgery.

She sighed and picked up a new sheet, knowing none of her hexagons would pass.

"Take a break for a second and grab me my hammer," said Heath. "It's sitting on the shelf right behind you."

Maria smiled and stood up.

Sometime I need to thank Maria again for this coat, Howard thought to himself as he slightly wiggled the fishing rod in his hands.

The first day of fishing weeks ago had completely

exhausted Howard, so much so that Jean had carried him back to the house that night. But now, Howard could fish all day without growing too tired if he was careful. He'd gotten good at getting the small volt skimmers on the list, but he hadn't had too much luck yet with the much larger creatures lurking at the bottom of the lake.

"Hey! Howard!" Jean shouted from afar, trudging through the snow towards him. "How are you doing?"

Howard waved his hand up in the air limply and then continued staring at the water. He had mixed feelings about Jean being around. He had good advice from time to time, but Jean's cheery attitude could sometimes be a little too grating on Howard's nerves, making it hard to concentrate.

For a moment, Howard tried to put in a little burst of energy into the fishing rod to attract a bigger catch, but he quickly found himself feeling faint. He eased up and rubbed his throbbing forehead. This tool worked just like his daggers, he thought, except his pair of weapons only took a little bit of his own energy to activate an electric current. The fishing rod, on the other hand, demanded a constant source of energy to work, but it could produce an incredible amount of electricity if its wielder were capable enough to feed it the necessary energy required.

"Catch anything good while I was gone?" Jean asked as he had a seat beside Howard.

"Nothing yet," Howard quietly replied.

CHAPTER THIRTEEN

"Let's take a break then," said Jean. "I brought some food from the house while I took a walk."

"Hold on," said Howard, "I'm still trying to get one of the ones near the bottom."

"Take a break, Howard," said Jean in a slightly sterner tone than before. "You need to rest once in a while or you won't catch anything."

"... Alright," Howard gave in. He didn't want to admit it to Jean, but he knew he had pushed himself a little too hard in the last hour.

Howard put his fishing rod down and spun around to face Jean.

"So, what are we eating today?" he asked, pulling a book out from his coat pocket to read.

"Nothing too exciting, I'm afraid," said Jean, offering Howard a small bag. "Just some dried firebulbs."

"Better than nothing," Howard replied, grabbing the bag and undoing its lace with one hand while flipping his book open with the other.

"They aren't bad, though," said Jean as he opened his own bag. "Pretty good with some salt, actually."

"Yeah," Howard agreed, picking several red bulbs out of the bag. They were tiny enough that a dozen or so could fit in his hand.

"What are you reading?" Jean asked.

"Just a history book Boss gave me," said Howard.

"What kind of history?" Jean asked next.

"Volgiev," Howard answered, turning the page. "I've been learning more about the rulers of this kingdom.

There isn't anything about the most recent king, but there is plenty on all the others that came before him. A Medov has always ruled, and each king has traditionally picked their successor, though they usually just pick their oldest son or daughter. To nobody's surprise, they've all been caretakers as well."

"Except the most recent two," Jean added, stretching his arms. "The current king is definitely not a caretaker, and his father was probably not one either."

"Yeah, and nothing I've read explains why," said Howard.

Jean nodded while grabbing a handful of firebulbs.

"I couldn't find Leon anywhere," he said, tossing the fruit into his mouth. "I stopped by the edge of the forest, but he was nowhere to be seen."

"He probably had to go deeper in to fulfill what's left on his list," said Howard. "He'll turn up later tonight like he always does with a bunch of stuff."

"Are you jealous he's getting ahead of you?" Jean slyly jabbed, grabbing another handful of firebulbs.

"I'm not jealous," Howard snapped back. "With a crazy spirit weapon like his, I'd be disappointed if he didn't find every whistle cone in the whole forest."

"Is it really that good of a weapon, though?" Jean questioned. "I know ones with plant spirits are very rare, but that's mostly because the weapons able to house such spirits are typically brittle. Boss doesn't even try making them. Frankly, Leon's cane seemed pretty lackluster to me when I held it. Even after it woke up and turned into gloves, there still wasn't much power coming from it."

"You have no idea what you're talking about," said Howard angrily, looking annoyed at Jean.

"Why's that?" Jean lightly laughed.

"I saw Tim use the cane once before. In his hands, it can destroy an entire —"

Howard stopped himself as he realized he almost said something he shouldn't talk about so casually, especially when it came to things like Ravnell.

"Destroyed what?" Jean asked, sounding genuinely curious now. "Something big? Like a cart?"

"Yeah," Howard halfheartedly lied, turning back towards the lake. "Thanks for the food, but I need to keep fishing or Heath will yell at us —"

"You're not telling me something important," Jean interrupted with a smirk. "I won't prod it out of you, but I would like to know the *real* reason that cane is so special. I figured by now you'd tell me."

Howard briefly glanced at Jean, but didn't reply, choosing instead to stare back at the water and think to himself in silence. A part of him wanted to share with Jean what he knew. They needed to find answers to all the things Glint and Tim had said that night, and Jean could be trusted in helping, Howard was sure of that; but he also felt he shouldn't talk about something so important without Leon and Maria knowing. It wouldn't be fair to them, he thought, especially not to Leon.

"You know," Jean spoke up, "I'm actually more curious to know how Leon got so good with that cane so quickly. I thought he would struggle a lot more with using it, but he's barely needed any advice. It might just be the spirit's doing, though. We really don't know much about forest spirits, do we?"

"That's because there are no forests in Pradow," Howard joked.

Jean chuckled hearing him say that.

"You're not wrong," he happily replied. "Here, let me show you how you catch one of the fat skimmers at the bottom. There's a trick to it."

"We still haven't found pepper leaves yet," Leon remarked as he checked his list. "It says they grow on a sleigh ... oh!"

The cane suddenly slipped from Leon's hand. As it dropped to the ground, the wood coiled into a ball and tumbled a few feet ahead.

"Did you find another one already?" Leon asked, walking up to the ball. He tapped it with his finger and then watched as the ball unraveled back into a cane. Leon then knelt down and started digging in the snow with his hands. It took him a minute or so, but eventually, he yanked his hands back up, holding a frost melon between them now.

"Good work, Mori," Leon told his spirit as he placed

the melon in a small sack. "I only need seven more of these."

Leon had never been this deep into the forest before. Normally, he stopped once he reached where the blue pine berries grew, but today he had decided to go a little farther. The whistle trees were taller, more densely packed, and their whistling sound was much louder and eerier to hear. Leon didn't mind, though. He was having too much fun finding frost melons to notice the change in the forest's tone. He had badly needed the fruit for Heath's list of ingredients, so finding so many so quickly spurred him on to keep looking.

Leon kept walking and the trees kept growing closer and closer together. After finding yet another melon, he noticed that it was starting to get late.

"We should probably go back …" Leon began to say, but then he spotted something red moving farther ahead amongst the trees. Not one to ignore something out of the ordinary, he craned his head to the side a bit to get a better look, but he wasn't entirely sure what he was looking at: It seemed to be just snow and a red rag of cloth. Leon took a step closer next towards it, but immediately stopped as the snow spun around, revealing a pair of glowing blue eyes. Leon then realized it was a snezy, just like the one he had seen in the alley, rag and all. It looked so similar that Leon was convinced it had to be the same one he'd met before.

The spirit did not stare back for long, deciding to

quickly hop away deeper into the forest, and Leon, consumed by foolish curiosity, followed right after it without much thought. At this point, the trees were packed so tightly that Leon was practically squeezing between them, forcing his way through. The forest was also growing eerily dark, as if warning bold travelers to not wander any farther, but Leon was far more interested in the snezy than his fears.

Just as the whistle trees seemed to have turned into a wall, they all of a sudden thinned a great deal, forming a glade in the heart of the forest. In the center stood a single tree with no branches or leaves whatsoever. It looked dead to Leon, like it were ready to fall any day. At the base sat the snezy, tapping on the tree with its mitten-shaped hand. In the open light, Leon realized it was a lot whiter than when he'd seen it rummaging through the trash.

The snezy looked to Leon, then back to the tree, and then a moment later, hopped around it. Leon smiled, thinking the spirit was trying to hide. Leon played along and walked up to the tree, but when he peeked his head around to the other side, the snezy was nowhere to be found. Leon looked harder, searching for where the spirit had gone.

"Hey, where'd you run off — ?" Leon began to call out, but all of a sudden, a heavy gust of snow blasted against his back, startling him. Leon spun around in fear and was shocked to see the face of an enormous deer staring back at him.

CHAPTER THIRTEEN

"Uh …" Leon was still not very knowledgeable on the subject of spirits, but he was sure that, like the snezy, this creature had to be one too.

Its size was truly impressive, standing at a height about half as tall as the trees around them, but the nature of its body was what made Leon confident about it being a spirit. Its coat was long, thick, and brown; it draped so far down that most of the spirit's legs were covered. Even more unique, though, was the bristly texture of the coat that made it look more like pine needles than fur. Its antlers had a rough, bark skin to them like branches on a tree, and its eyes glowed a beautiful bright brown. They studied Leon carefully as its nose exhaled another gust of deathly cold air in his face, making Leon shiver.

Eventually, the spirit lost interest in its visitor, lying down. It rested its head on its front leg and stared past Leon at the barren tree.

Leon was still nervous but also a little curious now to know what was going through the creature's mind.

"Is this your tree?" he asked the spirit absentmindedly, waving his hand at the dead tree.

The spirit looked at him for a moment, making Leon nearly jump back in fear, but then its focus returned once more to the tree. Leon began to feel pity welling in his heart as the spirit's eyes grew saddened, staring longingly ahead. Eventually they closed and the spirit seemed to have gone to sleep.

Gripping his cane tightly as the wood quickly

formed into gloves, Leon grew a serious expression on his face.

We need to do something, he told Mori.

He walked up to the tree and pressed his hands on its dead, brittle bark. There he then stood in silence, trying to think of some way he could help. Nothing these past weeks, though, had taught him how to revive a tree. Mori had helped him find berries and cones, but he had yet to come close to performing the sort of feats he had seen Tim do in Moss Hill —

"That's it!" Leon exclaimed. If Tim was able to rouse the moss awake by speaking to it, then Leon might be able to copy him. He didn't need a whole forest, just this one tree, so it might be possible even for him.

Closing his eyes, Leon focused as hard as could on the tree. His grip tightened and the gloves slightly melded with the bark.

"Wake up," he quietly said. "Wake up. Please wake up ... your friend is waiting for you, so you can't die yet!"

Leon could feel his energy being sapped from the gloves, but he kept pleading for several straight minutes. When it finally got to be too tiring, the gloves recoiled and formed back into a cane, falling to the ground. Breathing heavily with his bare hands shaking against the trunk, Leon looked up and down the tree but saw no new branches or leaves.

"Damn ..." he muttered wearily to himself as he slumped down onto the ground. Before he had a chance to rest, though, something pricked his hand all of a sudden, making Leon quickly scuttle back. Looking at the ground, he started to see large, leafy blades of green shoot out from the snow. The leaves were enormous, engulfing the trunk of the tree as they continued to grow out. Then, once the leaves finished sprouting, the tip of the trunk started to split open next. The bark peeled away, collapsing downward and exposing a bundle of beautifully bright red petals. They slowly unfurled in almost a spiral manner and revealed a white center filled with enormous, round, gooey-looking fruit.

Leon was absolutely amazed by what he had witnessed, so much so that he failed to notice that the spirit was up again, standing right over him. As it took a heavy step forward, Leon finally realized it was awake. He watched the spirit lean forward and gaze at the flower, sniffing hard. Then, it slowly lowered its head and bit off a piece of fruit.

Leon grinned as he watched the spirit enjoy itself eating. He then quietly picked up his cane and thought it would be wise to leave now on a good note, but as he turned around, the wind tickled his nose, causing him to sneeze. With his eyes closed, Leon wiped his nose with his hand. He then opened his eyes and was very surprised to see the spirit's face now right beside him, staring. Before Leon could react, the spirit then lovingly rubbed its head against him, almost knocking Leon over. It made little noises as it kept rubbing, sounds that Leon imagined were out of happiness.

"You're welcome," Leon laughed as the spirit then lay down, curling around him like a warm blanket. Leon rubbed his hands against the spirit's pine fur and enjoyed the feeling, finding it much softer than what he had imagined earlier. Leon eventually leaned his whole body against the spirit's fur and sank into it like it were a cozy bed. Then, looking up, he saw the sun above was getting close to setting, but Leon closed his eyes, thinking he could afford a moment longer with his new friend.

It was nearly nighttime, but the Wrivenworth camp was as busy as ever. A small caravan of horse-drawn sleighs had come to deliver not only provisions, but also a new shipment of prototypes that Evelyn had requested.

"Get everything off the sleighs," she commanded. "This will be the last shipment from my father — be careful with those parts! They will be impossible to re-place out here!"

Keith strolled about without a care as he watched laborers from the caravan unload crates as fast as they could. Several engineers, in the meantime, were huddled in a circle, shivering as they studied the limp body of one of the machines lying on the ground. They had been assigned the task of making sure each machine had arrived undamaged.

"Is the shoulder supposed to bend in like that?" one of them asked.

Another snorted hard and nodded.

"Yes, otherwise the gears might be knocked out of place if any impact is applied," he explained.

"Does that account for the cold climate, though?" a third man asked.

"The cold shouldn't matter."

"How can you be so sure of that?"

"Because that's what we've been testing."

"Yes, but ..."

Evelyn enjoyed this sort of minutia, but Keith found it all far too tedious. Having seen enough, he walked back to where Zeke was sitting.

"Bored already?" Zeke asked, holding a cigarette.

"Yeah," Keith replied, taking a seat. "There's nothing for me to do."

"You're probably right," Zeke agreed.

Keith kept his mind occupied with watching a man slowly stagger out of the sleigh closest to them. Once he'd managed to get himself safely to the ground, he immediately began coughing hard while leaning his hand against the sleigh with his back towards Keith. The fit soon ended, and the man shook his head tiredly side to side in what Keith imagined was frustration. He took a moment next to collect himself, straightening his hat and tightening the scarf around his face, and then he reached back into the sleigh and pulled a small crate out. He stared at it briefly, maybe checking to be sure it was right, and then turned and slowly walked towards Keith and Zeke.

"Excuse me," he said as he got closer, "do you know where I put this box full of bolts? They are the smaller ones for the prototypes."

"Over there by the tent," Zeke pointed.

"T-thank you," the man coughed.

"Hey, do these things have a real name yet?" Zeke asked Keith.

"What, the machines?" said Keith.

"Yeah, we keep calling them 'prototypes,' but that's not a real name."

"No idea," Keith shrugged. "I haven't heard anything about it yet. Knowing my father and grandfather, they're probably trying to think of something clever that will sell well."

"Yeah," Zeke nodded.

"Zeke," Evelyn shouted, "get over here and help Orval with a crate."

"Yes, ma'am," he shouted back. He then sighed, stood up, and slunk over to where Orval was.

Keith looked up at the cloudy sky and wondered if it was going to snow hard tonight. He was getting tired of this kingdom's dreary weather.

"The camp is so busy, isn't it?" he heard the coughing man from earlier say.

Keith turned his head to the side and saw him

standing there, taking in the view. Keith could see now that he was fairly old with wrinkles around his eyes.

"Aren't you a little too old to be here?" Keith jokingly asked, and the man chuckled.

"Do I look that old to you?" he asked, reaching into his pocket. He pulled a lighter and pack of cigarettes out.

"Yeah, you kind of do," Keith admitted. "You some kind of supervisor or something?"

"Kind of," the man answered. Turning his head away, he lit a cigarette and took a puff. Then, once he had tightened his scarf back into place, he continued, "I'm here to help make sure those machines follow orders —"

All of a sudden, he started having a coughing fit.

"You alright?" Keith worried. He didn't want Evelyn blaming him for killing someone.

The man waved his hand and nodded as he finished coughing.

"Happens sometimes," he said in a slightly wheezy voice. "Y-you're Silas's grandson, aren't you?"

Keith was surprised yet happy to be recognized.

"How'd you know?" he asked out of curiosity. "Did someone tell you?"

"It'd be hard to work for the Wrivenworth Company for as long as I have and not know what its owner's family looks like," the man explained.

Keith looked down at the ground as he heard that answer, feeling a little disappointed, but then the man added, "You look just like your grandfather when he was young."

Keith looked up at him and saw the man's worn eyes closed with a happy expression on his face.

"Hey, Keith," said Zeke, walking up to them, "your sister wants to talk to you."

"What about?" Keith asked back, but Zeke defeatedly shrugged.

"No idea," he replied, "but she doesn't seem too mad, so I wouldn't worry. Who's this guy? You know him?"

"He's the guy you just gave directions to a minute ago, remember?" said Keith mockingly.

"Yes, but who is he?"

"I don't know, I just met him like you did," Keith snapped, not hiding his annoyance at the question.

"Right ..." said Zeke, rolling his eyes, "well, what's your name?" he asked, turning to the man in question.

"Oh, I'm sorry. I should have introduced myself properly first. My name is Malcolm Riff," said Glint politely. "It's a pleasure to meet you both."

CHAPTER FOURTEEN

COMMOTION

L eon, are you listening?" Howard whined.

A day had passed, and Leon, Howard, and Jean were up early as usual, but instead of working on their lists like they normally would, they were walking together down a narrow, dirt path. It ran northwest of Heath's, snaking between the mountains and Whistle Forest. Leon and his friends had been tasked with picking up supplies from a nearby village while dropping off a few items Heath had asked to be delivered. Along the way, Leon had kept his mind occupied with transforming his spirit weapon over and over, going back and forth from cane to gloves.

"I keep telling you to stop fooling around with your cane," said Howard. "Were almost to Bednye village."

"Why does it matter if I practice?" Leon asked. "I'm not bothering anyone."

"It doesn't really matter to us," Jean spoke up, "but the people of Volgiev take spirits very seriously. We'd rather not draw any unwanted attention, so keep your cane normal for now."

"Alright, but why do Volgians care so much about spirits?" Leon asked, reverting the cane back to normal. "You've mentioned before that they think they're special, but why do they think that?"

Jean nodded, knowing what he meant.

"They believe a spirit named Adrok rules and protects this land," he explained. "The other spirits, in turn, are viewed as Adrok's kin, and therefore are revered too."

"What does Adrok look like?" Leon asked next.

"No idea," Jean replied. "Besides being made of ice, I've never heard anything else. It's like the whole kingdom is him, in a sense. Though, some people do refer to snezies as his children."

"Really?"

"Yeah, but I wouldn't take it too literally. They're small and childlike in how they behave, so that's probably why some people like to think of them as children. Anyway, almost any scholar you ask outside Volgiev thinks Adrok is just a legend. There are no historical records of sightings or proof the spirit exists, so everyone thinks he's just a myth or maybe an early king's spirit. Don't mention any of that to a Volgian, though," Jean quickly added with a slight grin, "or they will get really mad at you."

"Avaleer doesn't really have any myths like that," Leon remarked.

"There is Ravnell," Howard spoke up.

Leon looked at him, and Howard looked right back, making it clear what he was implying.

"The mythic city lost at the edge of the world ..." said Jean, "you could convince me it's real, but I'm not sure how remarkable it would really be."

"Yeah ..." Leon quietly replied. Howard had re-minded him of what Glint had said months ago, that Ravnell was real and Tim was the one who had de-stroyed it. Leon at the time had put little to no cre-dence in what Glint was saying, but now, after meeting several kinds of spirits and working with Mori, Leon was beginning to wonder lately if maybe there was some truth in what Glint had said.

What do you think, Mori? Leon asked with a slight smile, staring at the cane in hand.

"I can see the village," said Jean, pointing straight ahead.

Leon looked up and saw that they had indeed reached their morning destination.

Bednye was a tiny village sitting just north beyond the outskirts of Whistle Forest. Its residents dwelled in wooden log houses with quaint yet somewhat shabby appearances, especially when compared to Heath's home. Everything was covered in snow, and not a sin-gle person was milling about, making the village seem abandoned, yet a few houses did have chimneys let-ting off puffs of smoke, giving Leon hope.

"The shop should be over here," said Jean, pointing as he led them through the heart of the village. "It's been a few years since I last visited, but Heath sent me here several times in the past to make deliveries. You can also get a sleigh ride from here to the capital that takes about half a day."

They approached a building not much different

from the rest, making Leon wonder if Jean might have the wrong house, but Jean didn't seem to think so. He opened the door wide without a second thought and prompted Leon and Howard to step inside. They did so, and he closed the door behind them.

Right away, Leon noted that it looked to be a proper shop, having shelves and tall baskets full of food and other goods for sale. The food was mostly dried and easily preserved items, and the shop itself was not much warmer than outside. In the back was an old man with a large, thick white beard and mustache. He was wearing a heavy set of clothes; in his mouth was an inexpensive-looking smoking pipe. He was seated behind a counter and did not get up to greet his new customers. Instead, he tiredly eyed them over from his seat with his arms crossed.

"It's been some time since I was last here," Jean remarked as he walked up to the counter. "How are you doing, Mr. Rus?"

"Little cold," Mr. Rus replied. "You brought friends this time."

"Yes, this is Howard and Leon," said Jean, pointing to each of them in turn.

"I assume they are working for the master carpenter as well?"

"Yes, they're helping out."

Mr. Rus nodded and stood up.

"I'll gather what he normally orders," he said.

"Thank you, and we also have a few letters we need

delivered," said Jean, pulling several envelops from his coat pocket. He handed them to Mr. Rus, and the old shopkeep read them over to see where these letters would be going.

"Two to Avaleer, and one to Pradow ..." he remarked. "It'll cost a little more than before, especially for the one to Pradow."

"Not a problem," Jean happily replied.

"Good, I'll be right back."

Mr. Rus then went into the back of his store, leaving Leon, Howard, and Jean to browse on their own.

"What things do you recognize here, Leon?" Jean asked for fun.

"Well," said Leon, glancing at the shelves, "those are obviously whistle cones, and that jar is full of dried pepper leaves, I think."

"That's right. There's all kinds of food here, even a few things from Pradow like these apricots, though our home is a little too far north to grow them."

As Leon listened, his eyes drifted from item to item, studying them carefully. He tried guessing whether each one was native to this land or some place much farther away. Eventually, he came upon a basket filled with an all too familiar kind of dried mushroom, and Leon grimaced hard, knowing exactly what it was.

"What's the matter?" Jean asked, noticing the disgusted look on Leon's face.

"He really hates pungent mushrooms," Howard answered with a smirk.

"Oh?" Jean lightly laughed.

"I can't help it!" Leon exclaimed. "They're so chewy and taste like gunk —"

Suddenly, the front door snapped open wide, and a young child bundled from head to toe in layers of clothes stepped inside.

"Mr. Rus —" she began to shout (her loud yet nonetheless girlish voice gave her away), but she stopped upon realizing the shop had customers. She quickly slammed the door shut (nearly knocking an item or two off the shelves), and then quickly pulled her scarf off. Leon was surprised to see a cute face hiding underneath, but it was a bit soured by a serious expression as she stared at Leon, Howard, and Jean.

"Who are you?" she asked, not taking her eyes off them as she removed her hat next.

"Oh, my name is Jean, this is Howard, and he's Leon," Jean warmly answered, pointing to each of them in turn. "We came today to trade with —"

"I don't care," she bluntly cut him off. "You don't belong here. Get out."

Leon was taken aback by her attitude towards them, but Jean and Howard didn't act very surprised.

"Belle, that's no way to talk to customers," said Mr. Rus, having just returned with a crate in hand. "You know better."

Belle looked a little ashamed, staring down at the ground in frustration.

"Please forgive her," Mr. Rus continued, handing

the crate to Jean. "Her family passed away a year ago from an illness that plagued much of the village."

"I'm sorry to hear that," Jean replied solemnly.

"It's not your fault. The kingdom has never been able to do much for our ill, unfortunately. I've been looking after this little one ever since that tragedy, having her run errands for me. Belle, apologize."

Belle shook her head.

"No," she refused. "you'll get in trouble, Mr. Rus, if they're here."

"And why is that?"

"Because —"

Before she could answer, the door to the shop swung open yet again, but this time it was a pair of men in thick fur cloaks. Leon recognized right away that they were soldiers of the kingdom. Belle looked frightened, shrinking away to behind the counter.

"How's business, Mr. Rus?" said one of them.

"Slow," Mr. Rus bluntly replied. "What can I do for you two soldiers today?"

"Come on now, you know who I am."

"Yes, you were a nice boy when you were younger, Miron. So what brings you all the way back here? Feeling a little homesick?"

"I wish that were just the case. The kingdom has us patrolling everywhere, checking to be sure nobody is involved ... with any troublesome people ..."

Miron's voice fell as he eyed Leon and his friends over carefully.

"Who gave you three permission to enter the kingdom?" he asked, walking closer. "You're clearly foreigners, especially you two," he pointed at Jean and Howard. "Nobody with gold hair lives around here."

"The port authorities of Povask granted us access," Jean answered, stepping forward in front of Leon and Howard. "We are here with their permission to make trades with the kingdom."

"Any proof of that?" Miron asked, picking up a handful of pungent mushrooms.

"Yes, right here," Jean replied, pulling a sheet from his pocket and offering it.

Miron raised an eyebrow, seeming a bit surprised, but he put the mushrooms back and then took the sheet, unfolded it, and read it over.

"Well ... it looks like everything is in order," he said as he finished, handing the sheet back, "but Mr. Rus, why are you selling mushrooms like these?"

Mr. Rus looked confused.

"What's wrong with them?" he asked.

"Pungent mushrooms are an Avalean product, you can't get them around here."

"And?"

"Don't act stupid," the other soldier spoke up in a low voice, "you know we don't allow trade with the Avaleans. They kill spirits."

"Whether we trade with them or not doesn't matter to me," said Mr. Rus. "I got these mushrooms and everything else from markets in the city, so if you have a problem, go and check there. It's not my job to do yours."

Miron's partner scowled as Mr. Rus spoke, and once he was finished, the young soldier placed a hand on a small basket of dried fruit sitting on a shelf beside him.

"It's that attitude that has let the revolutionaries get this far," he said in that same low voice from earlier, yanking the basket off the shelf and onto the floor, spilling its contents.

"What do you think you're doing, you lumbering idiot?!" Mr. Rus snapped, stepping out from behind the counter. "Are you going to pay for those?!"

"Anton, we're not here to make a mess," Miron chided his companion.

"I don't care," Anton shouted back. "Disloyal men like him are why we keep having to patrol out in the middle of nowhere."

"Disloyal?!" Mr. Rus angrily repeated. "I've done nothing criminal! I buy goods openly sold at the capital's market. It is not my job to figure out what the lords ban or not! I don't know how to make it any clearer than that. Do you want me to write it down so you don't forget — ?!"

"Just tell us where you got all this contraband!"

"Oh, look at you! Quite the big word you used," Mr. Rus mocked. "Miron, is this really the best the kingdom can find? No wonder the revolutionaries are running circles around you all lately."

"Don't change the subject, tell us who sold these things to you, old man —"

Anton had reached out to grab Mr. Rus by the collar, but Leon had stepped between them, not willing to tolerate the soldier's terrible attitude any longer.

"What?" said Anton angrily. "You got something to say?"

"Yeah," Leon boldly replied, "you shouldn't pick on your elders."

Everyone in the shop was somewhat taken aback; Anton's scowl grew worse.

"You trying to pick a fight?" he growled. "Want me to arrest you and your friends?"

That threat did the trick, bringing Leon back to his senses.

"No," he said with far less bravado in his voice now.

"Good," said Anton; with no warning, he then slugged Leon square in the side of his head, knocking him to the ground.

"Leon!" Jean shouted, running over to check if he was alright.

"Is that any way to treat my customers?!" Mr. Rus shouted.

"I wouldn't have had to have done that if you just answered my question."

As the two men continued to argue, Leon remained sprawled on the floor. Not from pain, though. He was surprised he'd been hit, but he was thinking to himself how it didn't really hurt. Arching his head up, he saw the cane still in his hand. Was this thanks to Mori somehow, he wondered.

"Leon, are you alright?" Jean asked, helping Leon sit up.

"Y-yeah," Leon mumbled as he watched Mr. Rus continue to argue.

"We can't keep having people work with revolutionaries!" the soldier shouted.

"I told you several times already, I have nothing to do with them!" Mr. Rus shouted back. "How dumb are you?"

"Are you making fun of me?!"

"Yes, you poor excuse for a —"

"Maybe the girl knows something," Miron suggested out of the blue. "She works for you, doesn't she, Mr. Rus?"

Mr. Rus looked appalled by what Miron suggested. Leon was growing very angry too, far more than a moment ago, and his head was beginning to throb.

"You leave her out of this!" Mr. Rus shouted. "You want money or something? Spit it out?!"

"Just information," Miron replied. "Anton, take her to Kirill. She might know something."

"Right," Anton agreed.

"Stop!" Mr. Rus shouted, but Anton easily shoved him aside and walked towards the counter. Leon at the same time slowly stood up.

"Don't worry, we're not going to do anything bad," Miron tried to assure Mr. Rus.

"N-no," Belle nervously squeaked, stepping back.

"Come on, don't make me chase you —"

Before Anton was allowed to take another step towards her, Leon suddenly gripped the back of his cloak tightly. His hands were now encased in wood and his expression was as furious as could be.

Anton turned his head to see who had stopped him, and he rolled his eyes seeing it was Leon yet again.

"Trying to pick a fight — ?" he began to smugly ask, but Leon was in no mood to listen: Gripping Anton tightly by the arm with his other wooden hand, Leon jerked him off balance and then slammed him down onto the floor as hard as he could, making the floorboards crack and the whole store shake from the impact. For a moment afterward, everyone was perfectly silent, looking too shocked to know what to say.

"A-Anton?" Miron was the first to finally speak, not sounding very confident now. "You alright?"

Anton was too stunned to answer.

"That doesn't look good," Howard mumbled.

"Leon, calm down," said Jean, placing his hand on his shoulder, but Leon brushed him off. He grabbed Anton by the scruff of his cloak and dragged him straight to the front door. Leon pulled it open, picked up Anton like it was nothing, and then tossed him headfirst outside. Leon then turned and glared at Miron.

"Out," he growled in a low voice.

"S-sure," Miron complied, not wanting to be tossed. As he hurried out the door, several soldiers on horseback came trotting towards the shop.

"What's the matter with Anton?" one of them casually asked. "Drink too much?"

"He attacked Anton," Miron shouted while pointing at Leon.

"What?!" another soldier barked.

"This is just getting worse and worse for us," Howard nervously remarked. "Should we run, Jean?"

"Probably — hey!" Jean shouted as Leon brazenly walked towards the soldiers.

The soldiers dismounted and surrounded Leon.

"What do you think you are doing, boy?" one of the men asked.

"This guy was picking a fight with the old shopkeeper," Leon explained.

"So you knocked him out?" another soldier asked.

"We were just questioning about any revolutionary activity," Miron argued.

"By frightening a little orphan girl?" Leon coldly rebutted. "Are you really any better than these revolutionaries I keep hearing about?"

"How dare you," said one of the soldiers, rushing forward. He tried to take a swing at Leon, but Leon easily dodged and pushed him to the ground. Another soldier then immediately charged in next, and Leon punched him hard in the gut, making him crumble. A third then tried, and Leon tripped and slammed him sideways into the ground. By this point, the remaining soldiers still standing were not sure if it was wise to pick a fight with Leon.

"Enough of this," said Miron, producing a spear of ice. He then lunged forward with it, aiming to stab Leon in the shoulder, but Leon easily parried the spear's blade and grabbed the shaft with his wooden hand. He then pulled on the spear, yanking Miron forward. Leon then grabbed him tightly around the wrist.

"Let go of me!" Miron shouted, but Leon squeezed harder, making Miron wince and drop his spear.

Leon was in somewhat of a daze at this point, wondering why his head hurt so much now. He imagined it had to be because of the blow from earlier. The thought annoyed him to no end, making him loathe these soldier even more. He glared at Miron, and several black lines began to creep up his cheek, but Miron was too focused on his hurting wrist to notice.

"H-hey, I'm sorry for scaring her, s-so let go already," he pleaded, trying to pull himself free, but Leon wouldn't listen. "Come on, we didn't even do anything to her. You don't know her, right? She's just an orphan, so it shouldn't matter —"

Leon's glare worsened, and his wooden hand began to tighten even more —

"LEON, CALM DOWN!" Jean yelled in his ear as loudly as he could.

The world suddenly grew clear again in an instant for Leon, and he finally let Miron go.

"Leon, can you hear me?" said Jean in a slightly calmer, but still concerned voice.

Leon nodded while quickly looking around. Without any idea of why, he and Jean were surrounded by soldiers and a few villagers who had come to see what was causing all the commotion. Leon then turned towards Jean with a confused expression, unsure of what was happening.

"What is going on here?!" a man shouted from behind the crowd.

Everyone turned to see a somewhat elderly soldier riding a magnificently large black steed. The soldier had gray hair and a long, bushy beard, and he too wore a heavy fur cloak like the other soldiers, but, as a strong wind blew past him, the crowd could see how impressive his military uniform was underneath, revealing his high rank. As several more cloaked riders slowly collected behind him, the old soldier studied the crowd with stern eyes.

"Move aside," he eventually commanded, and the ring of people immediately parted, revealing Leon and Jean standing in the middle.

"Who are you?" the old soldier asked.

"Nobody, it's all a big misunderstanding — Leon," Jean quickly yanked Leon towards him, pushing his head down while desperately whispering, "Put your cane back to normal, now!" but Leon was too confused by this scene to understand. He stared around him, trying to grasp how he ended up surrounded like this.

He couldn't remember well what he had just done, only that he was incredibly mad.

"Master Kirill," said Miron, "he attacked Anton and then me. We were just questioning a local shopkeeper about any information regarding revolutionaries —"

"I gave no such order," Kirill spoke firmly, dismounting from his horse.

"Sir?"

"You heard me, boy. We're here today to train, not search for revolutionaries."

"Yes, but —"

"And Nestor Rus is an old friend of mine. You thought it wise to harass him in his store? Who do you think provides feed for our horses and food for us to eat when we travel the countryside here? You?"

Miron looked more and more embarrassed by the second as Kirill's words sank in.

"Leon," Jean spoke in a heavier voice, finally getting his attention, "turn your cane back to normal."

"R-right," he weakly replied; the lines receded and the cane transformed back into its original shape. That act didn't go unnoticed by Kirill, though, who grew an incredibly startled look on his face.

"Sir," said Miron, "he still attacked us —"

"SILENCE!" Kirill bellowed, dropping to a knee.

"S-sir?" said Miron, not understanding what had gotten into Kirill all of a sudden.

"The wood of his cane is alive," Kirill explained. "He is a caretaker. Bow your heads. Now!"

Everyone throughout the crowd finally understood and swiftly dropped to the ground in respect.

"You really don't need to go so far," said Jean.

"We must!" Kirill replied, keeping his eyes glued to the ground. "I am Commander Kirill Prystov. Forgive my foolish subordinates for what they have done today. I will discipline them later. If I may be permitted to ask, why has a caretaker journeyed to this place?"

"He's not — we're just traders ..." Jean wasn't really sure what to say anymore.

Kirill had nothing to say, keeping his head lowered in respect.

"Mr. Rus," Jean turned to him next, "how much do we owe you."

"Nothing," Mr. Rus replied, with his head bowed now too. "I'm already blessed to have a caretaker's protection. I can't ask for more."

Jean sighed, but nodded.

"Let's go," he said, gesturing to Leon and Howard.

The two followed right behind, passing the kneeling crowd. They hurriedly left the village, not saying a word until they were far enough away.

"What was that?" Leon finally spoke up.

Jean immediately stopped and spun around to face Leon, making Leon instantly regret speaking up so soon. Jean's expression didn't seem all that angry or upset, though, like Leon had feared, but Jean did look tired and a little frustrated.

"Everything that just happened is why I told you

over and over not to use your cane while we were there," Jean sternly lectured. "The people here revere the spirits, believing them to be divine creatures to be worshiped. They protect the land and keep its inhabitants safe. Caretakers, in turn, are seen as a special entity that commune with the spirits. To many Volgians, a caretaker is considered equal to that of a noble. Some even believe greater than that."

Leon was unable to say anything back at first, feeling too ashamed to speak. He hadn't been aware of any of this, and it all reminded him of how little he still knew of the world beyond Vellenwood.

"I ... I didn't mean to cause any trouble," he eventually said in a sheepish voice. "I just got so angry, and all of a sudden I was outside before I knew it."

"It's alright," said Jean, already sounding calmer than a moment ago. "I know why you got mad, and I can't blame you. Unfortunately, though, it may cause some headaches for us in the future."

"With the kingdom?" Howard asked.

"Yeah," Jean replied. "Let's worry about that later. For now, we need to get back to Heath's."

Leon and Howard nodded in agreement.

"I had no idea you knew how to fight like that, though, Leon," said Jean, beginning to walk again. "It was quite impressive."

"Huh?" said Leon, following after him.

"I bet you could really give Howard a run for his money."

"I doubt it," Howard spoke up.

"Oh, have you been practicing?" Jean asked with a bit of a sly smile growing on his face.

"No, but the cane was helping him, so —"

"You'll need to practice a lot more if you want to beat him," Jean teased.

"Listen to what I'm saying," Howard groaned back in frustration.

As the two continued to argue back and forth amongst themselves, Leon thought more deeply in silence on what had happened in the village. He was slowly piecing together his fragmented memories, recalling that he had indeed fought the soldiers, but he had no idea how he'd so easily beaten them. It had just been natural at the time ... eerily so. He then looked down at the cane in his hand and slowly understood what had happened.

Mori had helped Leon a lot in the past few months, including climbing and staying in the freezing forest all day, but he had never fought any creatures or used the cane like a weapon before. Leon could never forget the image, though, of Tim blocking that keeper's enormous claws with his wooden hand. Yes ... Mori definitely had the power to also grant strength, but more importantly to Leon right now, the spirit had done so without being asked , worrying Leon.

Hey, Mori, he spoke to the cane in his mind, *are you awake?*

The cane twitched a little in response.

If … if I ever get mad like that again, don't help me. We have to be careful or I might hurt someone. You don't want to hurt people, right?

The cane gently coiled around Leon's arm, like it were hugging him.

Good, Leon happily replied.

Maria had wanted to go to Bednye Village as well. She had thought that she would have been allowed to get out of the house for once, but here she was, stirring a pot in the kitchen while Heath sat on a stool, peeling a potato.

"This is a nice change of pace, isn't it?" said Heath as he mindlessly tapped his foot.

"Yes … quite the change of pace …" Maria sarcastically answered, not hiding her feelings on the matter.

"It's not that big of a deal," Heath tried to assure her. "The village is nothing special, and you still need to practice more."

"Yeah, yeah," Maria grumbled.

"Besides, you can't leave me all alone with that machine," Heath jokingly added.

"Oh, come on!" Maria shouted in exasperation. "All he does is pet Warren most of the day!" (Pendle, of course, was sitting silently in the living room as she spoke, petting Warren on his lap.)

"You can never be too careful with those things."

"Why are you so afraid of horolocks? You shouldn't know anything about them. It was the Wrivenworths who made them —"

"No they didn't," Heath corrected Maria, keeping his eyes on his half-peeled potato. "They stole how to make them. I don't know how, but they did."

Maria stopped stirring, looking at Heath confused.

"From who?" she asked.

"Someone who ... who shouldn't be around any longer," said Heath in an oddly subdued voice. "He's the only one who could ever build such things...."

Maria found that answer too vague, but before she could press the matter any further, the front door of the house suddenly swung open.

"We've returned," Jean happily shouted.

"Good to hear," Heath shouted back, standing up. "Maria, go see if they need any help, I'll be over in a moment."

"Alright," said Maria.

She walked to the front and found Jean, Leon, and Howard all sitting on the floor, taking their boots off. Next to Jean was a crate full of food and other items.

"Were you able to send the letters?" she asked.

"Yeah, both to Louis and your parents," Leon answered, struggling to pull off his right boot.

"Good," Maria replied with a smile.

"What's for dinner?" Howard asked.

"Skimmer and potato stew from the leftovers last night," Maria answered. "I've been helping make it."

"Well that's not good," Howard joked.

"Huh?"

"Yeah," Leon meanly added with a smile.

"Hey!" Maria snapped back at them. "There's nothing wrong with my cooking!"

"Didn't you burn the whistle seeds last time you tried making something?" said Howard.

"Nobody told me how to make them properly!" Maria angrily defended herself.

"They aren't hard," Howard jabbed back.

"Be nice, Howard," said Jean, now standing with the crate in his hands. "You're not exactly a great chef yourself."

Howard scowled at that while Maria smiled hard.

"To be honest, her cooking isn't actually that bad," Leon admitted.

"Really?" said Howard, not sounding convinced.

"Yeah, her and her mom know how to make a lot of good food," said Leon. "Anything with trout, baked bread, jumber pie —"

"Spore soup, roasted caps, baked fenloaf, stuffed bark sitters, and dried pungent mushrooms," said Maria, calmly listing one dish after another while a terrible grimace grew on Leon's face.

"Is that everything I ordered?" Heath asked, walking in from the kitchen just then.

"Yes, it is," Jean replied, raising the crate towards Heath so he could see. "Where would you like me to put this?"

"The kitchen for now. I assume nothing eventful happened."

"Well ..." Jean began as he and Heath walked back to the kitchen. Maria noticed then that Leon and Howard were looking at each other nervously.

"I hope he doesn't get too mad," Leon whispered.

"He probably will," Howard whispered back, having trouble untying his left boot.

"What happened?" Maria whispered jokingly, but she didn't expect them to look so serious in response. "What — ?"

"Leon, Howard!" Heath angrily shouted from the kitchen. "Get in here, now!"

Leon and Howard both sighed hard, making Maria all the more confused.

"I didn't even do anything wrong," Howard bitterly remarked.

Both boys sluggishly rose to their feet and then slowly filed into the kitchen where they found a slightly peeved Heath waiting for them, scratching his cheek while stirring a pot.

"Quite the mess you've made, Leon," he said.

Leon had nothing to say in his defense, looking down at his feet in shame.

"What happened?" Maria asked, putting a little more weight in her voice.

"Yes, why don't you tell her, Leon," Heath prodded. "It's not every day you get into a fight with soldiers, right?"

CHAPTER FOURTEEN

As what Heath said quickly sank in, Maria grew a mortified look on her face.

"H-how — w-whyyy?" she stammered, looking at Leon for an answer. "Why would you do that?"

"T-they ... were picking on the shopkeeper," Leon timidly explained, not willing to look her in the eye.

"So you got in a fight?!"

"To be fair," Jean spoke up from the corner where he was now sitting on the stool while carefully peeling a fat potato, "it's a little more complicated than that. Howard and I don't blame him for putting the soldier in his place. And you don't need to worry, Heath, nobody followed us back."

"That's good," said Heath. "I'm actually not that mad you got in a fight, Leon, so you can relax."

Leon was noticeably relieved to hear that, but that didn't do much to appease Maria. She expected a more thorough explanation later.

"I'm glad you protected that shopkeeper," Heath continued. "He and his family have done business with me for years, so I owe them a great deal. That doesn't change the fact, though, that you attacked soldiers of the kingdom."

"I'm sorry," said Leon, knowing his temper had caused this mess.

"Howard, grab the jar of salt in the cupboard," said Heath, pointing behind them.

Howard did as asked, turning around and opening the cupboard full of jars of seasonings.

"Which shelf?" he asked.

"Middle one, near the front, right behind the hazel flakes," Heath directed as Howard searched, "yes, that's it. Place it here on the counter beside me. Thank you."

Heath then opened the jar, took a pinch of salt, and sprinkled it into the pot.

"Now, um, what were we talking about?" he asked, looking at his kitchen aides' faces for a clue.

"Something about attacking soldiers, I think," Maria answered.

"Right!" Heath replied, tapping his wooden spoon on the pot's edge. "So attacking the soldiers isn't the issue."

Leon, Howard, and Maria all looked equally confused to hear that, making Heath smile a little.

"The problem ..." he continued, waving the spoon in the air, "is that they now think an unknown caretaker is lurking around."

"I explained to you guys earlier how important caretakers are to this kingdom," said Jean.

"I didn't get to hear about this," Maria reminded him.

"Right, well, you know that spirits are really important to people in Volgiev, right?"

"Yes," said Maria.

"Alright, so caretakers, who look after spirits, are considered just as important."

"That makes sense."

"And since Leon was caught using his cane," said Heath, "the soldiers will undoubtedly report to their superiors what happened. I imagine by tomorrow the King will hear about this."

Leon was shocked to hear that.

"Why?" he asked.

"Because caretakers are just that powerful," Heath answered. "So much so that you can think of them as a weapon."

Leon certainly didn't like the idea of being called that.

"If an unknown weapon appears from out of nowhere in your kingdom," Heath continued, pointing his spoon at Leon, "wouldn't you be concerned with who is wielding it? I would."

"They might think he works for the revolutionaries," Howard added, "or another country. Especially if he's attacking soldiers."

"Exactly. They are going to want to know who you are, Leon, and what you're doing here. To make matters worse, we're supposed to go to the capital next week."

This trip was news to everyone else, except Jean who didn't seem that surprised to hear it.

"Why are we going there?" Howard asked.

"Hmm?" Heath replied. "Oh, well, I need to deliver a violin."

"Is it the one you've been working on?" said Maria excitedly, loving this idea. "Who's it for?"

"That's still a surprise," said Heath with a bit of a grin. He then took a big sniff, and grinned even harder. "Food should be done soon," he said, putting the lid on the pot. "Maria, help me get all the spoons and bowls ready."

"The capital is filled with soldiers," Howard pointed out, looking at Leon as he spoke. Maria could easily tell what he was implying, and she didn't like what it meant.

"I assume you want me to stay home then, right?" said Leon, trying not to sound too disappointed.

"Oh, no, you're definitely going," Heath replied.

Leon, Howard, Maria, and even Jean all looked baffled by that answer.

CHAPTER FIFTEEN
UNEXPECTED GUESTS

A week had passed and it was now the middle of the day, but Maria for once was not trapped in Heath's workshop, drawing. No, instead she was fidgeting like mad as she rode in a small carriage. She was dressed up a bit more than usual, wearing a long green skirt, a white blouse to match, and a colorfully bright green, black, and white scarf draped over her shoulders. Her boots were no different, though, and her old coat sat folded on her lap, keeping her arms warm as her hands played incessantly with the coat's charms.

"Can you calm down already?" Heath growled, sitting across from her. From head to toe, he was covered in clothing, concealing his body in a way similar to how Pendle normally dressed.

"I can't help it," said Maria nervously. "Why didn't you tell me sooner who you were giving that fiddle to? Am I really dressed appropriately for such a thing?"

"Stop fretting," said Heath.

"But my coat is so old —"

"You look fine. Ilya won't care what you look like, so long as you appear respectable."

"This is a king we're talking about!" Maria shouted. "I've never met a king before!"

Heath just sighed and closed his eyes.

It wasn't long before they entered the city of Ledy. Maria found it far less impressive and less lively than Gildfoil, but it was still an imposing city. All the buildings were dull in color and covered in snow and ice, and very few citizens were strolling about. The roads were rather empty too. Maria wouldn't describe the city as dead, though, but perhaps sleeping instead.

"The palace should be in view soon," said Heath, keeping his eyes closed.

"Really?" said Maria giddily.

As the carriage turned, the Palace of Ledy came into view, and Maria found herself completely mesmerized by its beauty. From its symmetry to its size, every aspect of this royal palace was absolutely enchanting to her. Even more impressive, though, was the seascape behind it: The palace sat on the edge of a bay, and in the far distance, Maria could see blocks of ice as tall as skyscrapers floating along.

"Are those icebergs?" she asked, pressing her finger on the window.

Heath opened an eye and nodded.

"That place is called Glacier Field," he said. "It looks like that year-round."

The carriage driver slid the small front window open and said, "We will be arriving soon."

"Thank you," replied Heath.

Once the driver shut the window, Maria started fidgeting, feeling nervous again about meeting the king.

"Worrying ..." Heath yawned, "won't solve anything. We're not even going to be there that long."

"I know, but I can't help it!" Maria squeaked.

"If it's any comfort," said Heath calmly, stretching his neck, "I think you've met a few important people before."

"Huh?" said Maria, looking very confused by what he had just said. "Who?"

"Never mind," replied Heath. "I don't feel like explaining it right now."

The carriage briefly stopped at a side gate before being allowed to enter the palace grounds.

"Boys," said Heath softly, "you know what to do. Don't take long. Otherwise, you will need to find another way home."

The carriage soon came to a stop again, and a guard opened the door.

"Thank you," said Heath politely, stepping out. "Maria, don't forget the case."

"I won't," Maria replied as she quickly threw her coat on in a hurry. As she then leaned down to pick up the instrument case lying by her feet, she whispered, *"Be careful, you two."* She then stood up and stepped out as well.

As Maria exited the carriage, her eyes were immediately drawn to the palace. She was somewhat reminded of the way the museum in Gildfoil was designed, both in terms of size and grandeur, but the stone blocks of the palace were far larger and looked many times older than the materials of the modern buildings of the Avalean capital. She and Heath were by a side entrance with only a pair of guards watching an arched doorway.

One of the guards opened the door and a man that looked about as old as Jean poked his head out. Maria was somewhat surprised to see how ornate his clothes were: He was wearing a dark blue suit coat of sorts, but the collar and cuffs were embroidered with gold threads, forming a dense, detailed pattern.

"He's a palace steward," Heath quickly whispered in Maria's ear.

"Oh," Maria quietly replied.

"Are you two the employees of Master Heath?" the steward asked.

"Yes, we are," Heath answered. "We've brought the instrument as had been requested."

"Perfect, come inside," said the steward, pushing the door open wider. Heath and Maria did as he asked and walked past him into the palace.

"The King is very excited to see one of Master Heath's creations," the steward explained as he shut the door behind them.

"Is that so?" said Heath. "Master would be honored to hear that."

Maria was far too nervous now to giggle at what Heath had just said. As the steward led them through the large hallways of the palace, the gravity of where they were was really sinking in. Every inch of the walls and high ceilings was either painted, adorned with what looked to be priceless paintings, or gilded with gold trim. The furniture looked far too ornate to ever be sat on, and the floors too polished to be tread upon. The candle chandeliers hanging overhead looked so large and heavy to Maria that she could feel their weight looming in her mind.

Maria, Heath, and their steward guide walked through halls of every color, went up and down short flights of stairs, and constantly passed servants, maids, and other employees of the palace. Many eyed her and the disguised ermine as they walked by, Maria imagining because they were curious to know why such an ordinary-looking girl had been let into the palace.

Maria's fears worsened once they reached a tall set of red doors inlaid with panels of gold. They were open wide, allowing her to see a dozen men standing in pairs across from one another. They were dressed similar to the steward, but each man carried a sword at his side, leading Maria to believe they were guards. They stood ready to protect their king as he sat on his throne at the far end of the room. The king was a distinguished-looking man with a calm, almost indifferent expression on his face. He also wore clothes of the court much like those of his stewards', but his clothes were far more decorated, with cords, a red sash, and medals that made clear his high authority here.

Without giving Maria a chance to wrap her mind

around what was happening, the steward spoke in a booming voice.

"Presenting to His Majesty, King Ilya the IV, the assistants of Master Carpenter Heath."

With that said, the steward stepped back and gestured for Maria and Heath to enter.

"Don't be scared," said Heath, casually proceeding forward; Maria followed close behind.

They walked between the two rows of guards and stopped at the foot of the throne's steps where the king's personal steward waited. Heath bowed his head, to which Maria awkwardly followed, and they both remained like that as the steward spoke.

"Your Majesty," he said in a polite tone, "as you have requested, these two have come from far away today to present you with with one of Master Carpenter Heath's finest creations, a violin like no other. As requested, the wood for the body of the instrument was carefully selected from the many trees growing in Lady Emiliya's personal hunting grounds. After selection, the tree was carefully cut and its wood delivered to the fabled craftsman's home in Whistle Forest where Master Carpenter Heath began the difficult and intensive labor of crafting the perfect instrument befitting of someone such as —"

"You are far too long winded, boy," Heath interrupted him.

The steward looked aghast, the guards were confused, and Maria was terrified that Heath might have just done something very frowned upon in a royal setting.

"Sorry, but I don't have all day," Heath continued, raising his head. "You've grown quite a bit, Ilya. The last time I saw you, you were just a boy, I think, hiding behind your grandfather and brother when you all came to visit me at my home. The two of you boys nearly broke one of my chairs and kept asking if you could see Sosnog."

As Heath casually spoke, Maria noticed the king's somewhat indifferent eyes come to life.

"Do not address His Majesty in such a familiar tone!" yelled the steward. "And bow when presenting yourself before — !"

"There is no need for such formalities," King Ilya suddenly spoke up. "Let me speak with these two in private."

"B-but," the steward looked stunned, "I cannot just leave you unprotected —"

"Do not worry yourself, Ivoc," said Ilya, putting a little weight in his voice.

"S-s-sir?" Ivoc nervously stuttered, bowing low out of reflex.

"Leave us be," Ilya continued, "this man is definitely not a threat."

"A-as you wish," said Ivoc. He then reluctantly gestured to the guards to follow. They all filed out of the throne room, closed the doors behind themselves, and left their dear king alone with Heath and Maria.

CHAPTER FIFTEEN

After waiting a moment to be sure the doors didn't reopen, Ilya stood from his throne and walked forward towards his guests. Maria worried if she needed to back up in response, but Heath didn't move an inch.

"I had no idea you would actually come in person, Heath," said Ilya, standing eye to eye with Heath. "You must be so warm in all that clothing. If you'd like, you can at least take your scarf off for a bit."

"Thank you, but I'm alright," said Heath politely. "I have the instrument you asked me to make. Maria, if you would, please."

"Hmm?" Maria replied, somewhat mesmerized by their conversation.

"The instrument," Heath hissed. Maria then finally realized what he meant.

"Right!" she squeaked, quickly placing the case on the ground. She undid the locks, opened the case wide, and then picked it up, revealing a beautiful violin sitting inside.

Ilya slowly reached out and took the instrument in hand.

"Such fine work ..." he remarked as he studied it, "I don't know of anyone else who can put such detail into something like you can. I had this commissioned for my youngest daughter, Renata. Her birthday is soon, and she likes music, so my wife and I thought this might be a good gift for her."

As his focus remained on the instrument, Maria quickly glanced at the king standing so close now, and she finally noticed that his eyes were remarkably blue, something very uncommon in her life.

"I came in person today," said Heath, "because I wanted to talk to you."

"I can imagine why," Ilya admitted, placing the violin back in its case. "My family has ruled this land for centuries, and I know that you are considered by many of my ancestors to be our most esteemed advisor."

"No need for any flattery," said Heath. "You are not sure what to do about the rebels, right?"

"Has it become that big of a problem in your eyes?" Ilya asked with a somewhat saddened expression growing on his face.

"It has," Heath replied firmly.

"My brother Nikolai keeps trying to broker peace," Ilya explained, "but I can't bring myself to agree to the rebels' terms. They want the machines and devices our neighbors have, but Adrok will curse us all if I allow my people to use such things. The Prads are already paying for what they have done, and I'm sure Avaleer will one day pay as well."

Heath nodded as Ilya finished speaking.

"I understand the need to protect your people from the dangers of technology …" he said, "I've seen what such things can do in the wrong hands, but you have gone too far. You cannot freeze your kingdom in time when the rest of the world is ever changing. Especially when your people know it."

"But —"

"No, Ilya. You must listen, or you risk losing a great deal, more than I think you realize. The spirits don't care about machines or inventions."

"What — ?"

"That's right, they aren't upset by light bulbs or cars like you imagine."

"I'm aware of what upsets the spirits," said Ilya coolly. "The Avaleans destroyed their homes and replaced them with the factories and cities necessary to make such things."

"Yes, you're right, but so long as they are left alone, spirits will not care the least bit about what your people create. I tried to tell your father that, but he refused to listen, so here I am, having this same conversation yet again years later. There is balance in everything, so I implore you, be more open-minded and open your borders to the outside world."

"And become like the Avalean Empire?!" said Ilya angrily.

"No," Heath barked back, "become better than them! Become a kingdom that Avaleans, Prads, and the rest will envy!"

Maria worried if anyone had ever spoken so frankly to the king in his entire life. Ilya didn't seem to mind, though, listening carefully, nodding as he thought hard on what Heath meant.

"Is this why you brought an Avalean today?" Ilya asked next, narrowing his eyes a bit as he looked towards Maria.

While Maria was too frightened to say anything, Heath simply shook his head.

"She is a student of mine," he said, patting Maria on the shoulder. "Try not to scare her."

Ilya's expression softened.

"She must be very talented to learn your carpentry skills," he said.

"No, not carpentry," Heath corrected him. "I am teaching her how to be a caretaker."

Ilya looked quite surprised to hear him say that.

"She is just starting," Heath continued, "but I see some promise in her."

Maria couldn't help smiling from hearing him say that, enjoying his rare words of praise.

"An Avalean caretaker ..." said Ilya, still looking a little dismayed, "it's hard to believe. Our neighbors have treated the spirits so poorly for so long that I never imagined another caretaker would be born from amongst them again, yet here you are. Perhaps I really do need to be more open-minded. Young lady, what is your name?"

Maria was startled to be asked a question directly, but she did her best to properly reply.

"Maria Treckle, Y-Your Majesty," she answered stiffly, lowering her head like the stewards had done.

"I have a daughter near your age, Maria," said Ilya. "Someday, I would like her to meet you and Heath."

"I would like that," Maria replied, keeping her head bowed but sounding a little less stiff this time.

"While I have the opportunity, I'd like to ask you another question. Were you at any point in the village of Bednye recently? I received a report personally from the Palace Commander that a caretaker had been spotted there, and since they are so rare, I'm curious to know if you might be the person in question."

As the king spoke, Maria grew nervous again, knowing exactly who he was looking for, but Heath readily shook his head.

"No," he said, "until today, she hasn't left my home for weeks now," he calmly answered for her. "Right, Maria?"

"Yes," Maria quickly replied, trying her best to keep her voice calm.

"Besides, she is still learning, so I doubt she would have done anything worth noticing," Heath added.

"Right," said Ilya, nodding. "I'd been told it was a young man, but I wanted to be sure. As to what we were discussing earlier, Heath, I'm … I'm still not sure what to do, but once the Spirit Ball is over, and I have all the lords present here, I will discuss some kind of change with them. You are right that something must be done."

"Now you sound more like your grandfather," said Heath.

Ilya smiled brightly, as if he'd been given an incredible gift.

"We should get going," said Heath. "Your steward might go crazy if we take any more of your time today."

"Are you sure you would not like to stay the night? I could —"

"I don't want to cause you any trouble," Heath explained, pointing at his wrapped face.

Though looking a little disappointed, Ilya nodded in agreement.

"Thank you for coming," he said, patting Heath on the shoulder. "And thank you for making the violin for me."

"It was no problem," said Heath. "Let's go, Maria."

"Alright," Maria replied. "Wait, what should I do with this?" she asked, holding the violin case up.

"I could take it," said Ilya.

"No, let's pretend to do this properly," said Heath, already walking away. "Come here, Maria."

"Best to just listen," Ilya quietly chuckled.

Maria smiled and quickly bowed her head to Ilya, and then she ran after Heath.

Together they walked back in silence to the main entrance to the throne room. As they reached the pair of large entryway doors still closed, Heath, without pause, grabbed hold of a handle and yanked the door open. Ivoc, several guards, and even a few servants were all gathered on the other side, waiting anxiously.

"You can go back in, boy," said Heath, opening the door wider to show Ilya was perfectly fine.

"Are you finished — ?" Ivoc asked.

"Maria, hand him the case," Heath commanded.

"Yes," she answered, handing the case to Ivoc.

"Are one of you going to show us back to our carriage, or shall we show ourselves out?" Heath asked, tapping his fingers impatiently against the door.

"Y-yes, I will." said a different palace steward. "Please, follow me."

"Thank you," said Heath.

With the steward in the lead, Heath and Maria strolled back through the palace. Unlike before, they took a different route that briefly passed by windows looking out onto a courtyard. It was full of snow and trees with bark colored a pretty white that Maria had never seen before. They also reminded her of the other reason they had come to the palace today.

Pulling on Heath's coat to get his attention, Maria signaled with her hand for him to lower his head. Once he had done so, she whispered, *"Are Leon and Howard going to make it back in time?"*

Heath chuckled and put his hand on her head.

"I hope so," he calmly answered.

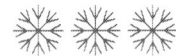

Maria and Heath were not the only passengers in the carriage today. While they both had ridden comfortably to the palace, Leon and Howard had snuck aboard, hiding under the seats inside storage compartments. The accommodations were cramped to say the least, but it was the only choice they had. Why? Well ...

"I don't like this idea at all," Maria had protested the week before. "What if they get caught?"

"Yeah," Howard agreed, looking eager to find any kind of excuse.

"The goal is for you not to," Heath replied, continuing to stir his pot. "I need Leon to collect flowers from the trees in the courtyard. If I could get them anywhere else, I would, but as far as I'm aware, they only grow in that single place. I need those flowers for an important request someone made."

"I understand all that, but why can't we just have them go in normal like us —"

"Because … as I've said before, I would then have to explain why I need the flowers and who Leon is, both of which would be a nightmare for me to deal with."

"But it's okay risking Leon and Howard's lives so you don't have to deal with something uncomfortable?" Maria coldly asked.

Everyone else felt a little cowed by her chilly tone, but Heath tried to remain strong.

"Look," he said, "We wouldn't have to be so secretive if Leon hadn't made such a scene earlier today, but now a bunch of royal guards know what he looks like." (Leon stared down at his feet in embarrassment, knowing he had nothing to say in his defense.) "I need those flowers, and this is probably our only chance at getting them. I promise you, if they get caught, nothing bad will happen. The boys just need to mention my name, and that will probably be enough."

CHAPTER FIFTEEN

Maria didn't look very assured.

"Why not send Jean too?" she suggested, but Heath immediately shook his head.

"I'm unfortunately busy with work tomorrow," Jean answered.

"Besides," said Heath, turning towards Leon and Howard, "I think this will be good opportunity for you both to see how well all your time spent training here has paid off. I really don't think it will be that bad."

Unable to fight against that confident look on the ermine's face, Leon and Howard quietly accepted their fate.

Once the carriage had stopped for good and Leon was sure the driver was gone, he pushed the lid of the compartment seat open. He stuck his head out and found Howard had done the same. After nodding at each other, they crept out from their hiding places and checked behind the curtain of a side window to see where they were.

The carriage had been parked just outside the palace stables. The carriage's horses were already un-hitched, and several stablehands could be seen busy walking about, sweeping the ground, moving bales of hay, and working on other carriages. Leon almost felt nostalgic in this setting, being reminded of his old barn home.

"There's no way we're sneaking inside unnoticed," Howard remarked as he tightened a scarf around his face. "I don't even see an entrance anywhere."

"You might be right," Leon agreed, tying a scarf of his own around his face in a pitiful attempt to conceal his identity.

"We could sneak around to another side," said Howard, "but even if we could get in, we don't know the layout at all — I don't know what Heath was thinking! This is ridiculous!"

While Howard was lamenting their situation, Leon studied the walls of the palace, looking for open windows. He couldn't spot any, but his search did give him another idea.

"I can get us inside without getting caught," he said confidently.

"Huh?" said Howard, surprised to hear that.

"We just need a distraction."

"I think I can do that," said Howard reluctantly, "but it's your fault if we get caught."

Leon nodded, and they quietly exited the carriage.

"What's the plan — ?" Leon began to whisper, but Howard raised his hand up, asking for quiet. Leon complied and silently watched with anticipation as Howard pulled one of his daggers out.

He first generated a charge throughout the dagger's blade, and then he reached into his coat pocket and pulled out a few raw firebulbs. As he gently pressed the tip of the dagger to each of them, Leon saw that the firebulbs were quickly beginning to pulse in the same manner as the blade. Once the berries were all fully charged, Howard took a wide step back from the carriage, reeled his arm back, and then threw the firebulbs as hard as he could towards the stables. The firebulbs flew through the air, and as they landed, each of them exploded, making loud popping noises that frightened the horses into a frenzy.

"WHAT'S GOING ON?" a man yelled angrily.

More of the stablehands started to clamor, and soon enough, they were all distracted with calming the horses down.

"Let's go," said Howard, pulling Leon by his coat sleeve.

Together they darted to a spot along the palace's exterior wall where a pine tree stood, giving them some cover.

"I held up my end of the deal," Howard whispered. *"It's your turn, Snail Boy."*

Leon smiled confidently and pressed his wood-clad hands against the wall.

"I learned a few new tricks too," he said, and then the wood latched onto the stone. It dug into whatever tiny cracks it could find in the wall, forcing the cracks to fracture further. In a matter of seconds, Leon's hands slowly clasped shut, pulverizing the stone to dust.

While Howard was mesmerized by what Leon had done, Leon didn't pause to marvel with him. He instead raised his hands higher and carved out yet another set of holes. Over and over he did this without pause, and Howard slowly realized what Leon had planned. Soon, Leon was steadily climbing the wall, using the earlier holes as a foothold.

"Hurry," he called down to Howard, who nodded silently in response. He followed Leon's lead and climbed right after him. They scaled the wall as fast as they could, never stopping out of fear that the stable-hands might spot them. Once they finally reached the top, Leon and Howard both sat down and breathed a sigh of relief.

"How'd you do that?" Leon asked, stretching his wooden fingers.

"The firebulbs?" said Howard.

"Yeah. Did Jean teach you that?"

"Sort of. It's just like using the fishing rod. I make the electricity flow through them, but they start to fall apart quickly, so you need to get rid of them before they pop."

"Interesting," Leon remarked.

"We don't have a lot of time," said Howard, stand-ing up. "We need to find the courtyard, get the flowers, and then get back in the carriage without getting caught."

"Yeah, we'd better get going," Leon agreed, stand-ing up as well.

They turned and crawled their way up the slanted roof, being careful not to make too much noise. They quickly reached the top where they were greeted by an unbelievable sight: All around Leon and Howard the enormous palace spanned, and in the far distance, gargantuan blocks of ice could be seen floating in the sea. Leon sat down on the peak of the roof and spent a moment gazing at the incredible seascape.

"That must be Glacier Field," he remarked, thinking back to what Heath had said during the carriage ride.

"I imagine it is," said Howard, already beginning to climb down the other side of the roof, "but unfortunately for us, we can't spend all day up here."

"You're right," Leon nodded in agreement.

He returned his focus to the task at hand and stared down at the courtyard below in the center of the palace. It was packed full of barren trees standing so tall that the tips of their highest branches rested on the roof. Leon and Howard carefully slid down to the bottom of the roof and stopped at its wide ledge.

"How do we get down?" Leon asked, leaning over the ledge.

"No idea," Howard replied. "Can't we just use the branches to get the flowers?"

"No, I need to get Mori near the base of the tree," Leon explained. "It only seems to work that way."

"If you say so, Snail Boy," said Howard, leaning his head back to stare up at the sky. He breathed deeply through his nose and then looked down at his feet while lightly stomping his heel.

"What are you doing?" Leon asked.

"Just making sure it's not slippery," Howard calmly answered.

"Huh — ?"

Before Leon could finish his question, Howard suddenly leapt from the roof, grabbing onto a thick branch just below them.

"Are you crazy?!" Leon angrily shouted. "What if the branch broke — ?"

"We don't have time," Howard shouted back, already working his way towards the trunk. "Jump."

"Fine!" Leon growled, taking a step back. He then dashed forward and leapt off the roof's ledge, barely managing to grab the same branch that Howard was hanging from. The two of them then worked their way down the tree.

"I'll keep a lookout," said Howard in a hushed voice once they reached the ground, *"You get the flowers."*

"No problem," replied Leon.

As Howard skulked about checking the windows, Leon turned and faced the tree. They all looked so old, but Heath had said they could bloom with Mori's help.

"Who are you two?!" the two boys suddenly heard, though the voice was much softer than that of any gruff guard who might be watching the palace. If that wasn't warning enough, a rather large shard of ice then punctured the snowy ground beside Leon's feet, inches from crushing his poor toes. He dove behind the tree, afraid the next shard would be aimed at his head.

"What are you two doing in the palace?"

Hugging his cane, Leon peeked his head out to see

who was speaking. To his surprise, it was a beautiful young lady standing on the other side of the tree, glaring at him with her bright blue eyes. She wore a long white hooded cloak with fabric so sleek that it blended with the very snow. The hood itself was lined with dark fur and hanging down, revealing the girl's long brown hair neatly tied with a big blue bow.

"Bunny ears ..." he mumbled to himself, squinting.

The girl swiftly raised her hand up and pointed her palm directly at Leon's head, but Leon didn't seem to mind in the least bit. He was far too focused on her bow at the moment to worry about anything else. The blue piece of apparel and the girl wearing it seemed oddly familiar to him, but he couldn't quite figure out why ...

"Who are you two?" the girl demanded. "Why are you trespassing — ?"

"Lily!" Leon spoke over her, having finally recalled where he had met this girl before. "You've gotta be Lily, right?!" You look so different!"

"Yes, I am Liliana Medov," she replied coldly. "Are you one of the rebels? Speak now!"

Leon started to laugh, sounding a little giddy. Regardless of the circumstances, he was delighted to see she was alright.

"What is so funny?!" Lily shouted angrily.

"I guess you wouldn't recognize us like this," Leon remarked playfully as he stepped out from behind the tree, undoing the scarf hiding his face. Though it took

Lily a second to understand what he meant, her tough expression melted fast once she saw that it was her old acquaintance Leon Skyler standing right in front of her.

"L-L-Leon?!" she stuttered.

Leon wore a grin as he pointed to the side and said, "The guy over there is Howard."

"H-Howard too?!" said Lily excitedly, turning to see him with his scarf off too, looking at her with an eyebrow raised. She sheepishly lowered her head, unsure of what to say.

"I want to talk to you about what had happened at Willow's Rest," said Leon, "but we don't have a lot of time, so that will have to wait for another day."

"W-what do you mean?" said Lily, trying her hardest to regain her composer. "Why ... why are you two here? How did you even get into the palace in the first place?"

"Let's get to work," Leon said as his cane melded with his hands, forming into wooden gloves once more. "This should only take a second, Howard."

"Alright, but hurry up," said Howard anxiously.

"I-is that a spirit weapon?" Lily asked, entranced by the sudden transformation of Leon's hands.

"We just need a few flowers off of this tree," Howard explained as Leon put his wooden palms against the trunk.

"That's not possible," said Lily. "These trees haven't bloomed in centuries. There is only one caretaker who can make … them …" She fell silent as she saw the tree's many branches begin to bud. The buds grew rapidly in size until all at once, they bloomed into stunningly pure white flowers.

"H-how …?" Lily mumbled to herself, looking absolutely amazed.

"Howard," said Leon, hunched over, breathing a little hard, "pick a few so we can get out of here."

"Sure," said Howard, looking a little too pleased all of a sudden to comply. "Hold still."

"Huh — ?"

Before Leon realized it, Howard leapt up onto his hunched back like a stepping stone, and then climbed onto a branch.

"That hurt!" Leon growled.

Howard tried to pull at the stem of a flower, but the whole thing immediately shattered from his touch.

"You can't just rip them out," Lily cautioned him. "They are as fragile as snowflakes."

"Yeah, you better stop breaking them, Howard," Leon teased.

"So how are we supposed to take them back, Snail Boy?!" Howard shouted angrily.

"What do you mean?"

"Even if I could pick them, they would all fall apart the second I put them in a bag!"

"Oh —"

"Princess!" A woman shouted from across the courtyard. "Who are those two?!"

"Princess?" Leon repeated; as the meaning sank in, a wave of shock overcame him. "Y-you're a — ?"

"Leon," Howard hissed, "we need to get out of here, now!"

"Hey, Howard," said Leon, looking at him bewilderedly without a care for what Howard had just said, "did you know she's a princess? I had no idea."

"I put it together earlier," replied Howard, staring hard at Lily, "when she gave her *real* name."

Lily averted her eyes, embarrassed that he had caught her in a lie.

"None of that matters now, though," Howard continued, dropping to the ground. "We need to give up on these flowers and get out of here as fast as we can before it's too late."

Leon was inclined to agree with him at first, but as he quickly looked over the tree one more time, an idea suddenly popped into Leon's head.

"I might have a way to fix our problem," he calmly said, tugging on the tree's bark.

"I don't know what that means, and I don't care," said Howard anxiously. "Just hurry up with whatever it is you're doing, and let's get out of here."

Inna stormed through the courtyard, but as she neared where Lily was standing, her pace slowed a great deal from seeing the tree in full bloom.

"L-Lily," she said, her voice almost trembling with awe, "h-how — how did the sacred tree awaken?"

"I — I'm not sure," said Lily softly, almost lost for

words. She turned to Leon for an answer, but he and Howard were both gone. Looking all about, she finally caught sight of them somehow scaling the far wall of the courtyard.

"L-Lily?" said Inna, surprised to see a slight scowl growing on Lily's face.

Lily had finally had enough of not being told what was going on.

"I'll be right back," she said coolly.

"Wha — w-wait!" Inna shouted as Lily then darted off. She went straight to the wall and was appalled to find it punched full of holes. As dust sprinkled onto her head, she looked up to see that it was Leon damaging her home. Even angrier now, she immediately started climbing. She wasn't very strong, finding it a bit hard to keep a firm grip on the wall, but she was determined to get answers. Once she reached the top, she saw Leon and Howard already climbing over the peak of the palace's snow-covered roof.

"Come back here!" Lily shouted.

Howard turned his head and saw Lily struggling to stand up straight, looking like she could slip and fall any second.

"What are you doing?!" he shouted worriedly. "It's not safe up here!"

"S-speak for yourself," Lily retorted under her breath, using her ring to help her firmly plant her feet in the icy snow.

Leon and Howard climbed over the peak, and Lily

crawled after them. She slowly made her way up to the top of the roof and found Leon and Howard standing at the bottom of the other end, talking to one another on the roof's ledge.

"You two have a lot to explain!" she shouted from atop the peak.

"Can't we just climb down the way we came?" Leon worriedly asked Howard, neither seeming to have noticed at all that Lily had said something.

"Stop complaining," Howard growled at Leon. "This is a lot faster, and you know it! I don't feel like being imprisoned because you're too scared!"

"Alright, alright," Leon groaned in defeat.

Lily didn't like being ignored, but before she had the chance to demand their attention, Leon suddenly turned and jumped off the palace's ledge without warning. As he disappeared from view, Lily's face filled with terror.

"No, wait!" she cried, trying not to slip as she then hurriedly slid down backwards on her hands and knees towards them. "You're not in trouble! Please, don't hurt yourselves!"

Lily's heart wrenched as she saw Howard readily jump next, but once she finally reached the roof's ledge and leaned over it, she immediately breathed a heavy sigh of relief: Howard and Leon were both clinging to a large pine tree growing right up against the palace's wall.

Lily was so thankful to know that they were alright.

CHAPTER FIFTEEN

As she watched the boys climb down the tree, she stood up. Undeterred by the frightening height, she bravely leapt after them. She fell into the tree's branches and clung onto them for a moment, breathing hard while laughing a little at what she had just done. She then awkwardly scaled down the tree, but towards the very end, her hands slipped, causing her to plop down into the snow at the bottom.

Rolling onto her hands and knees, Lily searched all around her until she spotted the boys running straight for the outer wall of the palace.

"Stop!" she shouted, but Leon and Howard paid her no heed. Lily found it quite frustrating to be ignored like that. As she got to her feet, she used her spirit ring to quickly mold a clump of snow in her hand into a fragile ball of ice. Once the ball was complete, she then trudged after the two boys.

It didn't take Lily long to reach the outer wall and find Leon and Howard already climbing it. Out of breath at this point, she stopped and flung the ball of ice in hopes of getting their attention. The ice shattered loudly against the wall over their heads, but the boys were too focused on escaping to care. Lily groaned at their lack of interest, but she continued to chase. By the time she reached the base of the wall, Leon had climbed over already and Howard was nearly at the top.

"You two aren't getting away!" she growled, following after them.

Lily climbed to the top of the wall and then lowered herself over the edge. Once she found enough courage, she let go and dropped down into the snow, awkwardly falling onto her rear. Breathing heavily, she looked up at Leon and Howard as they stood over her, patting snow off their clothes.

"Do — do y-you give up yet?" Lily struggled to say.

"No," Leon chuckled with a silly grin. "We don't have time to be trapped here. We'll have to talk more another time, but I'm really glad to know you're safe, Lily."

Lily blushed a little from hearing him say that, but before she could respond, Leon and Howard had already begun to walk briskly into the city. Lily's expression then saddened a great deal. She looked over her shoulder at the surrounding wall of the palace, knowing how important it was that she remain home.

"Princess," several voices began to shout from somewhere distant within the palace grounds.

They must be looking for me, Lily thought. She then turned her head forward again.

Leon and Howard had gotten much further, but they were still in sight. Lily stared at them and thought of what had just happened in the courtyard that had brought about all of this. How a boy had made one of the sacred glass trees of Volgiev bloom, just like Elm had done long ago ...

The voices of the guards were growing louder, but Lily still did not answer back. Instead, her expression grew serious once more. She knew she couldn't afford to let this opportunity slip away, not if she ever wanted to find the answers her troubled kingdom desperately needed.

Lily pushed herself up onto her feet and then ran forward as fast as she could, chasing after Leon and Howard.

Hello again my friend!

I'm glad to see you are still here with me. This story has gotten quite chilly, and the cold won't stop anytime soon. I suggest you wrap yourself in your favorite blanket and sip on some Brumstead tea. Maybe ... read a book. Just an idea, nothing more.

Keep warm,
Nim

P.S. Careful of any snezies you might see. They love to fool people.

Made in the USA
Columbia, SC
06 June 2021